One Door Opens

By Terrie Stevens

To Darlene Stevens
I would be only half the person I am without you..
Thank you

And Nelson
You are my anchor and wings…
Always and forever

Chapter One

Jenna scooted a few inches to the left. Aw, yes, this angle into his shop helped her spy on him.

How different her life could have been.

"Two children, a boy, and a girl and a dog. A big dog."

She continued her internal dialog, something she did far too often anymore.

"A brick house with a wood fence, and a minivan in the driveway."

Her heartbeat jumped while she watched him play with the children in his toy store.

"This is wrong on so many levels."

She turned her eyes away. She hated how she objectified this unfortunate stranger, but the lies to her mother made her mind hurt more.

"But what choice do I have?"

Her mother insisted she date, and how could she say no to a dying woman?

"Well, maybe this is the type of dating that is best right now." She surveyed her surroundings as people walked by her.

A familiar country song about pretty girls and summer days played overhead. The aroma of fried food wafted from the nearby food court. Jenna's stomach lurched and growled. In her before life, this mall represented lunches with her high school friends or where she bought new outfits for dates with real people. But that life ceased to exist five years ago; how quickly and drastically life could change at the drop of a hat, or in her case, the results of a medical test.

She adjusted her position again, and a plant brushed her arm. She let out a squeak and jumped. Across the hall, near the entrance to the toy store, a little boy laughed at her fright. She made a face at him, and he answered her with a quick flick of his tongue.

"Could I have had that?"

She closed her eyes and pictured herself feeding an infant, spaghetti in her hair, and mashed potatoes on her shirt.

"Yeah, and I can see it now. If things were different."

She giggled at her vision. When was the last time she laughed?

"Yesterday, you dolt. Quit being so over-dramatic."

Yesterday her mother told a terrible joke, and for hours they chuckled about it. Laughing came so rarely during all the chemo and radiation.

Jenna glanced back at the fine male form, sighed, and stood up.

"I think I've been gone long enough."

She gathered her few bags and strolled towards the exit. Conversations between families and teens crowded her mind as she passed the food court.

Jenna smiled. All these voices a welcome distraction.

She spied two women engaged in a serious conversation, their heads bent together, and she sat down near them.

"Oh May, I'm so sorry about what he said to you. He had no right."

"I know, but it's better I know now, rather than invest more time," May answered.

"Yes, I guess so."

The woman, not May, looked at Jenna and scowled. She nudged her friend and nodded towards Jenna.

"We need to go," Her friend agreed, and they gathered their things.

Jenna took a deep breath. "Well, now I guess I can tell mom I had lunch with friends also."

She rose and walked towards the exit each step taken with purpose.

"I don't regret my decision," her inner voice commanded, and she meant it, really.

She passed a maternity store and stopped. Her hands felt cold and clammy, and her breathing quickened. She contemplated what it would be like to create life as she watched the last stages of it in her new life.

The day would come, and soon. The time came at a high price of pain to her mother, but they celebrated the gift contrary to the original medical prediction of only three years. Each extra day Jenna included in her mental time capsules.

She walked out the door, and a blast of heat from the early days of spring encompassed her. In the last few weeks, her mother insisted daily she leave the house and do something normal, but normal was subjective. Normal was new cooking methods so her mother could keep food down. Normal was watching the clock and administering medicine. Normal was lying awake, listening to her mother's breath and dreading the day she didn't hear it anymore.

Yes, normal was subjective.

And her normal would change, sooner than later.

"How do I get ready for another shift in normal?"

She looked up at the clouds rolling in from the west and sighed.

"Okay, time to go back to normal."

Chapter Two

If Jenna didn't move, maybe time would stop.

Jenna struggled to see movement from the thin figure, while the clock on the wall ticked seconds away.

"Come on, mama."

Too much time passed since she gasped for air, followed by that awful gurgling noise. The soft humming of machines filled every corner of the room, but the sound long ago became another everyday household noise, like the creaking of a door opening.

Jenna shattered the oppressive quiet with a gasp for air.

"Breathe mama."

Nothing.

The dreaded soon was now, and Mama was gone.

"What am I supposed to do now? I'm not ready."

She needed to do something-Call the police or a doctor or something. Her stomach tightened, and her heartbeat doubled.

"I'm having a heart attack."

She placed cold fingers on her neck and took deep breaths to slow her heart down. She turned from the figure and walked to the window. She marveled at the young buds on the Lilac tree planted as a tribute to her father when he died. A few weeks from now, large groups of purple and white flowers would scent the yard and house; Mama would miss her favorite time of year.

"Who will I talk to, or cook for, or shop for now? What am I supposed to do?"

With her heart slowing, Jenna dialed 9-1-1.

An older female voice answered.

"What's your emergency?"

The voice shoved the "now" into reality.

"Oh, my God! Please send someone; my mother died."

Sobs overtook her body, and she fell to her knees. She fought for air. She struggled for breath while her lower spine vibrated.

"Ma'am? Ma'am? Are you safe? Are you in danger?" With each syllable, the volume of the voice increased. "You need to calm down so I can help you. I need an address. Ma'am?"

Word comprehension oozed into Jenna's mind like thick raw honey, and the voice opened the curtain hanging over her brain. She grabbed a piece of paper with essential information and read off her address.

"I'm so sorry, I thought I was ready for this, but I'm not! My mother has cancer, and now she is gone. What am I going to do now?"

"An ambulance is on its way." The wail of a siren penetrated Jenna's consciousness.

"Just take some deep breaths," the woman instructed her voice so much like her mother, an umbilical cord to sanity.

"Okay, where is your mother?"

"She is in her bed, a few feet behind me," Jenna couldn't bring herself to look at the still form. "We moved the bed into the living room about three weeks ago."

The approaching siren howled as the neighbor's dog sang along. Jenna swayed to the disturbing music until it ceased, and only the machines filled the void.

"They are here now," Jenna hesitated to hang up the phone and her connection with the operator. Jenna jumped as a pounding on the door echoed through the house.

She shuffled to the door, and two EMTs entered the house.

"We had a call from here?"

She pointed towards the living room in response, and the two men rushed to her lifeless mother.

"Keep it together. You can do this." Jenna closed her eyes and willed herself to wake up from this nightmare.

Questions were fired at her by a policeman she hadn't noticed come in. He introduced himself with some sort of animal name. Fox? Badger? Shepard? She couldn't recall.

"She said I should give you this."

She retrieved an 8.5 x 11 envelope off the table and stared at it. Her hands shook, and her mind zoomed from one snippet of thought to the next without allowing the first to mature. She rubbed her temple.

"Mom said these papers were important."

A memory flashed of her mother's hands when she handed Jenna the papers a few days ago. Her mother's frail hands shook uncontrollably at the time, just as Jenna's did now.

"Now, don't you open this," her mother's weak voice saturated her mind. Jenna closed her eyes while the officer pulled the papers out and nodded. He handed a few of the documents to his partner and placed the rest back in their paper jacket.

"These are for you."

He held the papers out towards Jenna, but she ignored him, and he dropped them on the coffee table. She turned to the bed, and she rubbed her stomach as the emptiness filled her.

12

Jenna needed this to be over, to escape this nightmare, even if only in her mind. Her gaze latched on to some of the artwork. Her mother loved to decorate and the contrast of the wall color and the paintings.

"Just breathe. Air in, air out." She closed her eyes — anything to avoid lashing out at the man touching her mother.

"Shouldn't you buy her dinner first?" She swallowed the words before they could exit her mouth.

His grope too intimate for her comfort.

Jenna turned away again;

"He needs to do his job."

He pulled the sheet over her mother's head, and she could no longer hold it in.

"She doesn't like her face covered. She's always cold but says she can't breathe with her face covered."

Jenna crossed her arms across her chest and squeezed her arms. She needed to stay in control.

Her mind, at last, accepted the loss, and the situation bludgeoned her. She dropped to her knees and tears broke through the safety damn. The animal-named cop caught her as she descended and wrapped her in his arms. He whispered in her ear.

"It's okay. I understand, but we have to do our jobs. It's going to be okay. Is there someone we can call to come over to help you?"

Jenna stared up into his dark eyes, unable to process the question or answer. She stood up, and with nonverbal consent, she allowed him to lead her to the couch. She sat down as the ambulance medics pushed in a stretcher. The lack of a knock caused Jenna to cringe and comment under her breath.

"You didn't knock."

No one noticed, or perhaps didn't care.

Jenna couldn't look at the cancer-ravaged body, and she dropped her head down. Her hair fell forward and created a curtain she could hide behind. This shell, this body, couldn't be the one who held her during heartbreaks and thunderstorms.

The police officers watched Jenna, and she squirmed under his stern gaze. Why was he looking at her like that? The paramedic placed the body into a black back and zipped it, the sound reverberated in the depths of her being.

"Oh mama," Jenna grabbed her stomach and fought the urge to vomit.

"What am I going to do now?"

She appraised each face as she looked for answers

Jenna dropped her head. Tears fell on her hands folded in her lap, and the wheels from the stretcher on the hardwood floor hurt her ears. She didn't want to think of her mother trapped in the confines of the black bag. A faint metallic taste coated her mouth.

"Can I call someone for you?" The animal-named officer asked again.

Jenna looked at him, her eyes blank, unable to think, unable to talk. She opened her mouth, and words fell out.

"I don't know; I don't have anyone."

He sat next to Jenna.

"Do you have a minister, a priest, or someone? The note said something about calling your minister."

14

He touched her arm, and the warmth of his hand comforted her. The face of the gentle preacher at her mother's church crossed her mind, and she nodded. She stood and walked to the little desk her mother bought years ago, an extravagant purchase for the single mother. She opened a drawer, and a pang of unexpected guilt fell over her. How could she get in her mother's personal space so soon? She fought through her intrusive feelings and dug into the drawer. Her head hurt, and exhaustion swept through her.

She located the minister's business card.

"Use this number when the time came," her mother instructed her. She handed it to the man in front of her.

"I guess you can call him." Her voice came out flat while she fought for control. Another onslaught of tears threatened another flood.

The officer picked up his phone and dialed the number.

She sat, numb, the chatter of voices floating in and out of her mind.

"He said it would be about half an hour, and I think I would like to sit here with you if you don't mind. We have a little time and no calls to run to."

His voice rolled over her like a soft pillow. He reached over and placed his hand on her hands. Her eyes pointed towards the appendage, but her eyes couldn't force Jenna out of her head.

His partner sat across from Jenna and flipped through something on his cell phone. Silence again packed the room, and Jenna yearned for any sound, even those damn machines. But those sounds died with her mother.

"It's okay, you don't have to stay," Jenna recited the words, but questioned her sincerity. Manners dictated what she said and did.

The men nodded in acknowledgment, but no one moved. Officer animal looked at his cell phone clock and smiled at her.

Jenna stood as she ran through the kitchen's stock.

"Would either of you like something to drink or eat?" her mother would be upset with her lack of courtesy

Both men smiled and shook their heads. Jenna plopped back down, relieved. She didn't have the energy.

"What am I supposed to be doing?"

"Nothing, you are fine."

Jenna wrapped her arms around herself and leaned forward while the men talked a little, while she treaded water lost in a sea of memories and worries.

She could do nothing but wait as time seemed to stop and speed up at the same time.

Something near the door drew her attention. She whipped her head around, and a memory of her mother played like an old home movie. Mama walked through it, her hands full of groceries bags. In the vision, her mother exuded strength and health, before the disease, robbed her of everything.

"Jenna, I told you, I'm too tired after work to have to do your chores too. You were told to take the garbage out and to rake the leaves."

The voice robust and clear.

Her eyes teared up.

"If I don't stop this, I'm going to drown."

Jenna turned back as the two officers studied her. She straightened her back and returned their stare.

"You know, I don't need babysitters."

"We know, but we are just worried about you, and the minister said he would be here very soon.

Jenna nodded and looked back at the Lilacs.

A light knock on the door pulled her back to the horror show she was living. Officer animal-name gestured for her to stay while he stood in one smooth motion. She sighed; he would take care of everything. She noted the creak of the door opening and made out the soft murmur of a familiar voice, Pastor Thomas. She turned to a mirror and spied on the men through its surface as they conversed. She witnessed the cop pat Pastor Thomas on the shoulder as they entered the living room and addressed Jenna.

The officer lowered himself to meet her eye to eye, his hand on her.

"We need to leave now."

The officer spoke in a tone reminiscent of an adult talking to a small child. His soft brown eyes comforting. There were more questions she should ask but couldn't think what they might be. She nodded, reached up, and patted his hand.

"Thank you." Jenna's voice not much more than a whisper.

Officer animal-name straightened up, and his partner joined him. Jenna repositioned herself on the couch and pulled her legs up to her abdomen. She held herself in a shallow hug.

"All your mother's wishes are in the envelope in great detail." The cop motioned towards the envelope on the table. "You may want to look at it when you feel better. She wrote her funeral and burial wishes in there for you. Pastor Thomas is here to help you with anything you need."

Jenna nodded an acknowledgment, and the two officers moved towards their exit.

Pastor Thomas nodded his thanks as the men left.

The minister lowered himself next to Jenna and laid his hand on her shoulder, almost on the identical spot where the cop's hand covered minutes ago. She didn't feel the same warmth.

"Thank you for coming." Jenna eyed the only father figure she remembered. She couldn't think of a time he wasn't a part of their lives.

"Would you like to pray for your mother?"

Jenna furrowed her brows and searched for words. A deep ball of emotions swelled in her heart, and tears filled her eyes. She could feel her heart beating faster, and a thin layer of sweat coated her forehead.

"Not now," she pleaded to herself. The thin line of control she clung to, snapped, and her rage consumed her. She jumped off the couch as an onslaught of verbal abuse vomited out in a tidal wave of anger. She let go, too defeated to combat the blitz or try to stop the flood.

"Seriously?" fell from her mouth, her mind a full cup running over. The minister lowered his eyes and folded his hands. Jenna witnessed his lips moved in prayer. She glared at him as he mouthed an 'Amen" and glanced into Jenna's eyes.

"I know that this must be hard. I know it is for me. Pamela was a wonderful mother, a wonderful admin, and a great friend."

"Yeah, and your God, your all-powerful God, the one YOU claim can heal anyone who believes hard enough, took her from me," Jenna spit out. "Yes, she was a wonderful mother, and I could tell her anything. Who am I going to talk to now?"

Her voice echoed in the stuffy silent air as she waited for an answer. Pastor Thomas looked towards the heavens and took a deep breath; his hands still folded on his lap.

Jenna paced in front of the man. He looked at her and spoke in a slow and deliberate tone.

"We don't have the abilities to understand His ways. I understand your anger, and that you are mad at God, but he has a plan. You are not the first person to ask these questions, and you won't be the last, but..."

Jenna's eyes bore into the man, and he stopped talking. Her deep quick breaths and fast heartbeats the only response she offered. Her hands curled into fists as she fought to take control back over her emotions; for her mother's sake. But it was too late, and she passed the point to stop them.

"Yeah, then find the answers! If he really is up there, loving humanity, well, he really screwed me over. He took the only person that meant anything to me, the only person that listened to me. I have no one else, and he took her. How can a loving God do something like that? Taking care of her is my life, and now I don't have that. How do I go on?"

The minister lowered his eyes.

"Your mother was a wonderful woman, and I know she would want you to be happy."

Jenna hit the wall. The loud pounding sound gave Jenna the chance to stop and take a moment. She took another deep breath and walked to the chair across from him. She dropped into its soft fluffy cushions.

"Yeah, I'm sure she would, but how am I supposed to do that?" Jenna felt a weight on her chest. She couldn't do this. She had no choice, and she surrendered; at least for this moment.

"I'm here," he put his hand on her knee.

"You don't have to stay, I'm fine, and I have a lot to do."

"Can I help?" A concerned expression crossed his brow. Jenna shook her head.

"I just want to be alone. I need to process all this. Don't you have someone else to go save?"

Pastor Thomas picked up the pack and pulled out her mother's final papers. He fished out a small envelope among the legal documents.

"Maybe we should open this and see what it says. Your mother told me she was going to write down a few things for you."

Jenna snatched the note from him and studied her name scrawled across the surface. A slight smile tugged at the corner of her mouth, looking at her mother's large loopy letters. She admired her mother's penmanship and emulated it in her own scribbles. The same hand which penned numerous notes of encouragement in her school lunches. Her heart swelled with memories and love. Even though as she grew, she chastised her mother for the notes, they lifted her up and provided her a sense of belonging and security.

She picked the tab and released her mother's last message to her. A familiar perfume drifted from the expensive stationery. She breathed in deep, and for the first time since this nightmare began, Jenna smelt sickness, it penetrated the room like the dark shadow as the sunset. The black letters danced around while Jenna fought the tears and shaky hands. She let out a breath and dropped her hand to her lap.

"Do you want me to read that for you?"

Jenna handed him the paper, stunned by his tenderness after her assaults.

He pulled out reading glasses and began.

"My darling daughter, I love you, and I know you are hurting right now, but please know, I'm out of pain now, and I'm sure I'm in a better place."

He paused and glanced over his readers at Jenna. She sat still, quiet.

"Go on."

He cleared his through and continued.

"And even though I can't hold your hand or give you words of wisdom anymore (as if I ever did anyway), I'm still near, and you can still tell me all the things going on in your life, no different than the last few months, though to be honest, I'm pretty sure that some of your recent adventures were made up for my benefit. I know you gave up your life to help me exit mine, and I want you to know I appreciated it, though I never wanted you to do that. I need to say I am sorry I didn't stop you from doing it, but I enjoyed our time together. I tried to tell you stories of my life, so that you remember who I was, though I would have preferred you remember me with hair."

A small sob escaped from Jenna's through, and Pastor Thomas paused. For a split second, a small smile shadowed her face while she recalled her mother's long blond hair, a contrast to her curly red mess. She nodded for the minister to continue

"I can't tell you how proud I am of you. You have shown repeatedly how much of a caring and special person you are. I know you can do anything you put your mind to, I only hope you use your powers for good and not for evil."

Another smile escaped Jenna's lips.

"I want you to have a happy life and make lots of memories. I know I will continue to live through you, so I need you to do the things I always wanted to do but let time get in the way. Don't let your life slip away as I did. Remember, life can get cut short in an instant, and understand life is not about making money or what you do, but about what you feel and how you spend your time. Make it count, if not for you, then for me."

Jenna pulled her legs up and wrapped her arms around her knees. She closed her eyes and imagined her mother's arms around her, just one more time. Her mother's arms were her regular place of refuge over the years.

"I want you to travel, and to fall in love and to have a family. You will make a wonderful mother, and you can tell them about me, and I will live forever, through those stories."

Jenna cringed. Could she ever live up to her mother's expectations? How could she ask her to do these things? She wouldn't even be here to argue with or object to her demands?

"I know it seems like I'm asking a lot of you right now but give it time. You will be okay. You are strong, and I'm counting on you."

The minister pulled off his glasses and rubbed the bridge of his nose.

"Are you okay?"

He watched her movements.

She returned his gaze, her green eyes clear for the first time since his arrival. She sniffled and shrunk further into the chair.

"I'm fine. Is that all she wrote?"

Jenna turned from his gaze and stared out the large plate glass window. Golden rays illuminated the outside world, and Jenna wondered why God seemed so happy.

"No, there is more." She relaxed and let his voice soothe her.

"I know it is going to be hard, but I have faith in you. I hope the lessons I have taught you will be enough, though I know when you hold your first baby in your arms, you will wish I was there. To think of you with my first grandchild, oh, what a sight that will be. And when you kiss their sweet little forehead, I hope you know I did the same to you and felt as if my heart would burst, as you will too. I will be looking down at you and smiling. I wish there was more time to write all the things a mother needs to tell her daughter and answer all the questions a young mother asks, but you will be fine, I promise. Just have faith in yourself."

He paused to clear his throat, and Jenna noticed the minister's tears. She turned away and looked at the family pictures on the fireplace mantle. Her parent's wedding

23

picture owned the position of honor in the middle, with assorted pictures of her life since birth on each side.

"So, my most precious heart, I'm sorry to have to leave you, but I'm tired, and I hurt, I want you to know I'm not scared or worried, my faith is strong, and I know that I will see you again in Paradise just as I know I will soon be able to once again feel your father's arms around me. Please, my wonderful kind, intelligent daughter, please, do not turn on God or on your faith. I know I did that when your father died, and it is easy to question why, but if your father didn't pass away, I might not have found God, and perhaps, our relationship would be different, not as close as we are now. Please, believe me on this one. God has a plan, and I believe that, even now. I can't tell you enough how much I love you and being your mother has been the best thing in my life. I wouldn't change a thing, even the fights. Please, if you are going to mourn my loss, please, try to do it quickly and get on with your life. Become the person God intends for you to be. Again, travel and enjoy what God has put on the earth. Remember, it was God who gave us more time then we were told."

The minister sat the letter down.

"She signed it 'mom,' and she also says there is another envelope in the kitchen desk drawer with important papers such as the deed to the house; title to the car and final wishes on burial and such."

Jenna concentrated on the images in front of her, her voice silenced by a loss of what to say. She picked up the paper and noticed several places tears smeared the ink.

24

"You know, Jenna, I remember when I met your mother. Your father recently died, and she came for answers, just as you want them now."

He took off his glasses and put them in his shirt pocket.

"I saw something in her that day, a strength. I saw her through the tragedy of losing her beloved husband, and I see the same strength in you."

He reached out and tried to place his hand on her arm, but Jenna moved out of his reach.

"You were a small child, and she was worried about how she was going to raise you and care for you."

He sat back in his chair.

"God spoke to me, and told me to offer her a job, which I did, and never regretted it for a minute. You became part of our family."

Jenna rotated her eyes and looked out the window.

"She was a devoted member of the congregation and an essential part of my staff. We are all going to miss her."

Jenna turned and noticed tears on his wrinkled cheeks.

"I'm fine, and I'm tired. I think I need to rest."

The man nodded and leaned forward, his elbows on his knees.

"Maybe I could make you something to eat?"

Jenna shook her head, stood, and walked towards the door. The minister followed her lead.

"I'm here if you wish to talk, or a shoulder to cry on."

"I know, but I'm fine and not interested in what you are selling," she opened the door and stood aside for him to pass.

He lowered his head and did her bidding.

A new silence crowded in on her. She missed the raspy breathing of her mother and the rhythmic beeps of the medical equipment. She took in a deep breath and tried to hear anything, even a siren or the wind, but no noise came.

Jenna refused to cry anymore and stumbled up the stairs, her body and mind ached. Despite the early hours of the day, she went to her room, changed to her pajamas, and crawled into bed. She looked at the ceiling and waited for time to pass so she could start this horror story over again in the morning.

"How could you do this to me, mother?" she yelled into the oncoming darkness. "What now?"

She rolled over and buried her head in her pillow.

"How am I going to survive?" she sobbed. "I can't do this. I don't know how to do this."

Chapter Three

A soft breeze passed through pine branches and created a mystical song outside Paul's window. He shut his eyes and let the melody invade his mind.

He placed his hands on the wood desk, littered with papers and empty coffee cups. The warm wood furniture piece reminded him of his former life, the lone item he saved from his old life after she bought it the first year they were married.

"I need some help today, God. The anniversary is almost here again."

He hoped no one could hear him and looked up towards heaven.

"I don't know why, and I can only pray that she is at peace with you now."

He placed his hands on the keyboard and looked at the screen.

"Okay, I need some words. Please, God, anything."

He reached up and rubbed the bridge of his nose, a habit she teased him about.

"You are going to rub a dent there." Her voice echoed inside his head.

He loved her voice, the sound lulled him to sleep in the late night and pulled him out of his dreams in the mornings.

"I would do anything to hear it one more time."

He picked up the worn leather Bible and flipped through the flimsy pages. He stopped and looked at the text, shook his head, and repeated his actions.

He drew in a deep breath and slowly let it out. He glanced at the non-descript clock on the wall.

"Well, at least I have a few days before I need this done 'cuz it ain't happening tonight."

He snapped the book shut and returned it to the desk.

He caught the image of a picture taken 12 years ago, the two of them together and happy.

"How long has it been." He asked the photo. His voice broke the quiet.

"Six years, 362 days, two hours, and 42 minutes." The answer gushed into his mind like an over-anxious high school student.

Nights like this, any sounds in the quiet house helped. Most of the time, he welcomed the silence of the night when he could listen to the ghosts, but tonight it was repressive.

He plopped into the chair and pulled the portrait closer. He stroked chips and dents in the silver frame. Six years, 358 days ago, the object took the brunt of his anger. He turned it over and found a dented corner.

"Where it hit the wall," he remembered.

His mind flashed back to the high pitched explosion of shattering glass, a poor symbol of his shattered heart. He rubbed his thumb over a scar on his finger the result of a cut obtained as he picked up the shards. The cut on his hand healed; the blood ceased to flow, and the external wound healed. Despite the years, his heart still showed the cracks.

Pictures of the small family dominated the walls among images of Jesus and posters of encouraging sayings. What would she think of the job he took or the small town he fled to after they were gone. Despite traveling miles away from their home, she still haunted him.

He grabbed the photograph and looked deep into the eyes of the woman. Her deep blue eyes twinkled in the sunlight. In front of her, a smaller carbon copy of the woman smiled the same smile.

"When I couldn't think of something to say, you were always there with suggestions. I think you would be better at my job than I am."

He gently replaced the photograph.

"But you aren't here."

This wasn't the life she promised him. She swore to be in his life forever, and she lied.

There isn't a day I don't miss the both of you."

He looked at the bible next to his keyboard.

"I don't know what is wrong with me today."

He dropped his heads into his hands and prayed.

"Father, I know you have a plan, but I don't understand why that day still haunts me. I don't know why she couldn't talk to me."

He raised his head and shut off the computer. The monitor glare lit the room in a blue glow until it blinked off, and darkness surrounded him.

"Well, at least it's Thursday, and I've got a few more days to get this done. It's just not happening today." He repeated himself.

He stood and grabbed his coat. He scanned the room. No one expected him anywhere or waited for him. What was the point? He walked out the door, his schedule already written, the same as every night. Go home, make dinner, turn on the TV, and fall asleep in his comfortable chair. At some point, get up and fall into a large cold bed.

Chapter Four

The alarm screamed out an offensive noise and shattered the security of the night. Jenna woke with a start, flailing towards the sound at the assault. Her heart thumped in her chest, and her breathing quickened.

"Oh crap, time for her medication."

She vaulted out of her bed. The soft carpet messaged her feet as reality set in. Her mother didn't need her pain pills any longer.

She wiped her forehead with a sweaty palm and leaned forward, elbows on her knees. She rubbed her temples and stared at the floor. Her stomach lurched.

Yesterday at this time, she helped her mother swallow her final morning pain pills. The frail woman's groans and retching competing for sound space over the machines. She fell back into her pillows and produced a week smile in a futile attempt to mask the pain before the medication kicked in.

In less than 24 hours, everything changed. Jenna's eyes filled with tears. How long could someone cry before they just ran out of tears? Would she eventually dehydrate into a pile of dust?

She descended back onto the pillows. How long before would before the reality didn't hit her like a crowbar? She was alone; mom was dead.

She looked at the clock.

She rolled over and sunk back down into the depths and descended into dreamless security.

A sunray crept into the room between a gap in the fluttering curtains. Small particles of dust caught in the beam performed a mysterious and ancient dance.

Jenna snuggled further under the large comforter, pulling the soft material up to her chin.

"You need to get up," she scolded herself, but the effort was too much. She followed the routine and hummed a song. Had parts of her mother joined the troupe? Her mom loved dancing and often waltzed around the house, arms around an invisible partner.

Jenna should move; the time came for her to leave this bed and deal with life. She groaned. Her body ached. The warmth and safety of this room made the future a surreal suggestion.

"I know, mom, I have to move. I need to eat. I need to figure out my life." She ran her hands through the dancers.

"Maybe I can choreograph."

She rolled over and paused.

Her stomach growled, and for the first time, the idea of food didn't cause her to want to throw up.

A groan escaped her throat as she rose to her feet. Her knees wobbled as she applied her weight on them.

"Okay, I will try. I will at least get out of bed and take a shower."

Water cascaded down her body and her mind shut down. Liquid fingers massaged her skin and scalp while steam rolled around the enclosure, dancing a ballet.

The shower started to cool, forcing her to get out. She slipped into clean clothes and stood straight for the first time in days. She wiped condensation from the mirror and studied her face.

"Who am I now? I don't even know me." She leaned in to get a closer look.

"Who are you?"

"Damn, what do I do now? I may have to find a job or something to keep me busy." She concentrated on the airborne particles floating in a beam of light above her.

"Oh, mom, what now? I don't have a clue who I am anymore or even who I want to be."

She slunk to the kitchen, cooked an egg, and looked at her mother instructions; phone the bank, the church, and someone to get the hospital bed.

"One thing at a time." She rubbed her temple and took a deep breath.

"Just one step at a time."

She dialed the number for the medical equipment supplier followed by the bank. Two men arrived and took the bed away. Jenna stifled a few tears as the act cemented her loss.

She picked up the phone for the dreaded final task.

"Hi, this is Jenna Caryl. Can I talk to Reverend Thomas?"

Too soon, a deep baritone voice filled her ear.

"Jenna, I'm so glad you finally called. I've been waiting for you to let me know when we could schedule your mother's memorial. She set it all up before her passing," he divulged.

"I know she told me in her letter. Why didn't you tell me when you were here?" She rubbed the back of her neck, messaging the giant knot which had taken residence there.

"It wasn't the time, and I knew you'd call when you were ready," Syrupy sympathy dripped from his words.

Jenna lowered her arm, her hand in a fist and her jaw muscle flexed

"I just think it would have been nice if someone let me know." The flatness in her voice echoing off the walls.

"Or even asked my opinion. That would have been nice too."

Silence dominated the phone line.

"Did you hang up on me?"

"I think you need to come and see me. I think we have..." An edge of hope shadowed his voice.

"How about now?" She burst in.

She glanced down at her paper. With a bank meeting this afternoon, she wouldn't be able to stay at the church very long, and she grinned. The minister consented, and Jenna ran out of the house within five minutes. She wanted this over.

She grabbed the papers and noted the two personal correspondence her mother wrote to her. She held her breath and touched the surfaces of them. Should she take them? She yelped as one of the envelops sliced into her skin.

"Well, that answered that question."

She left them where they laid and raced to the car to escape. Maybe getting out of the house would make her feel better.

She held the steering wheel tight, her knuckles a stark white color and she concentrated on the road. Shadows reached out to her from familiar places as she sped by them, blurs along her journey. Her eyes never wavered from the black pavement in front of her. She didn't need reminding, her mind overflowed with memories. She switched on the radio and lost herself in the addictive melody of a pop tune. She filled her lungs and let the air drain out

She turned a corner, and the whitewashed church loomed in front of her. Her foot refused to push down the pedal, and the car slowed. Memories poured over her and a pain shot through her shoulders. She parked the car and messaged her knotted muscles.

Mama called the congregation her "village." The church sustained her at every turn with faith, family, and employment.

When times were hard, the congregation brought food and help with bills. They came when her mother needed a shoulder to cry on and celebrated with her mother in her little victories.

The smell of rain overcame here when she opened the car door.

She concentrated on the large wood entryway.

She grew up under the congregation's watchful eye. Would they still be there for her? Did she even want them to be?

An ache in her back crept up her spine, and she put her hand on her lower back and pushed.

She conceded the people inside mourned her mother death, but not like she did. How could they understand? She slipped into the building, sweat trickled down her temple. The thick smell of wood polisher ambushed her senses. She slinked forward, and people emptied into the hallway; hands reached out in hugs and touches. Jenna pulled her arms around her and squeezed through the group. Voices bombarded her ears, and she dropped her head, and she longed for relief from the outpour. Why couldn't she just be left alone? She accepted a few hugs and bit her tongue when people offered prayers.

One by one, they offered her stories of her mother's kindness and compassion.

"Hi, Jenna." Pastor Thomas' voice directed her eyes to the man and pulled to safety from the sea of mourning co-workers. She followed him into the wood-paneled room. The smells of this room, wood, and incense, in the past, comforted her, but today it just piled more pain on her heart.

"How are you doing today?"

Jenna took a seat across from him. An image of Jesus hung on a cross behind him. Jenna glared at the figure while the minister pulled out papers and placed them in front of Jenna.

"This is what she wanted. She has written it all out, right down to the music and flowers."

Jenna nodded again. Could she object? Add something, or take it away?

"She paid for it all a while back so you wouldn't have to worry about a thing."

"Then why am I here?" she put her fingertips on the pile and pushed the papers back at him. He opened the file and pulled out a small white envelope, similar to the others.

"Because she also asked me to make sure you are okay. She worried about you," The reached over and placed one of his hands over hers. "She knew you didn't spend time with other people, and it troubled her. She didn't know how to tell you to go live your life."

Jenna pulled her hands away and set them in her lap.

"She also didn't know how to prepare you for this. She felt selfish for keeping you with her, but your presence made her feel both better and worse. You gave her strength on the hard days, a reason to keep fighting."

Jenna turned away and scanned the room, the man's voice droned on but became just background noise. An inspirational comic taped to the computer caught her attention. A boy sat on the fence with his dog next to him. She read the words

"We only live once," the black and white boy told her pet. The pet answered his owner, "Wrong, we only die once, we live every day."

She swallowed down a sob, and the man's voice drew her back in.

"She struggled knowing her illness kept you from doing the things people your age should be experiencing. She didn't want to rob your time as a young adult but also didn't want to rob you of time with her, knowing she wasn't going to be around much longer."

She turned and peered into his blue eyes.

"I'm fine, just let me know when you have an opening for this thing," The unemotional sternness of her voice surprised her, so unfeeling and business-like.

"Well, I'd like to let the congregation know since she was a part of our church family." Pastor Thomas pulled out a datebook and suggested a date two weeks from today. Jenna nodded. A tear dropped into her lap, and she swatted it away

"Are we through?" Jenna stood.

"Yes, but I'd really like to take you to lunch. Just you and I, and maybe we could just chat."

37

"No. I've got more things to do," she grabbed her purse from the floor. "I'll be in touch."

The minister stepped out from behind his desk towards Jenna.

"You know, I remember how scared, and alone your mom felt after your father died," he inched closer.

"So, when she told me her diagnose, she explained she never wanted you to go through what she did."

Jenna pulled her bag in front of her and covered it with both her arms.

"Yeah, well, she didn't manage to do it, did she? She may set me up financially, but emotionally I think she missed the mark."

The minister reached out and took Jenna's arm before she could flee.

"She wanted me to give you this."

He handed her an envelope, a twin to the one yesterday.

Jenna grabbed the offering, turned, and burst out of the room. People lined the hallway like vultures. She pushed past them before anyone could talk. She rushed to the security and sanctity of her car. She needed to lock the world out. She couldn't stand another person's sympathetic words or touches.

She put the vehicle in drive, and the tires screeched as she looked at the church in the rearview mirror.

She arrived at the bank early for her meeting.

She cuddled down into the bucket seat as people scurried by on their way to someplace else.

"When will I feel like myself again? I know I will, but when?"

A woman with a stroller pulled and pushed it up the curb. Jenna studied the process. The woman accomplished her task and scurried away. Jenna peered across to the passenger seat, and her mother's last note beckoned her. What possessed her mother to write it? How could she be okay? Five years and now what? Calls from friends stopped after too many canceled lunches and dinners. They didn't understand and even the people who sort of did, eventually grew tired of being stood up, but her mother needed her. The missed bridal showers and baby showers marked days she stymied while her friend's lives moved forward. She gave up everything to take care of her mother. Her mother begged her to hire someone, but how could she do that? This was her mother. She lost track of the multitude of lies she told to make her mother feel better. Were they really a sin? Her main concern grew weaker with each breath and needed her strength to battle cancer. She refused to hire someone; no stranger would do her duty. Her mother put her life on hold as a single mom, so how could she return the sacrifice and be there when Mama needed her. She reasoned it was just a temporary hold, but now with the grip gone, she couldn't just go back to the way things were.

She picked the letter up and admired the handwriting. The windows fogged up and erased the outside world. The sounds of ongoing life leaked into the car and Jenna ignored them. She turned the paper over in her hand before she finally opened it.

Her mother repeated words from the first letter and begged for her to rejoin life.

"I need you to take a trip, relax. You have given up living your life to care for me, and it is time for you to be selfish and take control. Please, go somewhere even for just a weekend."

Her mother found a new category to push, but how could she relax? How could her mother suggest it?

Minutes bled into each other, and a quick glance at the clock signaled time to go inside.

People crowded the bank lobby while the scent of lavender filled the air from an unseen source. She approached a well-dressed woman at one of the windows and gave her name. The woman led her into a down a small hallway lined with windowed offices. She chatted away, carefully teetered on her thin high heeled shoes. She turned into an office motioned her to sit. A trail of perfume remained much like the trail left by a slug. Across from Jenna, a slim man with a bad comb-over and thick glasses stared at her. The subtle papery metallic smell of money filled the office around her as a filtered light penetrated the room through a tinted window.

"Well, Jenna," he grabbed papers off his desk and threw them in a drawer. "Your mother was a longtime member of this bank, and I talked to her many times, especially in the last few years. I'm sorry for your loss. I know things got bad quick. Wonderful woman, just a wonderful woman."

He whispered the last words as if avoiding the ghosts and fates. He placed his fingers on the wood surface and drummed his fingers.

"She set you up nicely," He searched the desktop, moved shuffled some invoices, and smiled as he found what he was looking for.

"After your father died, she told me she never wanted you to go through what she did, so..." His voice trailed off as he opened the folder. He licked his finger and thumbed through the stack. He grinned, shut the folder, and handed the packet to Jenna.

"The house mortgage is paid off or will be in a week or so once the papers are filed." He turned and shifted in his seat. He proceeded to pile more papers on her and droned on in a dry soft voice. With each handout, he indicated where she needed to sign.

"It'll take time for the insurance money to get allocated, but then you will be set for a very long time." He reached into another drawer and pulled out another sheet of paper.

"She also has been putting money in a saving account to help tide you over until the other funds came through."

She placed the pen back on the desk and shook her hand to get the blood to flow back in it.

"So, what now?"

"Well, financially, you're set, but she did ask me to give you this."

He presented her with another envelope.

"Oh my gosh, are you kidding me?"

She recognized the curly handwritten name on the front, and an involuntary gasp escaped her mouth.

"This is just not the first one, not even the first one today." She accepted the envelope, thanked him, and forced a smile.

"Are we done?"

"Yes, but I must ask, are you okay?" He leaned towards her and stared deep into her eyes. "Your mother worried about you since you don't have family left and she wasn't sure about other relationships."

"I'm fine, dammit, I wish everyone would quit asking me!"

The words exploded out of Jenna's throat, and she regretted her lack of control. He stood up behind his desk as Jeanna rose. He didn't mean anything, and really the blame belonged with her mother; 'sorry' didn't change things despite how many people said it.

"Okay, well, yes, we are done. Thank you for coming in," the man extended his right hand, and Jenna accepted the gesture.

She rushed out of the bank, the new letter from her mother tight in her hand.

Safe in the car, she threw the letter on the passenger seat, alongside the previous note. She messaged the back of her neck and rolled her head around.

"Sorry mom, I just can't read another one of your letters right now." She punched the car into gear, and the tires squeal. She needed someplace to hide where she didn't see pity in people's eyes.

She arrived home and walked up the stairs to take a nap.

Chapter Five

Jenna descended the stairs towards the living area of the home. She stopped on the landing and scanned the area below her. The medical bed no longer occupied the space, but indents on the floor showed where it had been. She moved down the stairs and, circled around to her mother's desk.

"Might as well do this now." she opened the desk and pulled out the letters given to her by the banker. Tears clouded her vision.

"Mom, I'm not sure I can do this," she wiped her cheek and plopped down in a nearby chair. She put her hand on her stomach as it lurched.

A faint familiar perfume scented the area, and she felt sick. She leaned forward, and her eyes darted around the room. Everything appeared so familiar and yet so foreign.

"I have to get out of here," Jenna pulled air into her lungs and stood. She grabbed the back of the chair to steady herself as her head swam.

She regained her balance and rushed to the entryway. She felt another wave of nausea caused her to pause.

"I've got to get a hold of myself."

She reached for her bag. Next to it hung its twin. Images of an afternoon outing rushed through her mind, just an average weekend day, with her mother. They laughed as each picked the same bag and purchased them together like two best friends. Jenna grabbed both bags and rushed out the door.

She drove around the small town; every sidewalk overflowed with mothers and their young children. Jenna turned from the happy families. She realized a layer of wetness coated her cheek.

Signs of life faded into trees and fields as she continued to drive. She stopped at an intersection and forgot to go. Tears blurred her vision and created an impressionist painting of the surrounding area. She recognized the town's final crossroads, and her heart thumped in her chest. She gripped the steering wheel and willed her foot to hit the gas. Could she leave the only place she ever lived?

"On. Off. On. Off" the red light blinked a rhythm of heartbeats as they slowed and stopped forever.

She turned her head and studied each road. For the first time in her life, she questioned which one would take her to her future. She wrapped her arms around herself. Which crossroads took her to the happy ending her mother pushed for?

She looked right at the road. This one meandered along the river, and eventually back to the safety of her home. Along the way, breathtaking views of the river and mountains beyond made the extra travel worth it. As a child, she biked this path with friends and ventured into the murky waters. Memories of youth and friendships accompanied this memory but also emphasized how much things changed.

"I don't blame you, mama, but I do miss those days." Jenna let a tear fall.

She turned her head and looked left. Over the years many lives were lost to its twisty turns and drops, including her father. The forbidden highway and freedom pulled at her. No one could stop her or be angry if she tried. She closed her eyes and felt the cold air rush past her while she navigated the treacherous terrain. The smell of pine trees and dust polluted her sinuses.

"I wonder if he was thinking about mom and me? Did he feel pain? Is he with mom now?"

She looked forward, where the gray concrete rose and fell in a long ribbon as it disappeared with the limitations of sight. Despite 16-years of driving, she journeyed only a short distance down this path, never further than she could return the same day. Many of her friends got on the road and never looked back. Did she have that dream? She struggled to remember, but only sure that cancer robbed her of her dreams. She no longer remembered what she wanted from life; cancer stole her time and ambitions.

Behind her, ran the road home, to her security, or it did until a few days ago. What did she have anymore? Sure, she owned a car and a house, but no one to share these things. Her mother ensured her financial future, but what of her personal future? She rubbed her arms and gulped. At her age, she should have someone to share a life with.

Jenna pulled the car over and got out. She crept into the middle of the intersection and sat down. The smell of the pine trees brought memories of Christmas' and camping trips. She closed her eyes and brought up images of sitting around a fire with her church family.

She detected the faint sweet smell as a storm approached. She looked towards the horizon and the distance she spied dark clouds. She grasped an old tube of lipstick, fished out of her mother's purse.

"You are here," she wrote in her mother's favorite bright red makeup on the light cement. She felt wetness on her cheek, not sure if it came from tears or light rain.

Streetlights popped on around her as the evening approached. Shadows danced in the light breeze as the weather changed, and Jenna wrapped her arms around her. A chill ran up her back, and she returned to the car.

In the sanctity of the vehicle. Jenna picked up the first letter and held it in her hand. She studied it and ran her fingers over the letters. She felt the shallow indent where the pen scratched across the surface. Rain pelted the car with large juicy drops, and she released the contents/

"My Darling Daughter," the note began. "I know you have probably already read the letter that I put out for you when I passed, but I just can't stop myself from writing. I so want to be there with you, but I know the time will come when I can't be. This letter is about the future I want for you. First, I assure you that my funeral and burial have been planned well in advance and you don't have to do any planning. The church has my instructions, and the only thing I ask is that you just let them do as I have asked whether you agree or not. It is my wishes."

"How could you do that?" Jenna wadded up the note and threw it across the car. She put her head in her hands.

She startled when a honk interrupted her anguish. She whipped around looking for the source and realized she was the offender. She took a deep breath and reclaimed the paper.

"I was there for you for years, and you take away my last chance to care and love you and show you! How could you do that? When I was first diagnosed, I prayed for recovery but started to prepare for this day, just in case. The bills are paid off, the house and cars are set up to be yours after you meet with the bank and sign your name on the line."

Jenna looked out the window again. Could she live in that house without her mother? Could she overcome emptiness and ghosts?

"I also have a bit of money saved in a bank account for you and an insurance policy that is also currently stored at the bank for you."

Jenna stopped and scanned the pages. Her mother wrote about insurance policies and important people to be contacted before she signed it "Love, Mom."

She picked up the second letter and ripped open the paper. Again, the tome started with "My Dearest Daughter."

The note reiterated her mother's wish for her to be happy and to find love. "Go on a vacation" seemed to be the primary wisdom she imparted to Jenna. Jenna scanned the black letters, only reading a few words. She didn't need to read each word as it all blended together.

Near the end of the two-page tome, something caught her eye.

"Now my wishes for you, my beloved daughter. I need to know you will be okay and you live your life and not dwell in the past. I need you to take a trip, relax, clear your head, and plan a happy future. You deserve this after all the time you have given up and the life you have forfeited while you cared for me. Please, just go somewhere even for just a weekend. I know you, and I know you will wallow, and that is the last thing I need or want. Please, I can't beg you enough, do something out of character for you, and find your peace. I want you to smile again."

Jenna threw the letter next to her wrinkled sister on the passenger seat and looked out the window.

"What the hell was she thinking? I can't just leave."

"Why not?" a familiar voice filled the car. "She said you should, so what is stopping you?"

The blinking light rhythmically bounced its beams off the windshield, and Jenna again picked up the note.

"Go, have fun, live your life; be happy."

Jenna threw the paper on the passenger seat and started the vehicle. The purring engine collaborated with the signal light and screamed at her to honor her mother. How could she deny a dying woman's request?

"Shut up!" the silent car filled with her voice. She slipped the car into gear, and the vehicle moved forward. She stopped in the middle of the crossroads, the lipstick words under her. Which way? She did a U-turn and proceeded towards home. Raindrops like tears fell from the dark sky.

She arrived at home. She glared at the structure.

"You are now a house, not a home anymore."

Jenna walked into the house, flipped on the light, and threw both purses on the couch. She plopped down

The night wore on, and Jenna paced around the house. She meandered into each room and stopped. She reached the door of her mother's room and placed her hand on the knob. Dizziness clouded her brain, and her stomach jumped.

"Not yet."

She shut off the lights and returned to her room for the night.

Chapter Six

Paul kept the smile pasted on his face until Mr. and Mrs. Larson left. He picked up his pen and jotted a few notes on the paper in front of him.

"If you want to go to lunch, now would be a good time."

Paul raised his head to see his admin fill-in, Rachel, in front of him.

He nodded and put the pen down.

"I always wonder if they will listen to me and do the work that needs to be done."

Rachel smiled and turned back to her desk.

Why would they listen to him? He wasn't in a relationship, and his marriage ended in the worst way possible. He leaned back in the chair, his arms behind his head. He spied his framed degree on the wall and smiled.

He leaned forward and with the aid of his desk, stood up. He stretched, and an involuntary groan escaped his lips. He inhaled deeply.

"Yeah, I think I will get out of here and grab a bite." He didn't really have any place to go, but past experiences told him being here alone with Rachel could become very uncomfortable very fasts.

He glanced at his calendar and noted his next appointment in two hours. Large red letters wrote across the last week of the month "Mexico," and he smiled. He needed the trip despite the fact most of the days were filled with missionary work.

"Three weeks."

He knocked on the desk as he walked out the door.

Chapter Seven

Days blended together like a red sock in a laundry load of whites, days tumbled together and stained by hours of despair.

Jenna drove around in search of somewhere she could be alone and free of the ghosts in her mind. She clutched the wheel and pushed the pedal, but the rest ran on autopilot. Her head and body hurt from days with nothing to do.

She almost missed the small coffee shop on the edge of town but noticed it at the last minute and pulled into the parking lot.

The aroma of coffee and frying meat greeted her when she entered the small establishment. Large picture windows created a flood of natural light in the dining room while walls displayed artwork from local high school students. Jenna studied some of the art, some of the last names looked familiar, but she couldn't say why. A secluded booth in the corner beckoned her and once seated, she ordered coffee from a cheerful waitress.

She stared into the black depths of her coffee cup for answers. She squirmed in her seat as memories of moments exploded in her mind. She swished the coffee around in her cup and reminded her of a fortune teller with tea leaves. Was her future as black as this liquid?

"I can't just give up. I have to get out of this funk."

She placed the mug down as people turned and looked. She forced a smile as they returned to their meals. She shook her head. She wasn't home and needed to be aware of talking out loud.

She pulled out one of the letters from her purse and with a flick, the triangular clasp snapped open.

"Okay, mom, what more do you have to say?" she pulled out the stiff white paper.

"My darling daughter, at this point, you have probably read two previous letters. There is so much I should tell you and so little time. I know no matter how many letters I write, it won't replace me being there for your big life moments in person, but I know we have a loving God and he will allow me to see from Heaven."

Jenna gazed out the window. How could her mother believe in a deity who allowed so much pain in the end? A God who left a woman broke and alone with a small child? The constant knot in her stomach jumped. Jenna grabbed a glass of water and gulped the contents. She took a deep breath and slowly let it out.

"If there even is a God?"

"There is, and you apparently need my prayers," an older woman in the next booth cooed. "I'm sorry you are hurting, but he does have a plan."

She smiled as Jenna turned and scowled. Old eyes looked back with sympathy and care.

"Sorry," Jenna sputtered and lowered her eyes. The woman nodded.

Jenna gazed out the window and swatted away tears. The waitress came around with the coffee pot and refilled her cup.

She took a deep breath and picked the letter back up.

"By now, you have also figured out I want to make sure you were financially in a better position than I found myself after your father died. I don't know how much you remember; you were so young, just eight years old."

Her mother waxed on about how she needed more time, and her wishes for Jenna's future happiness. She shared memories of life as a young wife and mother, and adventures the family shared before the unexpected death of her father. She wrote of feeling love and loss, how even with pain, she stated again how much she loved the life she lived, and the memories.

"You were my sole reason for going on, the only thing that got me through your father's death. And while I believe you probably think you don't have anyone, what you don't know is that you have the village. You have people all around you, and I will be watching you."

The writing on the page became less legible, and Jenna recognized in the handwriting her mother's struggle and desperation; to write everything before cancer stole her writing ability.

Despite her hesitation, Jenna savored them. She folded the letter and slipped it into her back pocket for later.

She paid the bill and retreated to her car as the encompassing darkness set in. The onset of a summer rainstorm softened the view outside as a passing car's headlights created moving shadows inside of the vehicle. Raindrops pounded on the roof and produced a song. Jenna listened for any rhyme or rhythm in the beats. Was it a disco hit from the past or a modern backdrop for a famous rapper?

She reached for the ignition and pulled back. Where did she have to go? Time marched on and stood still all at the same time. She leaned back in the seat and inhaled. Tick. Tock. Tick. Tock.

She held the air for five beats and let it go.

"Oh mama, where do I go from here?"

She started the car and pulled onto the street, not sure of her destination, she soon found herself back in front of her residence.

Tiredness crept into her bones; only a climb similar to the Matterhorn stood between her and her bed. She paused on the landing and surveyed the living room below. The view familiar, yet so foreign; the same sight she saw her entire life. Her mother taught her reading, cuddled up in her mother lap warmed by flames in the fireplace. The same chair she sat in the last days of her mother's life.

Friends visited her, and they played on the same coffee table after school, while her mother baked cookies.

She experienced her first kiss with a boy from her sixth-grade class in the love seat, while her mother cooked dinner a few steps away.

She completed her climb and drifted towards her room. A faint smell of perfume floated from her mother's room and sent both a chill and comfort down Jenna's body. She touched the closed door and continued into her room. She undressed and slithered into the warmth of her bed. Jenna laid on her back, hands folded on her chest while she concentrated on the sounds of the house.

"In. Out. Repeat," she chanted.

She pulled the covers over her head so she could hide in the folds of the blankets and shut the world out.

"Okay God, you took my mom. You threw my life into a tailspin. You can at least let me get a good night of sleep."

Hours passed, and sleep evaded her again.

"Okay, maybe a warm glass of milk."

Jenna walked to the kitchen and stuck a glass of milk in the microwave. A bottle of her mother's painkiller pills perched on the counter.

"I bet one won't hurt." She fished a white tablet out and popped the pill into her mouth. Her limbs were heavy as the strong medication kicked in while she stumbled back to bed.

"Oh my God, what if I took too much?" She struggled into her bed. "No one will find me in time; in fact, no one will find me at all."

Jenna lost her battle to stay away, and the pill took her into a vibrant dream where her mother led her on a journey of color and lights.

Chapter Eight

Jenna awoke, her room bathed in red and orange, a whisper of her mother's voice resonated in her ear. She reached up and rubbed her forehead. Out the window, nature painted a morning masterpiece, but she turned away from the headache-inducing light. One hand stroked her tightened abdomen as she shielded her eyes from the abusive sun with the other. She rolled away from the window.

Red characters glowed from the alarm clock and reported date and time. Ten days passed since the death. Time moved on with her left in a whirlwind of nothingness.

"Oh, mom, I wish you were here to guide me."

She touched the three letters on her nightstand and ensured they were nearby. She grabbed one and reread it for the thousandth time. Her mother's words created a feeling of love. She pictured her tired and sick mother as she wrote words meant as a lifeline for future Jenna. In this letter, her mother included medical history information Jenna might need in the future.

Jenna kissed the sheet of paper and laid it back on the nightstand next to its sisters.

The light in the room turned golden as the sun broke the horizon. In a few hours, everyone would say a final goodbye to her mother. She rolled to her back and pulled the covers up.

Since the death, the phone rang, and doorbells chimed while she hid in this room, not moving. Today she couldn't avoid the hoards.

Would people come to her house? She meant to ask someone; one more of the many tasks still on her list too big to tackle.

Jenna dropped her legs over the side and groaned as she sat up. She needed to face the day and be the strong woman her mother kept writing about in her letters.

Jenna arrived at the church faster than expected. Outside the entrance, people hugged each other. She scanned the building for somewhere she could slip in undetected. She exited the car and smoothed down her black top and slacks. The outfit dated back to her younger days when she attempted to be a part of the "goth" kids in high school. She glanced at her reflection in the side mirror of the car and hoped it would be appropriate today. Her mother wouldn't care what she wore and would have approved even jeans and a tee-shirt, but she no longer could make those concessions for her.

A lone figure advanced towards her, and Jenna recognized the form of Pastor Thomas. He reached her and pulled her into an embrace. She stood stiff as the minister rubbed her back. He pulled back.

"We need to go."

He put a guiding hand on her back. Jenna moved forward and attempted to understand what he was saying. She reached up and rubbed her ear. Near the front of the chapel, he motioned her to sit.

A polished wood casket dominated the front of the sanctuary bookended by her pictures of her mother in happier times.

"I don't want to be here. Why is this happening to me?" Jenna's chin quivered, and she rubbed her hands together.

Green eyes stared out at her from the photograph, and Jenna heard the faint voice of her mother, 'move on and rejoin the world.'

"I know mom." She lowered her eyes and rubbed her sweaty palms on her slacks.

The service began, and Jenna slumped down, her hands still and folded in her lap. Person after person spoke of her mother's generosity and kindness. Stories told, prayers recited, while Jenna sat motionless and silent, just breathing. She stared straight at the coffin and avoided looking towards the speakers.

Men from the church came forward and picked up the box, and Jenna closed her eyes. Pastor Thomas approached her and placed a hand on her shoulder.

"We need to go out to the graveside now."

Jenna peered up into his eyes, her eyes dry and distant. She stumbled as she rose and grabbed the back of the pew.

"Jenna, we need to go," he repeated, and she obeyed.

They entered the small cemetery behind the church, and the minister said a few more prayers. Jenna gripped her stomach as a wave of nausea engulfed her. Soon her mother would be just another marble slab with a name and dates on it. People touched her arm and uttered words she didn't comprehend.

"Jenna, let me get you some dinner," Pastor Thomas pleaded. She shook her head, her eyes unable to pull away from the hole in front of her.

"No, I think I just want to go home now," she turned, and her legs started to move away from the hole.

"Okay, but I have something for you in the church." He put his hand on her elbow and directed her in a new direction

Jenna followed him to his office. She rubbed the back of her neck while he pulled open a drawer and pulled out a bible.

"Thanks, but no thanks," she raised her hand and turned to leave.

"Wait," He grabbed her arm, and she spun around. "This was your mother's, and she asked me to give this to you."

Jenna stared at the book, frozen, and after a few beats, accepted the gift.

"Why didn't you give it to me the other day?" she asked.

"I was instructed to give it to you after the funeral." He peered down at his now empty hands. "She insisted I do it this way. I tried to change her mind, but she was adamant. You know how convincing she could be when she wanted to be."

Jenna nodded. Her mother could talk people into things.

"Okay, well, thank you," she left, the bible held close to her chest with both hands. She scampered across the green cemetery and with each step, acutely aware she stepped on other people's mothers.

Jenna clicked the television remote, and it sprang to life. She threw the device on the bed and relished in the distraction. She rubbed her head. It hurt to think.

A soft glow from the TV lit the room.

The bible laid just a few feet behind her, separated by a wrinkle of the blanket.

An advertisement for a new cancer drug sent tears streaming down her face.

"What the hell? This is crazy!"

She rolled over, and the bible pressed deep into her stomach. She tugged the book from underneath her and tossed it onto the floor. The bible thudded as it hit the floor, and an envelope ejected from somewhere in the pages.

Jenna stared at the paper while canned laughter played in the background. She leaned down, snatched the item, and pulled it to her chest. Why did her mother keep doing this to her and how many was she going to find. She held her breath for a beat before she drew in a deep breath and dared to look at the note. She pulled it away and noted her name scrawled across the front.

"Oh, my God! What the hell are you doing to me?"

She moved to a sitting position and opened the letter.

"My darling daughter." Jenna rolled her eyes but continued.

"I know you're hurting right now, and I wish I could make the pain go away, but it is the curse of every mother to know their child is suffering and unable to make it go away. I know someday you will understand. It hurts when they are in pain, and you would do anything to make it stop if you could. I hope you have healed a little and perhaps you can even smile sometimes now. It's okay if you do feel happy. I know when I lost your father, it took me a long time to smile when I thought of him. Even years later I sometimes thought of something I wanted to share with him, and a tinge of pain hit me like a brick, not as bad, but still, there, it would always take me by surprise. I know you will get there also, but I know when you are in the middle of the pain, it's hard to think past today and towards the future."

Jenna crumpled the paper and threw it with the others. "What do you know?"

She slammed back into the soft mattress.

"And yet, you didn't prepare me, did you?" She laid looking at the ceiling, her hands curled in fists and her heart beating exploding in her chest.

How could she be mad at someone who hadn't left by choice?

In a single movement, she stood up and stomped across the hall. The door to her mother's room loomed in front of here. She rubbed the back of her neck with a sweaty palm and grabbed the doorknob. She paused before flung open the door and stood in the entryway. She stepped into the room, and the faint odor of floral perfume and dust filled her nostrils.

"This is my house now, and this is my room, and I should go in any time I want to."

She pounded the door as her initial opening bounced back at her, the thin wood veneer cracked, and the impact created an indent.

"We were a team, and you said you would always be here for me!" She passed over the entry way, he hand balled at her side. "But you didn't fight hard enough, did you? You didn't tell me what it was like. You could have warned me!"

Jenna marched across the tidy room and glared at her mother's nightstand. She picked up the last book her mother read before she could no longer concentrate. Her reading spectacles sat ready for service to finish the read. A glass of water sat untouched beside a pill bottle, the water surface dirty with dust and a few dead bugs. A lamp bought by Jenna at a craft fair years ago as a Mother's Day gift completed the items on the table. Jenna looked around; the room reflected her mother; the walls covered in serene beach paintings, and a frilly pink duvet covered the bed with matching curtains. Her mother loved this room and often called it her sanctuary.

Anger exploded through Jenna, and she threw the book across the room. It left a visible dent in the wall, but it didn't make her feel any better. She needed more. She picked up the little table and threw it across the room. The lamp crashed to the floor, and the sound of shattering glass filled her head. Water ran down another of the light pink walls from the drinking glass.

"You could have tried harder," she screamed.

Jenna reached across the bed and pulled the comforter spread. The sound or ripping cloth fueled her anger.

"You should have told me it would hurt like this" She scanned the room for her next victim.

She opened the closet door. Flashes of color as she pulled the neatly hung clothes from their homes and to the floor.

"What am I supposed to do with all these?"

She stalked to the dresser and yanked out the drawers. Panties and bras scattered across the floor like little animals looking for shelter. They joined the rest of the clothes, the floor covered in a plethora of garments.

"You don't know what this is like! You didn't lose your mother!"

Jenna waded across the room and pulled a heavy mirror from the wall. She heaved it against the dresser. Seven years of bad luck reverberated through the air.

"You left me an orphan! Did you think of that?"

Jenna paused, exhausted, and surveyed her work.

"I'm sorry, momma." She picked up one of her mother's favorite dresses and raised it to her nose. Laundry detergent and dust crossed her mind. Tears dampened her cheek. "I know it wasn't your fault."

Jenna threw herself across the disheveled bed and broke down sobbing.

"I'm losing it. I'm losing it."

Shadows moved across the wall. Jenna straightened back up, stood up and without a sound, walked out of the room. She shut the door behind her and paused. She lowered her head and slinked back to her own room.

"I am so sorry, mama, but...."

How could she finish that apology? Wasn't she at least a little justified? And it wasn't like mama would ever know anyway.

And didn't her mother do the same to Jenna's life, destroy it?

Jenna slipped under her purple comforter and grabbed the remote control. She began to surf through the channels again.

Chapter Nine

Paul flipped through the channels and landed on a music video. Nothing sparked interest, but it helped to have the distraction. He dug into his microwave bowl of chili, cheese, and sour cream. He wrinkled his nose and snorted when some large woman pushed her tushy towards the camera.

He searched for inspiration.

"Well, it is not coming from there." He shook his head and chuckled. He changed channels and settled on a popular sitcom.

He leaned back further into the blush sofa. He ran his hands through his thick brown hair and rubbed the back of his neck, his skin still slick from a recent jog in the nearby forest. Usually, that was enough of an inspiration to start this process, but tonight it yielded nothing.

He shook his head to clear away the anxieties. He couldn't let himself obsess over it; something would come. He looked back at the television screen as canned laughter filled the room.

"You would have loved this show."

He gazed over at a picture of his small family hanging on the wall above the set.

"But you just weren't strong enough to stay and find out."

He ground his teeth and held his hands together in front of him.

He bowed and said a silent prayer.

"You know what I need, help me with this anger. Amen."

He glanced at the photo one more time, though it was burned into his brain. He stood up and stretched. How could he continue to help people with relationships and the death of loved ones when he couldn't do it himself? He shook his head and rubbed his hands in front of him.

"Each person is different." He reminded himself. Going through the steps himself helped him to be better for those that needed him.

He crossed his arm in front of him as he separated the distance between him and the photograph. He stared into the women's eyes.

"Alexie would never have blamed you. I wanted to help you, but you wouldn't let me. I wish we could have talked and worked through it together. It wasn't your fault."

He dropped his head.

"I hope you're not suffering. It's just hard for me sometimes to think of a life without you in it, but maybe it is time."

He reached over, kissed his fingers, and touched the picture woman's lips. He turned away and turned the lights off, making it harder to see anything except the glowing TV.

Chapter Ten

The warm sun warmed Jenna's. She looked down at her knobby knees. She scanned the area as the scent of the forest filled her nostrils, pine trees, and fresh wet earth. Ahead, a path ambled around bushes and pine trees. She spied her mother's figure a short distance ahead of her.

"Watch out," her mother instructed. "I don't want you to get tripped up while you are looking back at me."

A breeze messed with her hair and Jenna could smell an impending rainstorm. She turned up and noticed angry black clouds. Jenna picked up her pace as darkness started to make the path harder to see. He mother's voice got quieter, and she picked up her pace, but the distance continued to grow.

"Jenna, really?" her mother begged. "Come on; let's get home before we get drenched."

Jenna paused.

"I don't want to go back," she screamed into the wind. "And I am not going to!"

She stomped her foot down and crossed her arms in front of her.

Someone grabbed her shoulder. She turned and looked into her mother's eyes.

"Jenna, let's just find someone that can help us get out of here," she cooed. "Please, let's not just get stuck here and lost."

Jenna looked up at the top of the trees, and for the first time, noticed no sound around her. She wondered where the birds had gone, or even the sound of the breeze through the leaves. She turned to ask her mother if she knew, and the woman was gone.

"Mama!" She scanned the area, her voice desperate.

"Jenna, this is just a dream, but I told you I would always be with you."

Jenna woke in her bed. Sweat coated her back.

"Mom?" she called out into the empty room.

She turned on the lamp and searched the room for whatever pulled her from sleep. Nothing out of the ordinary.

On the table, the partially read letter called to her and she began reading.

"I know it's hard to face life after a tragedy. When your father died, I had you, and that got me through. You needed a mother, but I was lost, alone, and scared. What was I going to do? I needed to feed and clothe you. Your father and I never looked beyond the next week. We were young and healthy and on top of the world. We both were young, immortal, and happy. Nothing was going to happen to us. Until it did. As I recovered from the shock, I didn't have the luxury of time to help me heal and get a new plan. Because of my experience, I made sure, and you have time to figure out your future and the resources to get by without the mechanics of everyday life. However, even after I found a job, we were okay physically, I needed more healing emotionally. I found it helpful to talk to someone who wasn't family or a friend, someone who didn't treat me with kids-gloves; Someone impartial who would encourage me to pick up the pieces and move on I am sure; you should do the same. Someone who would say the hard things that I needed to hear. As I write this, I worry about you. I don't want you to face this alone, so please, ask Pastor Thomas for a name or look one up on the computer, but please, even just one time, go and talk to someone to help you. I can see you now, rolling your eyes at me now."

Jenna laughed. Her mother knew her so well. She laid the letter in her lap and felt the isolation suffocating her. She recognized bits and pieces of rage that played in the background of her emotions. Maybe her mother was right. She wiped a thin line of sweat from her forehead. She closed her eyes and concentrated on breathing.

She grabbed the phone and pulled up the Internet.

"Grief counselor" she typed into the browser and names jumped onto the screen. Armed with three names, she started to dial the number before.

"Oh, crap." She caught a glimpse of the clock, and the time stopped her hands mid-dial. They probably didn't want an appointment call in the middle of the night. She would have to wait until the morning.

She jotted the three names and phone numbers down and turned off the lamp. Maybe she could still get a little more sleep before the sunlight signaled the beginning of a new day. Images of comic book psychiatrists with notebooks and couches started to float around in her mind as she drifted off to another dimension for the rest of the night.

Jenna felt her lips turn up with the sound of a bird's song outside the window. She opened her eyes to the new day. She rolled over and stretched. A soft groan of pleasure escaped her, and she sat up. She gathered her notebook and studied the names listed on the notepad next to the letters.

"Do I need this? Or was I just tired and vulnerable?"

She looked at the pile of letters next to the list.

"Maybe all this talking to myself is proof she is right."

Jenna glanced at the list again. Her heart fluttered in her chest, and her mouth was dry.

Okay, mom, this one is for you, but then I feel like I don't have to do anything else you are asking me to do."

The clock glowed red with the time, 8:30 am, and Jenna grabbed the phone and dialed the first number. A woman informed her there were no openings for a few weeks, and Jenna thanked her before she hung up without an appointment.

"One down, two to go, then I would say maybe it's a sign you were wrong," she scowled at the letters.

The second number yielded more success, and she hung up with an appointment that afternoon.

Jenna jumped in the shower and washed three days of neglect off her body. The pulsating stream of hot water massaged her shoulders and fell in rivulets down her torso. The water pushed out all thoughts. Too soon, she stepped out and dried off. She wiped the steam off the mirror and looked at her face.

"Maybe talking to someone would be nice. At least it is nice to have somewhere to be again."

She ran a comb through her hair.

"You know, you are possibly going crazy." She leaned in and looked deeper into her eyes. "I know this is crazy, but I almost think I'm looking forward to this."

Dressed and ready, she walked through the house and noticed the silence didn't seem to have the same eerie feeling. She entered the kitchen, and the sight appalled her;

70

the counters covered with dirty dishes, leftover containers, and fast food bags.

"I have to get a hold of myself."

Her mother raised her better than this. She pulled a pan out of the cupboard and remembered how much she enjoyed and took pride in cooking, but cancer changed that, making it more of a chore. After the diagnosis, food preparation included making sure it was soft and bland enough to be digested by her mother. She counted each ingredient for health benefits, calories, or cancer-fighting properties.

She opened the refrigerator and made a mental note; it was time to go grocery shopping. She avoided the task, afraid to run into someone or see something that brought the torrent of tears back.

"Not that I ever forget," she mumbled.

She took a deep breath and shook her head.

Jenna threw unidentifiable items into the garbage cemetery before she found two eggs and bacon. She fried up her meager breakfast and sat at the dining room table. She looked across the oak plank to the seat her mother usually occupied. The house rule crossed her mind; while they both lived in this house, they sat together for breakfast and dinner as a family. Jenna smiled and took her last bite of bacon. She put the dishes in the overfull sink. If she left now, she could splurge on a cup of coffee on her way.

Jenna gathered her keys and purse, and she contemplated anything she should bring with her. She stopped, ran up to her room, and grabbed the stack of papers. Could these be shared with a stranger? She put them in her purse and sighed. She closed her eyes and wet her lips as she held the bag tightly to her chest before she rushed out the door.

Her stomach fluttered, and she sat still in the driver's seat.

"This is not going to be so bad." She rubbed her crossed arms and closed her eyes. "It's not like this woman is going to tie me down and hold me there. I can leave at any time I want."

She pulled out her keys and inserted them in the car ignition.

"Have faith," she whispered.

She threw her purse with the letters on her passenger seat.

"Okay, mom," she whispered. "I get it, and I'm going."

Chapter Eleven

Jenna slunk into the lobby of the therapist's office, and a small bell chimed her arrival.

She removed the letters from her purse and stuck them in the back pocket of her jeans.

The faint odor of jasmine and vanilla filled her nose, and she inhaled the intoxicating aroma. Paintings of red poppies and purple lilacs tastefully dotted the plain cream-colored walls. A muted green carpet gave the illusion of walking in a garden. Jenna crossed the room and sat down in an overstuffed red chair that matched the color of the painted poppies. She picked up a three-month-old pop culture magazine and flipped through the glossy pages. A story caught her eye, and she stopped. She scanned a few paragraphs before she advanced to the next story. Jenna thumbed through a few more pages and stopped on a photo of a well-known actress and her mother. She replaced the magazine to its home and took a deep breath. She scanned the room and drummed her fingers on her thigh. The folded envelops pushed on her butt cheek, and she reached down and rubbed them.

"Okay, mom, this is for you."

A short, stout woman sauntered into the room, and despite her diminutive size, oozed with an air of confidence and security.

"Jenna?" the woman advanced, hand extended in greeting. "So nice to meet you. I'm Wendy Achondo."

The woman's face split in half with a giant smile. Thick-lensed glasses over-exaggerated her eyes, and a strand of blond hair escaped a messy bun and framed her face.

"Please come into my office and let's chat," she motioned to Jenna.

Jenna slogged into the small intimate office. Bookshelves overflowed with different books; the titles spouted information on various mental illnesses and conditions. Wendy directed Jenna to another overstuffed chair and plopped down across from Jenna in its twin.

"So, Jenna, tell me why you are here today?"

Jenna shrugged her shoulders and looked at her hands in her lap. She swallowed and rubbed her hands together.

"Well, I know you told me on the phone you were having a hard time with the passing of your mother."

Wendy grabbed a notebook from the desk behind her. "Would you like to start by telling me what you are feeling right now?"

Jenna nodded and talked about her mother. She shared her life story and her sacrifices while she dealt while her mother went through the last stages of cancer.

"And I keep finding these letters that she wrote." She pulled out the letters and held them in her hands. She took a deep-felt a lump in her throat.

The room fell in silence, and Wendy reached for them. Jenna looked at the extended hand before she allowed the woman to take them. Wendy opened and looked at the writing. She gently folded the letters and asked if she could copy the notes to read them more in-depth after the session. Jenna nodded and took in a long deep breath. Jenna concentrated on Wendy's every move and never let the notes out of her sight.

"From what I was able to read from a quick scan, your mother wants you to live your life. She keeps saying that over and over and in many different ways," Wendy handed the originals back to Jenna.

"I know, but I don't know what to do. I took care of my mother; that's who I am."

Jenna caught a glimpse of the councilor as she scribbled notes on her pad.

"She didn't care about that I wanted to have a say in her funeral, or where she was buried or who would talk," Jenna spit out. Her hands grew cold, and she rubbed them together. She could feel sweat starting to seep onto her forehead.

Wendy watched Jenna, no expression on her face.

"Well, you have valid points, but do you think she did that as a way of cutting you out or as a way of trying to make it easier on you?" Wendy put her pen down. "Even these letters speak to a mother who is protecting her child from the pain she knows you are feeling."

Jenna lowered her head. Tears started down her cheeks.

"I'm in my early 30s; I don't have a job; I don't have a family," Jenna brushed the tears with her arm. "I don't have anything because I gave it up to help my mother."

Jenna stopped talking. She took a breath, and a dark silence crowded the room. She held her tongue as her mind screamed for the therapist to say something. Wendy picked her pen up and wrote more notes. Jenna remained mute.

"Okay, Jenna," the woman looked up, "I understand what you are saying, and I have to ask, what do you want to do about it? Do you honestly believe that your life work is done? Do you think this is the end of Jenna? And if it is, where do we go from here?"

Jenna looked over at Wendy and her brow furrowed. She swallowed hard.

"I don't know what you mean," Jenna bowed her head, her hands balled in her lap.

"Well, the way I see it," Wendy leaned back and put her notebook on the desk. "You are in your early 30s; you don't have any obligations. You don't have anyone or anything holding you back from a very fulfilling life. You could wallow in the sadness and anger you are feeling, and you will, for a time. That is to be expected."

Jenna held her breath as Wendy paused and leaned forward towards Jenna.

"Or you can decide to celebrate your mother's life by doing what she asked you to do. Show the world who your mother was through your actions. I read she wants you to live. She wants you to be happy; to find your family."

"I don't know," Jenna looked towards Wendy through a curtain of red curls, her head still lowered.

"I guess I want to know what the future holds for me." Jenna looked up and faced Wendy.

"We all do," Wendy chuckled. "But none of us knows that, yet we still make happy lives."

Wendy leaned back in her chair. She rested her elbows on the arms of the chair and her hands clasped in front of her. Jenna suppressed a giggle as Wendy made her think of a kindly old grandmother.

"I don't expect you to walk out of here 'cured' or not still upset, and we need to address those things."

She leaned towards Jenna.

"You are going through a lot, and I want to help. You're going to have good days and bad, and I want to teach you the tools to get you through and grow."

Jenna nodded, a slight smile crossing her lips.

"You have most of your life ahead of you and have time to figure out who you are and what you want to do." She stood up, walked to her desk, and grabbed some papers. She circled back and sunk back into her chair.

"I know you're pissed off, and that's normal. You may even be scared, and again that is normal. But it is also okay to feel joy and happiness. You can let yourself do that. It is okay."

Wendy looked deep into Jenna's eyes.

"We need to find who the new you is going to be. With new goals and new aspirations," Wendy reached out and put her hand on Jenna's. "And one of your mother's constant request was for you to take a trip, get out and some time for you to reboot. Have you considered that?"

Jenna shook her head, enthralled.

"Well, maybe you should just think about it. Just think, that is all. Just see if you can picture going anyplace."

Jenna nodded.

The session ended, and Jenna stuffed a reminder card for her next meeting and brochure in her purse.

"See you in two days," Wendy followed Jenna out into the lobby. She put her hand on her shoulder.

"You are going to get through this."

Jenna smiled and returned to her car. She turned the radio on, rolled down the windows to enjoy the sunshine and started humming to an upbeat tune before she caught herself.

Chapter Twelve

Jenna paced between the poppy and the lilac paintings. She looked closer and hunted for anything she missed in the last four appointments. Without thinking, she stepped over the potted plant that two weeks ago, she tripped over. Now the meetings highlighted her week, and she considered Wendy, a close friend.

"I pay her to listen and help me," she reminded herself, each time she walked through the door.

Wendy opened the door, and her smile made Jenna feel special. Jenna walked past Wendy, into the office, sat in the same chair and started the conversation.

"So, for the first time, I have been thinking of the future." Jenna bounced around in the chair.

"That's great, and how are you feeling?"

"Scared and yet, excited," Jenna settled down into the overstuffed chair. "I really do feel like I can start thinking about what I want to do, or where I want to be."

Wendy stood up and moved behind her wood desk and pulled out a pamphlet with a pad of paper. She started to write something on the pad.

"Are you going to give me medication?" Jenna looked at Wendy; a scowl started across her face. The smile drained from her face as a lump formed in her throat.

"Oh, no, sorry." Wendy smiled at Jenna. "I'm not even able to do that if I felt you needed it, which I don't."

She finished writing and handed Jenna the pamphlet across the desk.

"If you feel you need some, I can suggest it to your doctor, but I had something else in mind."

Jenna looked at the brochure with the picture of a fluffy white dog on the front. She turned and looked at Wendy. Her brow furrowed and she put the leaflet in her lap.

"Seriously?"

Wendy laughed a little as she sat back down across from Jenna.

"I think an emotional support animal could help you," she stated. "I have been thinking about it, and I think you still need something to take care of."

Jenna looked down at the puppy and then back to Wendy.

"But I don't have a clue about how to care for a pet."

"You didn't know how to deal with cancer and how to care for someone so sick, but you did."

Wendy leaned forward and put her hand on Jenna's.

"You said that you were lost because you didn't have your identifier anymore, someone or something to care for, so why not find something that needs you. You have told me how good you were and how it gave you purpose, so why not get something that is small and needs your care."

Jenna nodded, and a slight smile started to cloud her face. Wendy leaned back in her chair and created some distance between the two women.

"And I realized you are attached to me more then you should, so I think we need to get something or someone for you to take away that sense of being needed that you miss."

"But a dog?" Jenna looked at the paper. "Don't they take lots of work?"

"Or a cat, or even a bird or fish, just something alive that needs you," she smiled. "I just think a dog would be good because they form such wonderful bonds with their humans."

Jenna fumbled with the pamphlet and smiled at the suggestion.

"Where am I going to get something like that?"

Wendy smiled, put her finger in the air. She handed her the paper she wrote the address and phone number on.

"That is a woman I know that raises emotional support dogs, and I called her this morning. She has a sweet little dog, about three years old, that is ready to be given a job," Wendy leaned towards Jenna.

Jenna smiled and looked closer at the picture of the dog. Would this really help her to get back on track with her life? It could be a solution.

"Anyway, she is the cutest little Pomeranian, black, brown, white, and tan." Wendy leaned back in the chair, a smile lighting her face with excitement. "Her name is Ziggy Zoggy Oy Oy Oy."

Jenna wrinkled her nose at the name.

"Wouldn't a bigger dog with a name like Sam or Butch be better?" Jenna suggested. "And that name? Isn't that like a drinking toast? A dog not named for a drinking toast?"

She looked at Wendy, amusement shone in her eyes. Jenna turned the paper over, and her heart skipped a beat at the shiny bright eyes of the dog.

"Or so small it could be easily hurt. I don't know that much about pet care."

"No, I think a little companion to go with you where ever you want would be better." Wendy reached over and put her hand on Jenna's knee.

"Tell you what," Wendy stood up and walked to her desk again. "I will bring the dog here for our session on Thursday, two days from now, and that can give you more time to think about it and maybe to do some research online. When you get here, if you are willing, you can play with her and see what you think. See if you can make it work."

She jotted down something on a notepad and taped it to her calendar.

Jenna stared at Wendy. She could barely take care of herself, why would Wendy feel she could take care of another living thing? She swallowed and felt slight moisture under her arms.

"No pressure, you don't like her, or you come in and tell me you don't think it will work in your life, no problem. I'll send her back to my friend's house, and she will go to the next person. No harm, no foul." Wendy stood up and waved her hands.

After a slight hesitation, Jenna nodded and agreed to meet the dog. Wendy walked Jenna to the door, and as Jenna left, little puppies ran around in her brain.

Once home, she booted up her computer and started reading all she could on emotional support animals and Pomeranians.

"Maybe this won't be so bad," Jenna sighed as she looked at the cute little faces popping up on her screen.

Jenna couldn't sleep. Today, she would finally meet the little canine. The last few days, she devoted much of her time to learn about the small dogs and what to expect. Yes, today, she would meet her new best friend. Videos on dog care and issues that plagued the small breed dominated the bookmark section of her computer.

In the corner of the room, a dog bed already sat and waited for its occupant.

She pulled up a video on her phone and laughed a little Pomeranian dance on the screen. On the nightstand, a picture of her mother watched her.

The research kept her busy and freed from the constant thoughts of her mother's death and helped her think of something other than herself and her situation.

"Well, mom, I think this is going to work."

Jenna picked up one of the letters and pulled it out to re-read her mother's words. She laughed at her mother's awkward humor, and her heart beat faster with the constant words of love. She appreciated the time and love these words represented, and she found a new appreciation for the notes without feeling lost and alone.

"Because today I won't be alone anymore."

She got up and started to get ready for the day.

"Though I probably never really was alone."

She glanced at the pile of letters, smiled, and grabbed her coat to leave.

Jenna arrived at the office early, and unlike her usual routine, she couldn't sit in the car and wait. She walked across the parking lot and looked over at a woman walking her dog. Over the years, she asked her mother for a pet but told it wouldn't be fair to the animal to be alone all day with no one home. Like all kids, she made promises, but nothing changed; until today. She bound up the stairs and burst into Wendy's office. Once in the lobby, she stopped and sat down quietly. She didn't want to ruin someone else's session with the counselor.

"Hi Jenna, you're early," Wendy opened the door to peek out after the tinkle of the shop bell over the door announced her arrival.

"I'm sorry. I have been thinking about it, and I think you are right. I need a new best friend, and I think that this dog could help."

Jenna moved up and down in the chair. Her hands placed on the cushions beside her on.

Wendy returned Jenna's contagious smile.

They walked into the office, and Jenna spied a small form sitting on a dog bed in the corner of the room.

"She's very well behaved, most of the time."

Wendy called the fluff ball over, and the dog cautiously walked over, sniffing along the floor on her stroll.

"Ziggy, come meet Jenna," Wendy scooped up the dog and walked over to Jenna.

The dog looked at Jenna with large brown eyes as her little nose sniffed the air.

"She is so small," Jenna reached out and rubbed Ziggy's head and ears.

"Can I hold her?"

"I think she would like that," Wendy handed the dog to Jenna.

Jenna reached for the dog but pulled her hands back.

"How do I do this?"

"It's okay, take your time." Wendy coaxed her. Jenna put her hands back out.

Wendy gently placed the animal in Jenna's arms. Jenna inspected the tiny, fragile body and marveled at how light the canine was. She held the pet close, and Ziggy stretched up. A pink tongue jetted out of the little black mouth, and it caused Jenna to giggle. The dog squirmed to get closer.

"Now, Ziggy, you behave." Wendy scolded the dog, and Jenna pulled her closer to her body.

Jenna pet the black and brown fur which dominated the dog's slight body. She suppressed a giggle as she looked at the dog's expressive face and the contrasting white hair under her nose and chin like a hipster's goatee and the black streak running up the back of each furry leg, reminiscent of women's nylons during World War II.

"Yes, she is even small for her family. I think they weighed her at just under five pounds," Wendy reached over and ruffled the dog's silky coat. "So, due to her size and markings, she can't be a show dog, but they found with her curiosity and great social skills, she would be a perfect emotional companion and scored high on the tests."

Jenna's heart slowed and the small creature snuggled in closer.

"You're just the cutest little thing," Jenna nuzzled into the dog's head, and Ziggy kept her head tucked in close.

Jenna searched for a clock as she counted the minutes until she could take Ziggy home. The dog cuddled into Jenna's lap and closed her eyes as the two women talked. Jenna's hands moved on the dog, her body relaxing with each stroke. This dog would indeed be her new companion.

As the session ended, Wendy stood and followed Jenna out of the office.

"But there is one thing that I want to make very clear, Ziggy is going to be your pet, not your world. We need to start doing something about you being around other people, but when you are ready to get out into public again, she will be there as a comfort, like a live security blanket. We need to make sure you don't get too dependent on her."

Jenna nodded acceptance, but she couldn't think past this moment. Wendy was right about this, so maybe there was something to what she said, after all, it was Wendy's idea to get Ziggy in the first place.

Chapter Thirteen

Jenna stopped at a pet store and overloaded on everything she thought the dog would need or want. For herself, she purchased a cute little purse/kennel she could hide the dog in if she needed to, and a pullover hoodie designed to carry a small pet in the front pocket.

"Just in case people are not happy to have me carrying a dog around." She hugged her new friend to her chest.

She anticipated scowls from people in places like stores and theaters if she entered with a dog, despite Ziggy's helper animal vest.

"I used to be one of those people. No need getting people all bent out of shape when it can be avoided, but not anymore." Jenna moved to the front passenger side of the vehicle and scratched under Ziggy's chin. She attached a dog safety harness, complete with a comfortable dog bed inside the car to the seat and buckled the dog in.

"Now you are safe, and I see no reason to have to take this out, ever. You are now my new co-pilot."

She threw bags of dog treats, clothes, and food in the trunk of the car. Ziggy sat and watched Jenna walk to the driver's side and get in, her little curly tail wagging at the sight of Jenna.

"Okay, now." She rubbed Ziggy's head. "Let's go and get you settled into your new home."

The two established routines including a shared mealtime with Jenna at the dining table, and Ziggy a few feet away on the floor. After dinner, they cuddled up on the couch and watched TV before they retired for the night. The dog bed sat forgotten in the corner of the room. Jenna pulled the dog up into her own bed every night, finding comfort when darkness overtook the room, and sadness crept back into her mind. Ziggy hushed Jenna's anxiety when the ghosts roamed the house.

She walked Ziggy around the neighborhood and found herself singing as she broke free from the prison of her bedroom's four walls; a sentence she condemned herself to after her mother's passing. She found the solace she sought and saw a bright future in front of her.

"How is it going?" Wendy escorted Jenna in for her session, and Ziggy followed close behind on a designer leash. The two women settled into their regular chairs and Ziggy jumped up into Jenna's lap.

"Oh my gosh, it is great!" Jenna pulled the little dog in her arms and kissed her. "She is just the best little thing, and you were right, I'm starting to feel more like myself."

Jenna nuzzled the little dogs head, and Ziggy tried to return her affection as she stuck out her pink tongue.

"So, are you ready to do more?"

Jenna stopped, and Wendy paused.

"I think it is time to take the next step."

Jenna loosened her grip on the dog, and Ziggy settled back into her lap. She bit her lip as she reached up and rubbed the back of her neck, her other hand still stroking the dog.

"I was right about Ziggy, and you are doing great, and I think it is time for you to figure out what you want to do with your life."

Jenna stared at Wendy, her happy expression changing to a blank look

"Not right this minute," Wendy reached out and touched Jenna's arm.

"But it is time for you to start to be around other people more. I want you to consider following your mother's wishes and take a short trip."

Jenna sat straight in her chair, her only movement the rhythmic movement of her hand on Ziggy. It was one thing to welcome a dog into her life, and quite another to leave the security of home and even another to be around people she didn't know.

"I don't know if I am ready. Can't we take one step at a time?"

"Look," Wendy stood up and walked to Jenna. She lowered herself down to be face to face with Jenna and placed a hand on her shoulder. "I know it is scary, but you were nervous about the dog, and see how that turned out?"

"I can't argue that." Jenna took in a deep breath and concentrated on Ziggy. "But that was so I would have someone to care for, a replacement for mom."

Wendy stood up, and her knees cracked. Jenna didn't change her gaze.

"How is going on vacation going to change anything?" Jenna looked into Wendy's eyes.

"You won't know until you do it," Wendy walked back to her chair.

"I also think you are doing so good that we only need to see each other once a week."

A lump formed in Jenna's throat.

"But mom only died five weeks ago. I'm still lost and not sure what to do with myself. Sure, Ziggy is helping me, but she is just a dog, and she loves me no matter what. People aren't like that. I'm not ready to not be able to come in here and talk to you," she croaked.

Wendy acknowledged Jenna's words with a nod.

"And you may be lost a while longer, but no one is asking you to make life decisions right now, just decisions for the next few weeks, or maybe even the next few months. I think you're stronger than you know."

She plopped herself down in the chair behind her desk, a reassuring smile across her pink lips.

"I think you can function now without me as a crutch, and you have Ziggy. You don't need me; you need to find friends that you share interests with. People to go have coffee or dinner with."

"We could go to coffee." Jenna dropped her head and looked at Wendy.

"I'm your therapist." Wendy dropped her smile, and a stern expression crossed her face. "You need to find someone to laugh with. Someone who doesn't have to say our time today is done."

Jenna took the hint and looked up at the clock. She started to gather her things.

"I will think about it," Jenna stood and walked towards the door, with Wendy following close behind.

"Please do," Wendy walked into the lobby on Jenna's heels. "Just a short little trip, maybe just a weekend to test the waters."

Jenna smiled, nodded, and walked out of the office. Outside, she took in a deep breath and let the sun warm her face. Ziggy gazed at her owner; her dark eyes concentrated on Jenna's every move.

"They have to allow you to come with me," She bent down and scooped the little dog up and hugged her close to her body.

She would call Wendy tomorrow and get some suggestions on where to go.

Chapter Fourteen

"I found these places for you," Wendy handed Jenna a stack of colorful brochures. "They are close so you can drive in about a day, but far enough you may want to consider flying."

Jenna took a deep breath and opened the pamphlets. Her eyes scanned the images, and Ziggy looked up at her with big eyes.

"What sort of things do you do at these places?" Jenna stared at the pictures of happy people.

"Oh, they are just a place to relax and refocus." Wendy leaned over Jenna's shoulder. She walked over and pulled out one more off the printer. She smiled as she handed it to Jenna. "This is the one that I think would be the best for you. It is a short drive, like half an hour to the airport, and the flight is less than an hour away. Then a short van ride to a resort situated in a lush forest."

Jenna gulped. Flying never crossed her mind, and she wasn't sure she wanted to start now. She looked down at the paper and stared at the glossy pictures of forests and waterfalls that called out from the pages.

"I know they may not be what you had in mind," Wendy sat down opposite Jenna. "But then again, I'm not sure what you had in mind, so I tried to figure out what would be good for you."

She leaned forward and touched the last paper she gave Jenna.

"The one I just handed you is quiet and away from people."

She turned her gaze up at Jenna.

"Well, away from people unless you want to be around others."

Jenna returned her gaze and forced a small smile.

You can sit and enjoy nature, get a message, or.." Wendy pointed to a picture of people playing some sort of game. "I would encourage you to go to one of their nightly mixers. It would be a great stepping-stone."

Wendy leaned back in her chair.

"And keep in mind, no matter what you do, you never have to see those people again, so why not put yourself out there. When you are done, if you haven't met anyone you want to talk to again, you come home and continue your life as it is."

More photos showed happy people as they milled around in a dining room in front of a delicious buffet and walked forested paths. Other pictures enticed with images of people reading under towering pine trees.

"All the brochures I gave you are dog-friendly so that Ziggy would be welcome there." Wendy paused while Jenna studied the paper. Could she do this? She put herself in the photo and maybe it would be okay.

Wendy continued her pitch, "the one I'm recommending is only a short distance outside of Portland, a short plane ride from here and then a short 45-minute bus ride to the resort. They have room service if you are tired and don't want to mingle with the other guests, or even if you are just overwhelmed by it all."

Jenna nodded and looked over at Ziggy and then back at the pamphlet. She smiled, readjusted in her chair, and nodded again. She raised her head.

"This may be okay," Jenna pulled Ziggy up into her lap.

Wendy bounced in her chair, and a smile dominated her face. She stopped and put her hands-on Jenna's arm.

"And I could set up someone for you to talk to if you get too stressed out. I met someone from that area at a conference last year, and he was exceptionally nice and accommodating. I bet he could be available if you need someone to talk to for a few minutes."

Jenna sat up straight, and Ziggy stood up, queuing in on his owner's mood change. Jenna looked at the pictures again.

"So, this therapist, he would be willing to make time for me if I needed to see him?"

Wendy nodded and leaned back in her chair.

"And how would I get to his office?" Jenna hugged the little dog closer into, her heart beating a beat faster.

"I'm sure the resort has cars and drivers. Or, he may be willing to come up there. We would make it work."

Jenna concentrated on her hand, going up and down on Ziggy's back, the repetitive action matching her breathing. In and out, front to back, repeat. She turned her eyes to Wendy.

"People go there for various health reasons, so they are prepared, but I can talk to them, discreetly, and let them know you just suffered a loss. I'm positive they will help make sure you get what you need, including a ride to town to see someone."

"What do you think," Jenna lifted Ziggy until they were face to furry face.

"I picked this place, and all these places, because they are very accommodating and will bend over backward to make sure you are safe, healthy and happy," Wendy leaned forward and patted Jenna's shoulder.

"So, I have no reason not to go." Jenna smiled and replaced Ziggy on her lap. This could be good.

"True, and even if I set it up, you know, you can cancel at any time."

Jenna stopped for a beat before she nodded acceptance. A small chuckle escaped her throat, and Wendy smiled ear to ear. Jenna took a deep breath.

"Yeah, this could be good." Jenna conceded as she rolled Ziggy over and scratched the dog's pink tummy.

"I can make a call and get this all set up for you." Wendy stood up and walked behind her desk. "I think you are ready and making a great decision. I can get it arranged for you to leave in two weeks."

Jenna's smile grew, and she again nodded. She looked down at the happy dog and a light sheen of sweat formed on her forehead. Was it okay for her to be feeling this so soon after her mother's death?

"Okay," Wendy chirped. "It's done. I set it up for Wednesday, two weeks from today."

"Thank you," Jenna placed the dog on the floor and stood up. Wendy pulled Jenna into a hug and held a little longer than usual. Jenna returned the gesture and hoped the woman understood how much this meant to her. She needed someone to push her and was happy she found just the woman.

"I will call you with more details in a few days," Wendy promised. Jenna stepped back with contrasting emotions in the unexpected personal contact.

Jenna left the office, the resort printout held tightly in one hand and Ziggy's leash in the other.

Chapter Fifteen

Paul threw a few clothes in a bag.

"What else am I going to need," he scanned the room and tapped information into his cell phones web browser. The temperature in Mexico popped up on the screen, and he shook his head.

"Mexico in the summer. What was I thinking?" He smiled. He hadn't been thinking, that was clear, but when the boss upstairs called, you went.

He walked to his closet and pulled out another pair of shorts. He threw them across the room to the open bag.

He glanced at the top of the dresser and spotted the picture of the woman and child.

"You always said we should take a vacation to Mexico, and here I am, finally going," he picked up the picture and looked deeply into the image. "We really should have done more traveling or more time together, but work always got in the way."

He chuckled.

"Even though I guess this is work-related, and I'm not sure this part of Mexico is what you had in mind."

He walked to the bag and placed the picture in the layers of fabric.

"So, I guess I will bring you with me this time," he said. "Though I think we need to talk."

He smiled as he pictured the older women of the church telling him it was time to move on and get married again.

He looked at his watch and jumped at the time.

He grabbed his bible from the nightstand and placed it on top of clothes. With his hands folded, he knelt next to the bed

"Dear heavenly Father, please let me walk the path you want me to walk and help me to show your love and mercy to the people I'm about to meet. Please let this trip be fruitful and help me to do your bidding."

He stood and took one more look around the room before switching off the light and closing the door.

Chapter Sixteen

Twilight always gave Jenna a surreal anxious feeling, and today was no different. She watched as the vibrant colors of life seemed to fade away into drab imitations of themselves, like a photograph sitting in the sun too long. Usually, during this short time, she kept herself busy and prayed not to be caught alone when the spirits of lives lost started to roam around.

Jenna walked past her mother's room and stopped. The last time she opened the door, she tore the space apart. The torrent of anger surprised her, but she felt better after the storm despite the fact the emotions rushed back; Nothing changed. She pictured the silk blouses torn and wrinkled, laid out on the floor in piles, broken glass covering the delicate fabric.

She put her hand on the handle of the door, and her heart thumped wildly. A small trickle of sweat trickled down her temple. She took in a deep breath and searched out Ziggy.

"It's time." Ziggy sat at her feet, her doggy dance from a few minutes ago quieted as she took a cue from Jenna.

"Yeah, well, you don't know how bad it really is, Tornado Jenna was a wild ride."

Ziggy cocked her head at her owner's voice.

Jenna turned the knob.

"I guess I'm going to have to do this sometime." She closed her eyes and held her breath as the door creaked open. A floral odor penetrated the surrounding air.

"I guess maybe I broke a bottle of perfume," Jenna forced an apologetic smile. The dog whined and stood on her hind legs to be picked up. Jenna shook her head at the dog.

"And from the smell of it, not one that she would have liked."

She reached through the narrow crack between the door and the jamb and located light switch. She pushed the button up, and light escaped from the room. Jenna peered in and caught the first glimpse of the mess.

"Well, I sure did a good job of it." She slipped into the room while Ziggy sat outside the door and stared at her.

"Chicken," Jenna smiled. The dog stood and wagged her tail and furry butt.

The destruction overwhelmed Jenna. She leaned down and picked up a pink sweater, one of her mother's favorite. She put the soft knit to her nose and took a deep smell of lingering perfume. A tear escaped and brought friends with it.

"I'm not going to cry," Jenna declared, and Ziggy tentatively stepped into the room. Big brown eyes looked up at Jenna in concern.

"I'm fine, girl." Jenna forced a smile on her lips and leaned down. She stroked the soft head.

She advanced, and her stomach clenched when she noticed the broken pieces of a crystal vase. She rubbed her face and neck with her hands.

"Oh, no."

Tears feel faster down her cheeks while she gathered the jagged pieces. She kneeled down and attempted to fit the pieces back together. Ziggy rushed to her side and again begged to be picked up. Jenna sat back and dropped the broken pieces into her lap. Ziggy crawled on to her legs and looked at the glass shards. Jenna picked the dog up, afraid for Ziggy's safety, and pulled the little body close to her.

100

"I gave my mother this when I was 16," she touched the slick transparent surfaces. "I gave it to her after I got my first paycheck. I was so proud of it."

She let the tears flow as she leaned over and put her arm on the bed. She dropped her head to her arm and took a deep breath. After a moment, she raised her head and surveyed more of the collateral damage of Hurricane Jenna. She crawled to a pile of clothing and touched the fabrics. Across from her, she noticed broken frames filled with photographs; her as a child with her father just before he had died.

Her hand hit something hard as she dug through the discarded fabrics. She pushed the clothes aside to uncover numerous books. Titles showed biographies her mother loved to read. She begged herself to turn away when other titles advertised herbs to fight cancer, cancer treatments in other countries, and books about the art of dying.

"They didn't work," she commented flatly and tossed the books to the corner. "And there is no art in all this. It's just ugly, and it stinks."

She found another image of her father and pulled it from the mess. She stared at the stranger's picture

"How many of my memories are just stories told so many times over the years?" She looked at Ziggy for an answer. The dog returned her gaze and tried to lick Jenna's nose, which produced a small smile among the tears on Jenna's face, and she kissed Ziggy's head.

She pulled the back off the broken frame, and an envelope popped out, her name scrawled across the white surface in familiar handwriting.

101

"Another one?" she groaned and scanned the room. How many more would she find?

Jenna unsealed the letter and began to read.

"My darling daughter, I wonder how long it took you to find this letter, but this is about your father."

The letter talked of her parent's meeting and courtship, a story Jenna knew well and never tired of hearing. It continued with the young couple getting married and starting a family.

"I wanted to have a daughter and tried for years, each month so upset and depressed when I got my period, but then, one day, I didn't, and nine months later, you were here. We were so happy. Nothing could have prepared me for what happened. I loved him with my whole heart, and then he was gone. He was a good man, secure and brave. He would have done anything for you, and I never knew just how much weight he was carrying on his shoulders until it was too late. You are a lot like him, brave, intelligent, and giving."

The note read like a love letter to her lost love, and Jenna devoured it. For the first time, she finished one of her mother's messages without falling into a puddle of tears. She looked at the end of the note and how the handwriting looked tired and sad.

"So, I hope you take these stories and the ones I told you as a child and remember a man that wanted so much to be with us, but couldn't outrun his demons. He should not have been on the road that morning, but he was. Despite it, you and I survived and grew; we have a great relationship that may not have happened without the shared tragedy. I love you, and I know he loves you too, please, never forget him or that love."

She folded the letter and replaced it in the envelope. What demons did her father fight? Her mother never mentioned this part of the story, and now it was too late to get answers. Was he trying to get home faster? Was he drunk when he rolled the car? She decided to let her father rest in peace and in the arms of her mother.

Ziggy crept into Jenna's lap and laid her head on Jenna's leg. Jenna pet the dark fur.

"Yeah, I see why people like you dogs," she rolled Ziggy over to scratch her tummy.

"I need to start picking this up," she picked up the dog and scrambled to her feet.

Jenna placed the dog on the bed and proceeded to clean up the room. She threw broken trinkets into the trash, each one thumped in the container, and Jenna's heart stopped for just a second. After an hour, Jenna laid down on the freshly made bed with Ziggy. She closed her eyes and smiled. Silence encompassed the room, except for her breathing. A soft pink glow bathed the pink walls as the sunset outside the window

Surrounded by her mother's things, she dozed off and dreamed of her mother and father. They held hands as the sky darkened.

The moon cast shadows on the wall as Ziggy paced and whined. Jenna woke with a start.

"Oh my, you need to go out," she sat up and stretched. "And I think we forgot to have dinner last night. Let's go and see what we can find."

Jenna walked down the stairs and let Ziggy out. She spied the resort papers on the counter as she came into the kitchen. She picked them up and again looked at the happy people.

"Okay, mom, I get it. Sold!" She looked up at the ceiling and smiled.

Ziggy let out a yap saying she was ready to come in.

"So, I have set you up with a ground-level room with a little fence around the back patio area so Ziggy can go out and do her thing, which you will be responsible for cleaning up, but I'm sure that won't be a problem."

Wendy smiled, and her excitement washed over Jenna.

"You are going to have such a good time." Wendy walked behind her desk and pulled out some papers from her drawer.

Jenna smiled and wondered if her mother would be as excited about all this as Wendy was.

"These are the names of people that could help you if you need it. I know the therapist that I found is a minister, but I talked to him, and he understands your situation with religion right now and is fine with it. He promised to be there and no preaching or asking to pray."

She folded the papers and stuck them in an envelope.

"I had hoped the two of you could talk before you got there, but he is going out of town for a few days."

Wendy scanned her desk, picked up more items, and included them in the packet.

"If he doesn't answer just leave a message and he will call you back. I also put my business card in there in case you are in a situation where you need me." Wendy's voice spilled out fast and furious. "I also have a letter stuck in there about your situation if for some reason you can't tell someone yourself. You are more than welcome to read it, nothing too personal, I promise."

Jenna signaled she understood and grinned. Wendy crossed over to Jenna and handed her the thick envelope.

"Now, do you need anything that I can help you with?" Wendy reached her hands out to Jenna.

"I'm fine; a little nervous but fine, I promise," Jenna put her hands in Wendy's waiting ones.

Wendy looked deeply into Jenna's eyes.

"I am so very proud of you," Wendy proclaimed. "I know we have only known each other for eight weeks, but you have come so far, and it makes me feel good."

Jenna let go of Wendy's hands and pulled her into a quick hug. They separated, and Wendy went back behind her desk

"Do you have your ride to the airport set up?"

Jenna nodded.

Wendy walked back to and leached down to give Ziggy a quick scratch behind her ears. She stood up and put her hand on Jenna's shoulder.

"Remember, I'm still here, and I'll see you just as soon as you get home and please, try to meet people and try to interact with someone. We need to try to help you with your social skills. You need people."

Jenna agreed and left. She couldn't believe how excited she was. The last few weeks were a thick fog, and now she was headed to her first real adventure.

Chapter Seventeen

Jenna walked through the jetway and into the terminal of Portland International Airport. She struggled to not throw the little dog around too much in her canvas and mesh prison. She turned and glared at the jet and the happy face on the tail.

"I don't know why he is so happy," she shook her head. "If that is an idea of what it's like to fly, I may stick to places I can get to by car or boat. I have been on roller coasters with fewer bumps."

Jenna stopped and looked around, trying to figure out where she was and where she needed to go. People rushed past her.

"What am I doing here? Why am I doing this?" She sat in a chair and pulled the kennel in her lap. Ziggy's nose stuck out one of the holes and Jenna touched it.

Cooking food mingled with body odor and perfume the area. Jenna stood up and walked past a grouping of seats that faced out towards the runway and planes. Each area sported a podium with a reader board announcing exotic-sounding places. Jenna squeezed through lines of people waiting to board planes bound for sunshine and beaches like Orange County, California, or Mazatlan, Mexico. As she trod on, gates became fewer and gave way to a parade of continuous shops offering souvenirs and food.

"I sure hope I'm going the right way." she stopped and looked in all directions for some sign. "I thought it said to go this way to baggage."

She continued forward, and the shops started to dwindle, and more waiting areas occupied space.

"Oh dang it, this can't be right."

A small whine came from the kennel as she paused and scanned her surroundings.

"I know, I'm trying." Tears began to blur her vision, and she wiped at her eyes with the back of her hand.

A group of teens came towards her in shorts and bright, colorful tee shirts with familiar characters on them. She moved to let them pass and noticed a few wore hats with ears on their head. Squeals of happiness pierced Jenna's ears. She took in a deep breath and turned to follow the group.

"Hey, Mike, that's our flight over there!" one of the teens yelled, and she stopped. She scanned the area for someone to help her, but after the teens, the hallway lacked travelers and airport employees. Overhead speakers broadcast arriving and departing flights, and she sat down alone with the chairs, podiums, and speakers.

"Okay, I have to figure this out." she set Ziggy's kennel in the space chair next to her, and the dog let out a little whine.

"Oh, baby, I know. It will be okay."

Jenna pulled the fluffy dog out, not sure if it was okay, but if it weren't, well, then someone would have to find her to let her know and then she could get help to find her way out of this place.

"I know, I will figure this out," she held the dog close to her body and kissed his head. "I'm sure someone will be by soon. I mean, don't they have planes that land on this part of the airport too?"

Jenna dropped Ziggy in her lap and her head in her hands. She concentrated on breathing. In. Out. In. Out. She needed to get a hold of herself. Ziggy laid down and got comfortable.

"What am I doing here. This is way too soon for me even to be trying this," Jenna groaned. "What do you say we just go back the way we came, maybe find someone at one of these gates and go home?

Jenna raised her head and looked out the window at the parked plane. The face on the tail seemed to mock her, laughing at this woman in her 30s that couldn't even get around an airport.

She turned from the window and scanned the empty corridor again.

"But then we have to get on a plane again. She quietly reminded Ziggy of the flight attendants' little speech of how bad some things could go. She shivered as she whispered into Ziggy's ear to remember the ride.

"I swear I didn't breath the entire way. I'm not sure how that metal tube stayed in the sky, and I'm not sure I want to test faith a second time."

"Okay, new plan." She clapped her hands as she tried to change the mood. The little dog jumped and ran back towards her kennel. "We are going to figure out how to get out of this spider web and then find a taxi, go to the train station and head home."

She fought tears of frustration and just watched the planes taking off and landing. She cried enough in the last few months that she should never have to cry again. Ziggy moved back to her lap.

"Are you okay, miss?" Jenna took a deep breath before turning to find the owner of the voice. Ziggy let out a little yip and low growl.

Jenna's eyes met two deep-set green eyes staring back at her. She pulled Ziggy in tighter and smiled.

"Whoa, uh, hi little guy. Sorry to bother you, but you look like you might need some help," the man stepped back a few inches.

"I'm fine," Jenna snapped.

"I don't mean to bother you. I just want to make sure you are okay or see if I could help," he smiled, and Jenna felt a warmth towards this kind stranger.

Jenna sat up straighter and looked past the eyes to the well-shaped face and shaggy brown hair. He appeared to be close to her age. She could feel her heart beating in her chest, and her palms felt clammy and rubbed them down her thighs.

"I said I'm fine," Jenna wiped at her cheek and ran her hand through her hair.

She attempted a glare, but couldn't get her face to cooperate.

"Okay," he raised his hands in surrender. "I wasn't trying to interfere."

He smiled at her, and his eyes twinkled. He turned and started to walk away. Jenna looked around at the unfamiliar surroundings.

"Okay, so I may be a little lost," she called out.

He pivoted to face her with a smile and sauntered back towards her.

"Oh great, now he is going to be smug," Jenna thought. She hated the fact she needed help.

"Well, let me help you then," he reached out his hand to her to help her to her feet.

"Oh my gosh," Jenna let her guard down a little. "I'm so lost, and my dog needs to go outside."

"Okay, well, I was just going to baggage, and the dog area happens to be on the way," he flashed a toothy smile, and Jenna's body relaxed.

"By the way, my name is Paul."

"Hi, I'm Jenna," she uttered and put her hand in his. She held Ziggy close to her body.

"Hi, Jenna," Paul leaned past her and grabbed onto the kennel. "Let me help you carry that, okay?"

Jenna nodded and smiled a genuine smile. She looked down, afraid to meet his eyes.

"Thank you, that is so nice of you, Paul. I was beginning to wonder if I was going to have to make camp there."

Paul chuckled, and her cheeks warmed.

"I'm sorry, I don't travel much," Jenna walked beside the man and noted that he was a good five inches taller than her. "In fact, this was my first time on a plane."

"Well, I hope it won't be your last," Paul matched Jenna's step. "I love traveling, but don't get to do it nearly enough. I just came back from Mexico."

Jenna blushed as she imagines of him in a small swimsuit, filled her mind and her cheeks became even redder.

"I'm not sure how I feel about it, the jury is still out" Jenna looked down at the floor and hoped he didn't notice her rosy appearance. "If you asked me about 15 minutes ago, I'd have told you I would never get on one of those metal tubes again, but you know, maybe someday."

The two walked down a small hallway with a security guard stationed at the end.

111

"Okay, whew," Paul replied with a twinkle, "we're out of the secure area and back in the real world."

He stopped after a few more steps, and Jenna did the same. He pointed to set of doors and told her she could find a nice grassy patch to let Ziggy out. She thanked him and took the kennel from his hand. Paul reached out and scratched the dogs head.

"I love dogs," he commented. "And you do have a cute one there."

"Well, thank you," Jenna hesitated. Her smile grew wider.

"After you let Ziggy pee if you still need to get baggage, the carousels are over there. Just read the signs above them, and they will tell you the airline and the flight, and you should find yours without a problem," he pointed towards two large areas with people circling one of the many luggage carousels. "And if you get there and it isn't there, there should be someone to help you."

Jenna thanked him for the third time and watched as her knight skipped off to find his bags and get back to his life.

"So what do you think?" she pulled Ziggy up close to her mouth. "I think he is like a fireman or something. Probably very happily married with a dozen kids."

Ziggy looked up at her owner and her little pink tongue jet out. She hit her target of Jenna's cheek, and Jenna let out a slight giggle.

"Yeah, I get it; you need to go out."

Ziggy let out a little yip as Jenna walked towards the door.

Chapter Eighteen

Jenna gathered her one bag and completed a form for her lost second baggage. She walked towards a pair of glass doors, the kennel in one hand, and her bag trailed behind her. Tucked under her arm, she juggled a bag with two overpriced cheeseburgers, one loaded for her and one plain for Ziggy, under her arm. Outside, she found a grassy patch and sat down. She quickly called the resort for her van while they both wolfed down the meal. Ziggy started to explore the area as far as her leash would allow.

Jenna pulled her surviving suitcase close to her explored the items inside to see what she was missing.

"Dang it," she searched the pockets, her hands jetting into and out of each. She threw the bag a few inches away from her and took in a deep breath. Ziggy stopped and watched her as she closed her eyes and dropped her head into her hands.

"I don't have your papers." Ziggy wandered over next to her and sat down. Jenna put out a hand and scratched the dogs head. She couldn't prove her little dog was a medical need. She laid back into the grass and looked at the sky.

"Oh, crap!" She covered her eyes with her arm. Along with the Emotional Support Animal papers, she didn't have the number for Wendy's associate. She sat up and gripped her stomach as it churned. She rocked slightly.

"I am going to be fine. I'll call her in the morning when she's back at work."

Ziggy stood and sniffed Jenna. She looked at her owner's face and wandered a few feet away to smell a dandelion.

Jenna took a deep breath in, and slowly let it out and repeated as she remembered the tools.

"I can endure anything for a short time.

Jenna looked at her phone and slumped as she noted the battery was running low.

"Of course," she took in another deep breath.

"I'll call Wendy in the morning and have her email me the papers," She arched her back. "I have pictures of them on my phone if nothing else."

Ziggy bounced around the grass, and Jenna closed her eyes.

"You found grass," a voice boomed above her.

Jenna shielded her eyes from the sun and looked up. A dark figure stood between her and the sun, and she recognized the outline of her hero, Paul.

"What are you doing, stalking me?" she laughed.

Paul planted himself next to her on the grass.

"Naw, I gave up stalking for Lent," a glint in his eye caught Jenna's attention and sent a chill through her.

"Shouldn't you be out of here by now." The words stumbled out of her mouth. Ziggy returned and crawled into Jenna's lap

"You would think, right?" Paul scanned the cars as they arrived to pick up travelers. "But that's what happens when you trust your transportation to and from the airport to your teenaged nephew." He chuckled and turned his gaze back at Jenna.

Jenna's cheeks warmed, and she smiled. She looked towards her lap and hoped he didn't notice her blush. She picked a blade of grass and played with it.

115

"He will be here shortly," Paul leaned back on his hands with his legs extended in front of him. "I would have asked my sister, but I told her son that if he did this, I would pay him."

Ziggy jumped from Jenna and strolled over to Paul. The dog looked up at the man and crawled into his lap. She laid down, and the man began to pet her. Jenna crossed her arms in front of her. She cocked her head and studied the pairing. They looked good together, and she grinned again, her cheeks starting to tire, though she couldn't stop.

"I think I am going to have to dock his pay," Paul scanned the cars again. "But he is overall a good kid."

Jenna nodded. His presence felt good, and she silently thanked the late teen.

Wendy would be proud of her as she attempted to make small talk. She asked where he was from, and he told her of his small town, about an hour drive from here.

"Though my sister lives in the city and I left my car there while I was gone," he picked a dandelion and tickled Ziggy's nose with it.

Jenna chatted about her home in Northern Idaho and made sure not to step over the line of too personal, so avoided questions about marital status and family, despite her longing to know more. After a few minutes, Paul jumped up and explained that he spotted his car and needed to run.

"Well, thank you for keeping me company," Jenna got up, as Ziggy jumped around, devoid of a lap to nap in.

"I'm delighted I got to meet someone so nice."

Paul smiled, returned the compliment, rubbed Ziggy's head one last time, and disappeared.

Jenna looked at her watch and realized her van would be here soon. She gathered the kennel, her one bag, and walked down the sidewalk to the place she was to meet the driver. Ziggy ran alongside Jenna on her leash, the dogs little legs a blur of fur.

Paul ran up to the car and opened the door.

"Sorry, I'm late," the kid stated.

"No problem," Paul reached into his pocket and retrieved his wallet.

"Tell you what," Paul pulled out a $20 and held it for the youth. "I think you should go and get some lunch and come back in maybe half an hour."

The boy grabbed the cash, smiled, and nodded.

Paul shut the door on the car and walked back to the patch of grass. He spotted the auburn-haired woman and smiled. She sat with her back to him, looking out towards the oncoming cars just as she was when he left a few minutes before.

"The wrong car," he touched her shoulder. The woman jumped back and turned around.

"Oh dang," he jumped back as the face didn't match the one he expected. "I'm so sorry; I thought you were someone else."

The woman smiled and offered to be his someone else if he wanted. Paul smiled and raised his hands in surrender. He thanked her for the offer and walked away to flag down his nephew when he came back around to pick him up.

Jenna arrived at the pickup location. She walked up to the van driver confirmed her identity to the driver. He

117

loaded her bag into the back of the vehicle as she picked up Ziggy and stuck her in the kennel. She stepped into the vehicle, and a sigh exited her lips. She edged towards the rear and claimed the backbench as her own. The driver entered the van, and after a few announcements about safety and rules squeezed himself into the pilot chair.

"Okay, folks," he exclaimed into a microphone, and the coach sprung to life. "The ride is going to be about an hour and a half. If you want me to let you know some of the nice things along the way, let me know."

Jenna counted ten other people on the bus, and the vote was unanimous for the guided tour package.

The bus moved into traffic.

"Okay, we are off. My first vacation," she whispered into the kennel. "At least the first time I don't have to sleep on the ground and hope the tent doesn't leak if it rains."

Jenna listened to her fellow vacationers chat with each other while the bus bumped along the road. Ziggy let out a little whine, and Jenna pulled her out and onto her lap.

"For now, but if someone says something, you have to get back in there," she stroked the dog's fur, and no one said a word to her about it. Jenna took a deep breath and let the dog settle in for a nap. Her shoulders relaxed, and she shut her eyes. A couple near the front happily let everyone know they were celebrating their 35th wedding anniversary while the couple just behind them were on their honeymoon. A family of four occupied the other side of the bus, the mother and father sitting close together and holding hands while their late teen daughter and younger teen son didn't engage with anyone while they played on their cell phones.

Jenna listened to the mother talks about the family taking one last vacation before her daughter started college in the fall. The final couple revealed they won the trip from a radio station and prayed they could get some time alone after leaving their twin two-year-olds with the husband's mother. Each person seemed so excited and happy to be able to leave their regular lives behind. The mother looked at Jenna and asked questions about her life and why she chose to come. Jenna didn't know how to respond. Should she tell them she was in mourning her mother, or would it seem too soon to be doing something like this? Should she say her therapist sent her on this trip, or would the comment send out red flags about who she was? She chose to give noncommittal answers and hoped she could figure it all out.

She stared out the window at the passing scenery. She wiped her hands on her jeans and put them between her legs to warm up. She envied those who could talk to strangers and thought back when she could do the same, but that was before the sickness and isolation. She chose to be her mother's caretaker and the decision cut out those around her who couldn't understand the struggles she dealt with. How could she get to that person from the past?

The troupe passed beautiful waterfalls and drove along the massive Columbia River while their host talked about the Native American's who had occupied this area and the Lewis and Clark Expedition. Jenna stared out the window, wondering what her mother would think of all this and was surprised when Paul popped into her thoughts. She recalled he lived an hour from the airport, and she fantasized looking down at the cars and seeing him.

"Seriously, he could have gone north, south, or even east, I suppose." Ziggy looked up at the sounds of Jenna's voice with bright brown eyes. "Besides, I just met the guy and probably will never see him again."

The teen boy moved to the seat directly in front of Jenna, his legs still in the aisle.

"I like your dog," he smiled at her four-legged companion.

"You want to pet her?"

He nodded and reached out his hand. Ziggy looked up at Jenna before she turned and licked the boy's hand. He giggled as the tiny pink tongue wet his fingers.

The two talked about the dog, while Ziggy ventured out to get closer to her new friend. Jenna picked her up and offered to let the boy hold her. His parents watched from their seat and smiled to let Jenna know it was okay. Jenna reached into her bag and dug out a dog treat. She handed it to the boy to give to Ziggy, who politely took the goodie offered and flashed him her doggy smile.

"I think she likes you," Jenna's smile penetrating her face.

"And I like her," he rubbed her head.

The bus climbed higher, and the air got murky.

"Sorry folks," the driver voiced over the speakers. "I know it looks bad now, but we'll be clearing this soon. There are some forest fires in the area, but this happens every year, and the resort is in a valley protected from the fires and smoke, so your visit should still be relaxing."

The bus pulled off the main road and onto a smaller back road. Jenna looked out the window at the hazy air and assured herself there was nothing to worry about. Not long after the turn, the bus slowed as a line of identical vans caused a backup. A look of concern and confusion crossed the driver's brow. He picked up the mike and talked to the group.

"Well, not sure what is going on here," he admitted. "Usually this road is smooth sailing, but we are close, so don't worry."

He put the mike down, and they continued the crawl towards the lodge. A short time later, a bus full of people passed them going the other way.

"Okay, we are almost there," the driver's voice betrayed his attempt to sound happy and sure.

Half an hour passed before the bus pulled into the parking lot of a large log cabin type building. Jenna marveled at the tennis courts that peeked from the other side of the building, and a river run pool snaking along the side wall of the complex, complete with a waterfall. In the middle of the river, a hot tub sat on a medium-sized island. A man flagged the driver, and the bus pulled over.

"I will be right back," the driver exited the bus and walked up to the man engaged in an animated conversation. The two men returned to the bus, and the driver returned to his captain's chair. The other man took the mike and addressed the crowd, the smile on his face forced, and contrary to happiness.

He introduced himself as Peter Nobis and informed the group the forest fires changed direction and were near the resort.

"So we are being forced to vacate." The crowd sighed.

His smile stayed on his face while he explained money would be returned and any other fees people paid if they chose to change their plane tickets to go home. He offered discounts on future stays at the resort.

The group looked at each other, worry in their eyes.

"Don't worry, everyone. I know it is not ideal, but we are relocating to a little town down the road. The hotels are full, but people are getting invited into homes, and we will be asking people to stay in beds at the local high school gym."

His eyes shoed sincerity as he attempted comfort to the people.

"I'm so very sorry about this, and they are saying it should only be a few days until we reopen and you all can come back and start the vacation of a lifetime. We don't know, but I have heard that they have the fire 53 percent under control."

He gave the driver an encouraging smile and a pat on the back as he left the vehicle. He walked to the bus behind theirs to deliver the same speech to the next set of disappointed travelers. The driver turned the key, and the engine roared to life. Three more people boarded as the happy chatter turned quiet.

Chapter Nineteen

The group arrived at the high school where volunteers directed people into smaller groups and from there to rooms for the night. Each person filled out papers about allergies and medications.

Jenna ended up in a room used for health classes. Posters on the wall advertised good eating habits and saying no to drugs. Makeshift blackboard walls separated the area into smaller areas, each square with a cot and decorations on the blackboards. In Jenna's space, someone had used colored chalk and drew flowers.

Jenna opened the kennel she draped with her coat so no one could see the little dog and take her away. She wasn't sure what they would do, but she couldn't prove her need for Ziggy with the papers in her other bag and he phone dead.

She pulled the dog closer to her and laid down on the makeshift bed.

"Hi everyone," a voice filled the room from a speaker in the corner.

"I know this is not ideal, and I am sorry you are all going through this. I know it is late, and I know that most of you are probably tired, so I am going to make this short."?

Someone in another part of the room coughed, and Jenna rolled to her back, Ziggy on her chest.

"We have a small assortment of foods for those of you that are hungry, and we will be leaving nonperishable foods out for those that would like something to eat later."

Jenna closed her eyes. Maybe if she went to sleep, in the morning, she could go back to the resort. Her stomach growled, but she didn't have the energy to go and find something to eat.

"Starting at six, we have breakfast served until 10."

Jenna drew in a deep breath and held onto Ziggy as she squirmed to be free. She cooed in the dog's ear, and Ziggy settled down.

"If there is anything that any of us can do, please do not hesitate to ask. I wish you all well and promise we will do all we can to make this as painless as possible."

The lights were dimmed in the room, and Jenna lost herself in thoughts which lead to dreams.

A shrill cry from the hallway startled Jenna and forced her to vacate her dreams. The furry little body next to her sensed her awakening and gave out a little whine.

"It was just a baby with her mother," Jenna stoked the shaking dog.

She held the dog close and sat up as she pulled a sweatshirt from her bag with an oversized front pocket for pets. She pulled it on and gently coaxed the dog into the pocket. She straightened out her blanket and made sure her luggage was securely under her cot and out of sight.

The aroma of fresh-brewed coffee and bacon enticed her as she put on her shoes.

"Okay, I understand, you need to go outside," Jenna scanned the room to see who was near. Soft snoring came from the "room" next to hers. She formed a belt with Ziggy's leash and tiptoed out of the school. On the other side of the building, she dropped Ziggy on the ground, snapped on her leash. She gave the dog a little freedom to explore, and the dog ran a short distance and relieved herself. With her business done, Ziggy started to sniff around and explore the small patch of grass.

Jenna looked towards the sunrise; the yellow orb tinted by the nearby forest fires to a blood red-orange. The smell of burnt wood scented the air, and rushing water nearby broke the silence. The music reminded her of the river in her backyard and eased her mind. After a short while, she gathered and stuffed the dog, back into the pocket. Jenna returned to the cafeteria.

The line for the breakfast buffet grew as people wandered in from the different sleeping rooms. Cheerful rested faces met the weary vacationers, and shoveled eggs, sausage and rolls onto plates. Jenna stepped into the queue, and her stomach growled as the smell of frying meat that perfumed the room. Ziggy whined and attempted to stick her head out to see what was going on.

"Not now, you be good, and I'll give you my sausage," Jenna pushed the dog, but the dog squirmed more.

"Ziggy, be a good girl, please," Jenna whispered and stuck her hand in the pocket with Ziggy to calm her down.

Jenna reached the front of the line and received her meal from a happy grandmother-type woman. She found a spot at a table by herself and sat down. She dug into her eggs and picked little pieces off with her fingers and slipped the tidbits to Ziggy. People stumbled in, some in pajamas and some dressed in street clothes and the room filled up. A few people pulled luggage behind them, waiting for cars to pick them up and take them to the airport. A speaker turned on with a loud squeal, and people moaned from the noise.

"Good morning, friends, I hope you all slept at least a little. I know this is not the best of circumstances." Jenna turned to look at the speaker.

"I just wanted to give you some information about what is going on today and the status we have received from the Forestry Department."

The crowd quieted to hear the news. As if by divine intervention, the crowd parted and Jenna caught a first glimpse of the man at the podium. She blinked twice and rubbed her eyes, making sure she was awake when the speaker took on the form of the same man she fell asleep thinking of. His jeans and tee-shirt from the airport replaced by khakis and a dark blue polo shirt, but she didn't doubt it was him. She couldn't. What were the chances this was real?

"This is not the vacation you planned, I am sure, but please be assured, we want to help with any needs. One of the people in blue vests would be happy to find answers if you have any questions." he leaned over and conversed with someone before he continued.

She breathed deeply as more details of the man came into focus. He smiled, and her heart skipped a beat. A thin layer of moisture covered her upper lip.

"Also, we have a couple of buses for anyone who wants a ride back to Portland, though we hear from the television that the fire is 65 percent contained."

Paul moved, and the microphone let out a loud squeal. He dropped the mike down to stop the noise and searched for someone in the wings. He mouthed some instructions and nodded back at them. He reapplied his smile and covered the mic while he carried on the conversation with other people on the stage.

"Oh, he is so cute." A young voice penetrated Jenna's thoughts. She turned and looked into the eyes of a girl about seven years old.

"Can I pet him?" the child raised her hands towards Jenna's pocket.

Jenna stepped back a few inches to readjust her mindset. She gulped and put her hands down to her pocket. Ziggy's head and front paws pocked out as the canine inspected the world around her.

Jenna plopped down in a chair and got face to face with the child. She gazed back towards the stage area, but the view from this angle was blocked. She scowled and straightened her back.

"Sure, her name is Ziggy."

"I really want a dog," the girl stroked the dogs head, her attention on Ziggy and not Jenna.

The child made a face and cooed at the dog.

"I bet you are the best dog in the whole world."

Jenna stood again and brought the dog suddenly face to face with the girl. The youngster's high-pitched squeal of joy filled the gym as Ziggy's little pink tongue found a bullseye on the tip of the girl's nose, and she burst into a happy giggle. Jenna dropped back down into the chair, worried the noise would bring unwanted attention.

"Maybe I'll get a dog when I find my forever family," the child exclaimed oblivious to anything but Ziggy. The words struck Jenna's heart. She glanced at the youngster.

"Forever home?" Jenna struggled to keep her voice steady. She swallowed and put her hand on Ziggy's back.

127

"Yeah, my mommy died when I was five, and my granny lives somewhere I don't know." The girl looked up at Jenna, a smile on her round face. The child's blue eyes pulled Jenna in.

"I'm Jenna.".

"My name is Molly," the girl flashed a toothless smile and held her hand out to shake. Jenna took the hand and held it.

"I, um, I'm an orphan too," Jenna and for the first time, the reality ambushed her. A tear escaped her eye, and she batted it away.

Molly tilted her head and watched Jenna.

"I'm sorry. It wasn't long ago, and I'm still adjusting," Jenna whispered. She scanned the room and pulled her arms close into her sides, clutching her hands in front of her.

"It's okay," Molly placed her hand on Jenna's. "I remember when it first happened to me, and I cried all the time."

Molly leaned in and went nose-to-nose with Ziggy.

"But you have this wonderful little doggy with you," Molly smiled. Ziggy responded with a quick flick of her pink tongue and licked her new friend.

"I remember I was scared and sad, but I'm not now. I've got mama Patty and Pastor Paul and my best friend, Jenny..."

The girl prattled on about people in her life. Her voice sang the words in a made-up melody while she danced along.

"I hope I can get there someday," Jenna stopped and held her breath. The little girl named 'Pastor Paul.' Could it be her Paul from the airport?

"So, Molly," Jenna touched the girl's arm. "I have to take Ziggy outside. Do you want to go?"

Molly jumped up and down and then stopped, looked at Jenna, and looked down at her feet.

"I don't know you, and I think I would be in trouble, so I'll just wait for Ziggy here," Molly plopped down on the bench. "I hope that is okay?"

"It is fine," Jenna smiled and stood up. "You're a smart girl, and you're right. Going with me would have been wrong even if you wanted to be with my dog."

Jenna touched Molly's shoulder.

"So tell you what, if you are still here when I come back in, you can play with Ziggy for as long as you like, and you and I can get to know each other. How does that sound?"

Molly nodded, smiled, and stood up.

"I just have to go and tell mama Patty where I am and what I'm doing, but I promise to be back really soon, is that okay?"

Jenna nodded, took the little girl's hands in her own, and nodded.

"I'm glad I met you, Molly, and I think Ziggy feels the same way."

Molly ran off into the crowd, and Jenna could still hear the giggle. She pushed Ziggy back into her pocket and made her way to the doors.

Chapter Twenty

Jenna walked towards the gym and stumbled into a group of people lined up by one of the buses, luggage in hand; Jenna spotted the family from the ride up among the group.

"Hi there," Jenna smiled at the family. "What's going on?"

"We won the lottery," the boy jumped up and down.

"Well, the lottery of getting out of here and to the airport," the father placed a hand on his son's shoulder. "People signed up if they wanted to leave, and they pulled names out of a hat, and we were lucky enough to be in the first group."

"Signed up?" Jenna turned towards the building.

The mother touched Jenna's arm.

"Oh honey, I'm sorry, did you miss that part of the announcement? You could go in and see if maybe someone decided to stay or if they can fit one more person on."

"It isn't my time yet," Jenna shook her head and touched the woman's warm hand. She noticed Paul in the parking lot with some kids and grinned. He tossed a ball to one of the boys and yelled something as they all cheered.

The woman followed Jenna's gaze and smiled.

"It's all good. I'll get out on a later bus."

The mother leaned in and gave Jenna a hug. Jenna closed her eyes and wrapped her arms around the woman's shoulders. The hug felt like a mother's hug, and warmth penetrated her body into her heart.

Jenna said goodbye, and they boarded the bus. Other people slipped by her and onto the vehicle,

She waved one last time as the bus pulled out and Ziggy stuck her head out. The dog flashed a panting smile.

"I honestly believe I'm going to be fine and be happy again," Jenna declared while she walked back to the side door of the school.

Jenna heard loud cheers from the cafeteria, and Ziggy whined in her pocket.

"Okay, you're right," she lifted the dog out of its cloth prison. "I need to let you be and stop trying to hide you. If it comes down to it, maybe Pastor Paul will remember you, and we can appeal to him."

She pulled the leash from around her waist, belt style, and put the dog on the floor. Ziggy sniffed around the base of the lockers that lined the wall.

"There can't be anything good to smell around here," she pulled on the leash and continued towards the sound.

In the gym, she spied kids of every age involved in some game involving giant balls and teamwork. In the stands, parents cheered and shouted encouragements to their children. Pastor Paul stood in the middle of the action as the referee.

Jenna's back straightened at the sight of him, and she felt a trickle of sweat at her temples. Her heart thumped in her chest, and she reached up and touched the area just below her neck. She took in a deep breath and watched.

His clothing changed from his business casual and to street casual, dressed in jeans and a tee-shirt. He looked more like their first meeting like the first time, and she sighed at the vision of the man who woke electricity in her body. Ziggy quietly barked and began to wander into the gym, wanting to be a part of the game.

Jenna reached down and scooped the dog up in her arms.

"Shhhh, we still don't know your status, and I don't really want to have to deal with that right this moment," she whispered in the dog's ear.

Kids ran up and down the court, the smiles on their faces contagious to the spectators. A whistle blew, and activity halted. Paul raised his hand in the air to get attention from both players and spectators.

"Well, after a hard-fought battle and two very dedicated and talented teams that I wish I could work with every day." His voice echoed around the room. "I have to say that it is a tie."

People and players moaned and screamed, and Paul once again rose his hand.

"Okay, I get it," he laughed. "So, I think we need to take a quick break, and then we can have a winner take all session in about an hour. How does that sound?"

The group cheered and the bleachers cleared.

Jenna watched people crowd around the charismatic minister.

"He is quite the guy," Jenna jumped as a voice behind her interrupted her thoughts.

Jenna turned and faced a woman who appeared to be slightly older than her.

"Uh, yes, he is," Jenna studied her features, short-cropped blond hair and aqua eyes. "Are you his wife?"

The woman laughed and shook her head.

"Naw, though don't think that the yentas in this church haven't tried on many occasions to set us up," Her eyes twinkled and emphasized the woman's broad smile. "But he just isn't my type."

"Um, sorry, but your not mine," Jenna said and turned back towards the gym. The woman behind her chuckled.

She watched as Paul picked up a child in each arm while other youngsters laughed and jumped in and out. The two women stood there, and Jenna squirmed a little.

"And this must be Ziggy," the woman nodded towards the dog. She leaned down to put the furry head, and Jenna circled back around.

"I'm Patty," the woman stood and extended her hand. "I have a little girl in my care that can't stop talking about your dog. I think she is in love."

Jenna smiled and took the woman's hand. Patty motioned to move out of the doorway as people left the gym.

"Oh, Molly, yes, she talked about 'mama Patty.' That must be you."

Patty nodded and pulled Jenna into a hug.

"I was hoping I would get to meet you, and we are all family here."

"And make sure I wasn't a perv or something," Jenna commented with a smile.

"Well, you never do know who is here in this sort of situation," Patty watched the people flowing by them. "And I do love that little monster."

"How about you and I go and get some coffee? I know this little place about a block away if you don't mind the walk," Patty started to walk down the hallway, and Jenna nodded consent, quickly falling into step with Patty.

Chapter Twenty-One

The sunshine peeked through the smoke and created a surreal painting. Patty stopped at a large van with the words "Mountain View Home" scrawled in a simulated child's handwriting. She opened the door and retrieved a bag between the two front bucket seats.

"Here, this is probably a good idea," she handed a medical mask to Jenna and slipped one over her own head. "I wish I had a small one for your dog, but only people ones. Sorry, Ziggy."

"I'm sure she will be fine on a short walk, and when we get there, she is usually pretty good at hiding in the pocket of this jacket."

Patty chuckled.

"I wondered why you were wearing a sweatshirt this time of year."

The women talked about the fires and the weather as they walked a few blocks. At the coffee shop, and with Ziggy hidden, they sat at a table in the back of the cafe.

"So, who wants to start?" Patty poured cream into her cup.

Jenna gestured for her to start and Patty began.

"I was once upon a time a nun," she stated. "But God had bigger plans for me."

Patty paused and watched for a reaction. Jenna nodded, and Patty continued her life story. She shared a story of finding God at an early age while she stirred her coffee. She talked about her calling to do his bidding and thought it meant joining a convent. After a few years, and just before final vows, she didn't think it was right anymore. She needed to be somewhere, but she didn't know where and God wasn't done, yet. She hiked through Europe and Asia and visited religious sites, which made her feel closer to God. She aided and provided what she could to those in need. Eventually, she ended up back in the USA, and one day she found herself here and put down roots.

"It was quite an adventure, and I knew what needed to be done when I walked into this town," she sipped her hot liquid.

"And what was that?" Jenna leaned forward to take it all in, her breathing fast and shallow, enthralled in the story and the storyteller.

"My childhood was less than perfect," Patty stared into her coffee. "I had an abusive father and a co-dependent mother."

The oldest of three, she attempted to shelter her younger sisters from the horrors of their life.

"I hear one of my sisters is well and happy," a small hint of longing crossing her eyes. "I think she is a teacher. She blamed me for some of the things that happened when we were kids. Once she turned 18, she ran from the house and never looked back. I used to try to call and write to her, but she always just returned the letters and never picked up the phone. I don't even know where she is now."

She lowered her eyes to her folded hands on the table. Her breathing slow.

"My other sister, the baby, wasn't strong enough to escape the past and took her own life in her 20s," she paused, and Jenna watched Patty's lips move in a silent prayer for her lost sibling. "I remember the last time I saw her, and I knew she was in trouble, but I was young and lost myself, so I didn't know what to do."

Patty looked out the window.

"I'm sorry for your loss," Jenna stirred her coffee.

Patty reached over and placed her hand on Jenna's.

"I have a feeling I'm not the only one here with a loss," a reassuring smile creased Patty's lips. "After that, my father got worse and ended up in jail after killing my mother. That was about 20 years ago."

Patty pulled her hand back to her side of the table and fast-forwarded her story to the present.

"I knew there were lots of kids in foster care or orphans, and all I could think of was how to save them since I couldn't save my sister. I realized most of them lived in terrible situations even now, and thought about how out here, nature is so healing. Most of them were like me and never got a chance to experience nature."

Patty's demeanor improved, and the twinkle in her eye returning.

The waitress came by and refilled their cups while Patty explained the values and healthy living in a small town.

"These kids fall into the category of 'hard to place.' Most of them have been through more than most adults will in their lifetime." Jenna marveled at this woman who seemed so strong

"I just feel that they need a place where they can see what caring really looks like and maybe grow into better people. A place where community means something and everyone around genuinely cares and loves one another."

Patty took a drink.

"At first, I received resistance from some of the town people, but I promised to never take a child that was over 10 or dangerous. After that, they rallied around me and even helped to build a home where the kids can become better members of society," Patty took a deep breath. "I convinced the judges in some of the big cities nearby to give me a chance to change lives, to let me take their charges to a little town they probably never heard of. Well, let's say, some were happy to be rid of the kids, and others were reluctant. But once the program was up and running, and they saw our accomplishments, it got easier. It hasn't always been easy."

She looked down and wiped a sudden tear while she talked about children she failed and sent back into the system.

"But I've had more successes than failures," she raised her head. "And that was 12 years ago."

Silence filled the booth as Jenna absorbed the story.

"Wow, that is quite a story," Jenna looked back towards her companion. "Mine isn't quite eventful and full."

Jenna told stories of school and her time at college where she earned a degree in liberal. She talked of mixed feelings when her next step to a major university was trampled on with one small word, Cancer. Her mother insisted that she go to school and Jenna's lies saying she didn't make the cut to get in.

"I don't think she ever believed me, but she didn't call me out on them," Jenna wiped away a tear. "I watched my friends fly away to colleges all over the country, and I just kept telling myself that when mom got that clean bill of health, I would go back and have the life they were having.

But things didn't get better, and the healthy report card never came. After a while, they stopped calling, or maybe I stopped answering. I don't remember, but I do know, I soon found myself getting up, going to work at the local grocery store, coming home, and taking care of mom."

She explained how she gave up her job when things turned critical. Instead of liberal arts, she found herself in classes about hospice.

"And then last April, she died," Jenna whispered.

Silence expanded between the two women and Ziggy squirmed in Jenna's pocket.

"I think she needs to go outside," Jenna announced, and silently thanked the small dog for breaking the tension.

"And I need to get back. I'm sure that my co-worker Jeremy and some of the kids are about to send out a search party."

They stood to leave, and familiar face entered.

"Paul!" Patty yelled and waved at the man. She grabbed Jenna's arm and pulled her towards Paul.

"Let me introduce you to one of the good ones."

Paul's face lit up, and he walked towards the women.

"Oh, my goodness, Jenna?" his eyes shined with happiness.

He opened his arms and wrapped them both up in a hug.

"What are you doing here, and where is your dog?" he searched the floor.

Jenna opened her pocket, and a foxy little face stared up at the three. Jenna motioned for them to go outside, and Paul asked them to wait and walk back with him.

139

"But first I really need some coffee. These kids are wearing me out," a big grin and twinkle in his eyes showed his true feelings on the subject.

The women stood by the door. Jenna put a leash on the dog and placed her on the ground. Once out the door, Ziggy ran to a bush to relieve herself.

"How do you know Paul?" Patty looked at Jenna in amusement.

"Believe it or not, he was my knight in shining armor at the airport," Jenna blushed. "It was my first time flying, and it wasn't a good experience. So there I was freaking out, with Ziggy needing a bush, and it was like he just appeared. He helped me to find my way outside."

Patty praised Paul and his helpful nature but abruptly stopped as he walked towards them.

"No use for him to get a bigger head then he already has," she winked at Jenna, and the two women giggled.

Paul asked the current subject of the conversation, and laughed when Patty casually commented, "Well, you, of course."

The women put on their masks and Patty apologized to Paul for not having one for him. He shrugged it off, and the trio began their walk back. Jenna snuck glances at Paul and studied his features closer. Occasionally, she thought she caught him doing the same, or at least hoped she did.

Patty and Paul talked about children at the orphanage. Meanwhile, Jenna lost herself as she fantasized about a big family of her own and questioned if it was in the cards for her. Ziggy trotted in front of the group, proud to guide the pack back to safety.

The word "money" caught Jenna's ears, but she wasn't sure in what context. She had money, and more then she needed. Maybe she could help in some small way. She felt her purse on her shoulder and thought of the money her mother left her. What she carried was a tiny fraction of what was waiting for her when the dust settled from her mother's passing. Maybe she could give Patty and Paul some to help out.

"Or maybe I could move here and help." She pushed the thought from her head. "But I just met these people. Why would they want me here? But what is waiting for me back home?"

Her mind played ping-pong with the ideas until her name brought her back to the group.

"What do you think, Jenna?"

"Uh, sorry, I wasn't listening," she pulled at Ziggy's leash.

"No worries," Paul looked at her, and Jenna hoped he couldn't hear her heart beating so fast in her chest. "It was rude of us to leave you out and talk about work, but it was just a question about what is better, to be morally right, or to have a loving heart and accept the situation."

"Loving heart every time," Paul smiled and nodded. His eyes approving of her answer, and he stared at her. Jenna turned away as her cheeks got warm.

A guilty look colored Paul's features as he glanced down at his watch. He explained he was late on lunch set up and rushed off.

The women watched him walk away.

"Nice," Patty spoke with a sly smile. "I know it is a sin, but I do like watching him walk away. Someday he is going to make someone very happy."

Jenna continued to stare but quickly turned away.

"You know, I don't know that I've seen him this happy and relaxed in a very long time," Patty shot Jenna a sly look. "And I can't imagine what has him looking like that."

"Well, he seems to be a very generous man and one that wants to help, so maybe it is that he can help so many people," Jenna felt a lump in her throat. "I watched him with the kids, and he seemed happy to be playing with them."

"Yeah, but I talked to him just before the buses arrived from the resort, and he was stressed out about what he was going to do to help all these people, and I know this morning he was a little better, but still stressed out. I think at the coffee shop was the first time I have seen him relaxed," Patty winked at Jenna.

"Well, I know it isn't anything about me since we have met a total of twice and he barely spoke a word to me just now," Jenna turned away from Patty and started to walk.

"Well, I know the way he looked at you spoke volumes," Patty caught up with Jenna.

"I think you're looking for something that just isn't there," Jenna stopped, but couldn't seem to control the smile on her face.

Ziggy went to the end of her leash as she tested her limits and looked up at her owner as if to ask if she could get to that one bush.

"I'm delighted that we had that time together," Patty put her hand on Jenna's arm. "And I know it is selfish to hope you are stuck here longer, but I would sure love to do it again."

Jenna nodded, and for the first time in many long months, she reached out and initiated a hug.

Chapter Twenty-Two

Paul couldn't believe his luck!

He sat down in his makeshift office and put his hands on his stomach. He looked up and mouthed a 'Thank you.'

His mind refused to let go of the woman he met at the airport, and he dreamed about her at night. On the drive home, he cursed himself for not getting a phone number or some way to find her. Even as he unpacked his suitcase and the picture of his wife and child fell out, his thoughts were of Jenna. Each night he said a special prayer for the woman with the little friendly dog.

"Okay, I think I'm back," he checked his hands to see if they were steady now.

He stood and walked into the hall as one of the church member's daughter rushed up to him.

"Pastor Paul," she grabbed his hand and pulled at him. "I really need your assistance."

He smiled and let her lead him off.

Jenna couldn't stop smiling. Happiness was an elusive emotion the past few months, and Jenna felt a tinge of sadness clouding her beautiful day.

She allowed Ziggy to lead her around the parking lot and into the grassy area. They stumbled upon a park-like area, and Jenna sat on the grass. She released the dog to explore, and Ziggy zeroed in on a butterfly. The canine bound after the insect but missed, and the yellow-orange bug flew off into the sky.

"I know, it sucks when that happens," Jenna laughed at the comical little dog.

Jenna closed her eyes and took in a deep breath, feeling the smoke-filled air fill her lungs.

She picked a blade of grass and shred it. She looked down the road towards the coffee shop with his smile tattooed on her brain and memories.

Lost in thought, she didn't notice the child who crept up behind her.

"Hi," a voice broke her fantasy.

"Molly, what are you doing here?" Jenna dropped the grass and wiped her hands on her jeans.

"Mama Patty said I could come and play with Ziggy if it was okay with you," the child looked at Jenna sheepishly, and moved closer to the dog.

"But she said I have to ask you if I could pet Ziggy since you never pet a dog that you don't know well without asking first."

Jenna smiled and nodded at the girl. She studied the girl and wondered who someone so young could survive the tragedies of her life with such grace and stability.

"Mama Patty also told me if I really wanted, maybe I could talk to Mike over at the Animal Shelter and volunteer there doing things like walking dogs," she plopped down on the grass next to Ziggy. Molly picked a dandelion and teased Ziggy with the flower, and Jenna copied her and picked a dandelion. She looked into the yellow petals. Could she be so carefree in time? She pulled a few of the petals from the flower and thought of the childhood game "He loves me, he loves me not."

The dog jumped up and gave the girl a lick on the nose

"Ziggy, you know better," Jenna scolded the dog.

"It's okay, really I'm fine," Molly pleaded, and Jenna detected a worried sound in the little girl's voice.

"Really she didn't hurt me at all. Please, don't be mad at her."

Jenna hit a chord with the child, and Molly crawled closer to Jenna. Ziggy looked at Jenna and crept into Molly's lap. Jenna reached out and touched Molly's arm.

"It's okay, I'm not mad at Ziggy, but she has to learn her manners so that she can be out with people and not get hurt or hurt someone," Jenna put her hand on Molly's back and gently rubbed.

Molly nodded, her body relaxing as she hugged the small dog body.

Tension hung in the air, but dissipated into the haze which seemed lighter and less suffocating.

A blast from a bell filled the quiet air and made Jenna jump.

"What was that?"

The girl giggled at the adult's fright.

"That is the lunch bell," Molly stood up and brushed grass off her pants. "That means we have to go in and have lunch now."

Jenna stood up, scooped up the dog, and put him her pocket.

"Does she like that?" Molly's face scrunched up.

"I don't know," Jenna shrugged her shoulders. "But I know that it is best for her to be when we are in the building in case some people are afraid of dogs. Also, if she was on her leash, she is so small that people may not see her and step on her."

Molly nodded and grabbed Jenna's hand as they walked into the building.

"You know, if Ziggy has to come outside and you don't want to go, I can do it for you," the child volunteered. "I'm old enough, and I promise to watch her the whole time."

Jenna nodded and promised to keep it in mind.

The constant aroma of coffee and hamburgers filled Jenna's nostrils made her stomach growl. Molly pulled Jenna forward and prattled on about something while pointing to a group of kids. Nodding at the child, Molly let go of Jenna's hand and ran towards the group.

"Hi everyone," a female voice rang out from the stage. "This is just your afternoon update."

Jenna scanned the room for Paul and Patty, but they were nowhere to be seen. She noted the number of people dwindled from this morning and wondered if they had found ways home, or were just in other parts of the building.

"The report from the fire line is that the winds have shifted and there is a good chance that the resort will be allowed to reopen tomorrow. Which, for those of you on vacation interrupted, should be back on the massage table by tomorrow night and the resort has given me permission to let you all know that not only will you be eligible for money back, but they are throwing in some wonderful surprises for those of you that are remaining and finishing your stay with them."

A few people clapped.

"For those of you interested in going home, we have another two buses leaving in about an hour for Portland, one to the airport and one stopping at the train station on its way to the airport," the woman at the microphone raised her fist in the air in happiness. "We need to see how many people want to leave and where they want to go, so if those of you who are interested could you please fill out a piece of paper with your name and destination, either the airport or train station, or even the bus station or a hotel, we will read through them and set up our plans. If we have more people that want to go then seats on the vehicles, we will be drawing names like this morning and set up another bus later in the afternoon or early evening."

She turned the microphone off as another woman jumped up on the stage and whispered in her ear. A squeal filled the room as she turned it back on.

"Oh yeah, and make sure to put how many people are in your party on the paper," she added.

Done with her duty, she moved off the stage, and into a crowd of people who waited with more questions.

"Hey, has anyone managed to track down Pastor Paul?" Someone yelled into the cafeteria.

Looking around the room, Paul and Patty were still absent.

Jenna looked down at Ziggy to make sure she was okay, and the little dog looked up with a sleepy look, worn out by her time playing with Molly. She put her head back down and closed her eyes.

"Dang it would be nice to be able to just sleep like that," she commented.

She got her lunch and sat down at a table while she daydreamed about life.

"Um, ma'am?" a young voice forced her to. "Do you want to fill this out so that you can be on the bus later?"

Jenna looked into the bright eyes of a girl in her 20s and graciously accepted the paper and pen. She put the form down on the table and posed the writing utensil to start writing her name.

"Do I really want to leave?" she put the pen down. She turned and looked up at the stage, the place she first saw Paul again. "What do I have to go home to? Maybe I could still have some time to think at the resort."

She scanned the posters on the walls and wondered what life her would be like. She picked the pen back up and started to write her name.

"Do you really want to get back on that plane?" She put the pen down.

She folded the paper in half and shoved it into the back pocket of her jeans and stood up.

"It may be sort of boring around here, but at least I'm alive," she thought about the smiling man on the tail of the airplane who promised a smooth flight and lied.

Jenna finished her lunch, cleared her space, and walked out towards her makeshift sleeping room. She bumped into a sandwich board set up in the hallway with a paper taped to it. She looked closer and read a list of things set up for the stranded vacationers.

"Wow, we can go and see a movie," she touched her pocket and felt the dog move. "Or there is a prayer service in about.."

Jenna looked down at her watch.

"..in about two hours or we can go and find out how to knit, crochet or quilt with the women of the church."

She scanned down the list.

"Now if they put on there a private session with the Pastor, that I may be interested in." An unwanted smile creased her face.

"It could be arranged if you need it," a voice answered.

Jenna spun around, embarrassed by her personal conversation being overheard.

"No, really, I'm fine," she uttered, her cheeks burning. "I was just, well, I was just."

The other woman's smiled and raised her hand to let Jenna know that no further explanations were needed.

"Don't worry about it, honey, we have all had the very same thought," she teased. "He is a handsome man."

Jenna quickly moved on to her room and crawled into her cot. She pulled the blanket up around her shoulders and hoped she could take a short nap, but her mind was wide awake and not about to shut down. Jenna shut her eyes anyway, and somehow sleep finally won over her overactive thoughts.

Chapter Twenty-Three

Jenna awoke and shuffled to the cafeteria. She spied Molly coloring in a book and joined her.

"Does Ziggy need to go outside?" the girl sat up straight, her eyes wide. Hearing her name, the dog stuck her head out with her mouth open in a smile.

"Well, probably," Jenna replied. She glanced at the dog and back at the child. She pursed her lips and scratched her arm.

"Do you think you can do that by yourself?"

The child's eyes sparkled, and she nodded fervently.

"Oh yes, and I promise to not let her out of my sight, ever."

"Okay, "Would you like to take her out?"

Molly's face lit up with the opportunity, and she jumped up. She ran off, explaining she needed to go ask mama Patty or Jeremy.

"I will be right back, don't move," she yelled over her shoulder.

Jenna watched a few people as they circulated around asking if anyone knew where the minister was.

"That man is never where he is supposed to be," an older woman snapped to a group of church workers around her. "But he is a good preacher."

They agreed and continued their search.

Molly returned with permission, and Jenna fished the dog out of her pocket. She attached the leash while the child danced around Jenna. She reached out for the strap, and Jenna put Ziggy on the floor. Jenna smiled and the girl's exuberance. She handed Molly the control of her best friend and Molly squealed in a high-pitched voice. She coaxed Ziggy out the door and into the sunlight that was winning the war against the smoke. Ziggy looked back at Jenna and panted a smile.

Jenna followed at a distance to give the child the idea she was in total control. She watched Molly walk the dog to the edge of the parking lot, and made sure not to let her charge out onto the concrete until both ways were checked at least two times for moving vehicles. Jenna could hear the cheerful chirping of the girl as she talked to Ziggy.

Molly led Ziggy to a nice patch of green and sat down next to the dog. Jenna exhaled her breath as she observed Molly as she played with the fluffy ball of fur.

"You are such a good dog," Molly rubbed the dog's stomach while Ziggy tried to lick her. "I wish I could play with you every day always."

Molly picked a blade of grass and teased the dog's nose as the dog jumped around, trying to take it away.

"They look good together," Jenna jumped at the familiar voice behind her. "I wish we could have a dog at the home. I really believe it would be good for all the children, but then we have to worry about allergies and find the money for vets and such, and we barely have enough to make the bills we already have."

Jenna turned around and faced Patty. She witnessed the longing on the woman's face to make this child's life the best she could.

"Not that she isn't doing better, but when she is with that dog, she just seems like a kid her age should," Patty's voice caught with emotion. She pulled air into her lungs and reached out to Jenna's arm. Tears showed in Patty's eyes.

"How is she normally?" Jenna turned and watched the little girl and dog.

"She is more withdrawn, more to herself. Sometimes I just hope she is not having constant memories and terrors of what she went through, but your dog has made a difference."

She looked like any other child seen in a park, but something nagged her about what the child lived through.

As if she read Jenna's mind, Patty started to tell Molly's short story. Born to a heroin-addicted prostitute in

Portland, no one knew why the woman decided to try to keep the girl.

"But I'm so glad they did," Patty beamed as she looked at Molly.

She grew up with her mother turning tricks in the next room for her unstable pimp boyfriend.

"Child protective services got involved and took her away when she was about two, but somehow they let the woman have her back a year later," Patty's face betrayed her look off contempt.

She folded her arms in front of her as she told how at least one man abused the child, and now any signs of anger put the child into a highly stressed state. Jenna teared up, thinking to Molly's reaction when Jenna corrected Ziggy's behavior. She hung her head and listened.

"One day there was a call to 911, and the police showed up to find Molly sitting next to her mother's body," Tears welled up in Patty's eyes. "They figured some john slit her throat over a disagreement in payment. It probably happened at least a day before someone heard Molly crying and called the police."

Tears streamed down Patty's face, her cheeks growing red. Her lips curled in a snarl.

"I heard about the case from a friend. I knew I had to get Molly out of the situation and take care of her. When we got her, she wouldn't talk or even eat. She sat on her bed and looked at the wall crying for her mother. We thought she was lost," Patty let the tears loose and batted them away. "That was three years ago when she was just six years old."

Jenna's heart raced as she watched the merry girl chase a butterfly while Ziggy ran around barking and dancing at her feet. Jenna put her hand on her chest on her neck and shivered.

"When she started to respond, we were ecstatic and has made wonderful progress. But she still has problems getting close to people or interacting with other children" Patty smiled through the tears. "But to see her with your dog..."

Patty stopped, not sure how to complete that sentence.

"Well, to see her with your dog, she is a little kid again. She is happier than she has ever been and just playing and enjoying the day. This is a gift from God I could never have even prayed for."

Molly's joyful squeals polluted the air while the facts of her life hung in the air.

"So, I guess I need to thank you," Patty wiping her eyes with the back of her hands. "Thank you for letting her play with that little fluff,

and thank you for being here. God does work in mysterious ways."

Jenna stood, unsure of how to react or what to say until her mind could formulate the words.

"I'm just happy that I could witness this, it helps me," she turned and reached for Patty's hand, but Patty wrapped Jenna up in a hug. Jenna gave into the embrace and felt the warmth of her new friend.

The women separated and watched the child and dog in silence.

"I wish there was more I could do or say," Jenna brushed her wet cheeks with her free hand.

"You know, I've known you like five hours," Patty linked her arm around Jenna's arm. "And I have to say that I'm convinced you were sent here for a reason. I have faith that you were meant to be here, and I hope you are not leaving soon because I believe you could do great things here."

Jenna smiled and turned back to the girl and dog. She scanned the scenery. What would it be like to live in such a friendly and beautiful place? She pictured her lonely house back home and questioned what kept her there. The people and places she grew up with no longer applied to her. She rubbed her eyes and thought about growing up in the town, but everyone had left her there alone. She leaned into Patty and smiled.

After half an hour, Patty moved over to the child and dog.

"Molly, I think it is time you let Jenna have her dog back, and maybe she will let you play with Ziggy again later," Patty put her hand on the little blond head. Molly squinted at Jenna, and Jenna nodded while Molly fought back the tears.

Molly slowly held the leash out to Jenna, who smiled and asked Molly if she could hold the leash until they were back in the building. Molly jumped up, a smile spread across her face. The trio crossed the parking lot to the school.

Inside the building, Molly handed the leash to Jenna, thanked her, and walked off with a promise she could see Ziggy again.

In the cafeteria, someone posted a list of the people who won seats on the departing bus. Jenna reached into her back pocket and felt the card safely still with her.

155

"Hello, folks," a woman stood in front of the room and addressed the crowd. "We have posted names and what buses you will be on. We ask that you try to be at least 15 minutes early. We will be seating families together first and then couples and singles."

Jenna scanned the room for Paul and didn't find him. She reached down to take Ziggy's leash off, and for the first time didn't try to hide her. Ziggy spotted Molly across the room and ran towards the child.

"Ziggy, you come back here," Jenna scrambled after the dog, but Ziggy was on a mission.

Molly disappeared around a bend, with the dog hot on her heels. Jenna trailed behind and hissed at the dog. She slipped around a corner and caught up to the fluff ball. She scooped Ziggy into her arms and Ziggy cowered submissively.

"You are a rotten little animal," Jenna reattached Ziggy's leash to her collar.

A girl in her 20s rushed past her from a doorway on her left; the girls face a rosy red glow from exertion as her hands smoothed down her wrinkled blouse. The faint smell of sweat followed her like a personal cologne. Wisps of light auburn hair sprung loose from a ponytail.

"Oh, excuse me," she rushed past Jenna.

Jenna peeked into the room and spotted a male figure's back as he tucked in his shirt. He turned around, and Jenna recognized the face of the man she couldn't get out of her mind. Paul's face showed the same redness of exertion, and he also sported the faint smell of sweat. Jenna observed a line of sweat along his hairline.

"Uh, Jenna," he smiled at her. "Hi, how are you doing?"

156

Jenna stumbled out of the makeshift office and looked at the floor. Anywhere but at this man she misjudged. She begged forgiveness and made up an excuse to explain her presence. Ziggy wagged her tail at seeing Paul, and Jenna felt betrayed by the small animal. Finally, Jenna asked if she could sign up for the next bus.

"Oh, I'm sorry you are leaving us," Paul continued to button up his shirt, and Jenna caught a glimpse of hair just below his collarbone.

"Yeah, well, you know. See you later," she turned and rushed down the hallway. She only stopped after she exited the building. She leaned against the brick wall, the sound of her rapidly beating heart drowning out all other noise. Her breath rushed in and out of her body, and her knees threatened to give out.

"I have got to be wrong," she winced as she pictured the pretty coed rushing from the room. She closed her eyes and thought about the details. Everything happened so fast.

Was she fair to Paul? He seemed surprised to see her, but not in the way someone caught with their hands in the cookie jar. Why should he be feeling guilty? The girl was young, but not so young, it was a crime, only a sin. She knew him, but not very well, and perhaps he did nothing wrong. He was a man, and she was a pretty young lady, but deep down, Jenna knew on some level, it wasn't right.

Jenna put her arm up over her eyes, while Ziggy squirmed in her other arm.

"Oh Zigs, please tell me that I'm wrong," she hugged the dog. "Maybe I'm wrong. There could be another reason."

She held her breath and forced herself to picture anything else, but once seen, she could never unsee.

Something was off. Paul played their last interaction over in head. Things went well on their walk back from the coffee shop, though she seemed distracted.

He sat down behind his makeshift desk, as Patty walked into the room

"Hey you," she moved over to him and gave him a hug.

Paul sat down, and Patty sat opposite him.

"Okay, spill," she folded her hands and placed them on the desk.

"Well, I thought Jenna and I were friends," he ran his hand through his hair. "But when we walked back from the cafe, she seemed distant, and now she was in here talking about getting a bus home."

Patty sat back in the chair and asked him to explain what happened. Paul stood up and started to pace as he talked about going out for a run, and how Rachel, one of the members of the young adult group, joined him. They returned to the school, and she used his bathroom to freshen up and change her clothes. After her, he went into the bathroom and changed from his sweats to something more presentable.

"And after that, Jenna came in to ask about the bus schedule," he dropped into his chair, his hands held out in question. "She just asked about the bus and didn't want to do a lot of small talk."

Patty shrugged.

"Maybe she was just tired or in a bad mood," Patty smiled at Paul. "You are probably just reading way too much into this. Of course, she wants to go home. This is not the best vacation, after all."

"I don't know, but something seemed off," he admitted. He shook his head and took a deep breath.

Patty smiled as she stood up. She patted him on the shoulder and told him to keep his chin up.

"You never know what God has planned for you, and what path he wants you on," she proclaimed as she left the room.

Paul looked at the door and shook his head. He gathered his things and left the room to go inspect the evening's activities.

The evening bled into night, and soon, Jenna laid in her cot with Ziggy cuddled in close.

"You know," Jenna stared up at the ceiling. "You really don't know the situation."

She rolled over and in vain, tried to think of anything else. Maybe the girl was older than she appeared, and they were in a loving, committed relationship. He never claimed he wasn't involved with anyone and perhaps she just wanted him to be single for her own reasons.

She rolled over on her back, and she listened to the whispers between one or two of her roommates.

For the second night in a row, Jenna fell asleep with Paul on her mind, though tonight so different than the night before.

Chapter Twenty-Four

Paul stopped by the church to pick up a few things on his way back to the school. Paperwork littered his desk, and he glanced at the stacks of sheets. The pile grew, but he didn't have time for it right now. He grabbed the top page and scanned it. A mark in the corner signaled it as read and answered, but something in the words drew him in.

"Dear Pastor Dorward," it read. "I don't know if you remember me, but we met at the Pacific Northwest Mental Health forum in Seattle a few months ago. I have a client I may require your help with. My client, Jenna Caryl..."

The letter informed Paul of the death, the anxiety of travel and Ziggy. Paul stared at the paper as it sunk into his brain. He shook his head, and he folded it between the pages of the book he came to retrieve. He opened the book and looked at it one more time. What were the chances?

He walked out into the rising sun. A surreal glow surrounded him as the smoke receded into little bits of wisps. He strolled towards his truck.

There was something special about this woman, and her presence brought joy to his soul; a joy he thought died with his wife. He witnessed her stares and wondered if she felt it too.

Would this new discovery throw a wrench in things? Paul climbed into his truck. Should he tell her?

Jenna dragged herself into the cafeteria for breakfast, with Ziggy on her leash following close behind. She spied Paul across the room, smiling and joking with a group of people. He spotted her and waved, and she dropped her gaze to the floor. He left the group and crossed the room.

"Jenna," he picked up his pace as she turned to leave. "I was hoping to talk to you for a minute. Can we go to my office?"

Jenna nodded as Paul grabbed a plate, filled it with breakfast goodies, and led her down the same hallway she had fled from last night. He directed her to sit in a chair opposite him, and he slid behind a large oak desk.

"Welcome to my temporary office," he waved his arms around, a smile spread across his features. "I promise you that it is not nearly as cozy as my real one, but then it will do in a pinch. I don't know how much you saw when you were here last night."

Jenna scanned the room. A whiteboard dominated one wall, with a shopping list scrawled down the center. Other walls were covered with shelves stocked with large cans of assorted vegetables. She looked back over at Paul.

"You know, I've thought your name was really familiar to me and couldn't figure out why, until I stopped by my real office a little while ago," he smiled and retrieved a paper on the counter behind him. Jenna sat stone-faced.

"And there it was, you name, on a fax I received from Wendy Achondo," he offered her the paper. "I guess she is your therapist?"

Jenna nodded and sat still. Was he planning on using it to keep her quiet? She picked the dog up off the floor and held her close? She could feel light perspiration on her brow.

"Anyway," he shrugged and put the paper down. "She wrote to me and asked if I could be available if you needed to talk to someone."

Confused, Jenna looked over at Paul.

"I'm a trained psychologist, and I guess you have my name also, just in case," he read the paper. "And I just wanted to touch bases with you and see how you are doing."

He smiled and waited for Jenna to respond.

"I'm fine. What did she say in there about me," Jenna refused to show anything she was feeling.

"You are welcome to read it but to paraphrase, you are first and foremost a very nervous traveler, and you recently suffered a loss you're dealing with and maybe having a hard time doing that," he looked up into her eyes and once again she struggled not to get lost in the green depths. "She mentioned Ziggy as an emotional support animal, so I guess she can spend more time out of your pocket now."

Jenna looked down at her hands, a child in the principal's office. Ziggy readjusted herself in Jenna's lap.

"Look, Jenna, you have nothing to worry about," he stood and moved closer to Jenna and sat on the edge of the desk. "I want you to know I'm here for you and I also want to say thank you for helping Molly."

Jenna's head snapped up, and she caught an authentic look of caring in his eyes.

"Patty came to me and told her about how that adorable little beast in your lap has done in the last few days what very few people have accomplished in the last nine months," His gaze pierced Jenna down to her being. "And for some reason, Patty told me what a good person you are, not that I needed her to point it out."

He moved from the desk and crouched next to her. He took her hands in his.

"I could tell even during our short time at the airport that you were someone special," he looked down and the floor and then back into her eyes. "I even told my nephew to go get me a coffee and come back and then went back to see if I could find you."

He chuckled and looked down at his feet again.

"But you already moved on, and I regretted not getting your information, so I could call or write or text or whatever is the right thing to do now."

He smiled at her, and she felt drawn in by his charm.

"Just like that pretty young girl," she thought.

She broke from his gaze and hoped he didn't see the rosy tint to her cheeks. Ziggy jumped down on the floor and laid down next to her feet.

"Anyway," he stood and moved back behind the desk. "We really don't know when they are going to allow people back to the resort."

He sat down and folded his hands on the desktop.

"And I guess I wanted to ask if you wanted to get back to Portland, or if you would like to stay here?" The question hung in the air.

She took in a deep breath and looked around the room. Yesterday, she wanted to stay, to get to know Paul better and find a way to help Patty. Only a few days passed since her arrival, but something about this place made her want to stay. But, that was yesterday, and today she knew more than she wanted to.

"The reason I ask," Paul leaned forward, "is Patty wondered if you would like to come and see the home? I saw in Wendy's letter that you were a caretaker for your mother and when she passed, you didn't have anyone to care for anymore and maybe felt a little lost."

Jenna turned and looked at Paul, her lips pressed together. She concentrated on breathing and rolled the question around in her head before answering.

"Oh my goodness, I would love to go," she stood up, ready to bolt out the door. "But only if Ziggy can come."

She looked at the little dog, and Paul smiled and nodded a nonverbal "of course" as he walked towards the door.

He dramatically swept his hand towards the door and stated he needed to tell a few people where he was going. He described the older four-wheel-drive SUV for her to find, and she nodded with a broad smile dominating her face. She watched as he got lost in the crowd and she exited the building to go and find his car.

"He is taken, and this is just to see my friend again," she told the little dog who stared up at her with her doggy smile. "He is not interested, and that is fine. I can do this."

She found the truck and leaned against the door until she saw him coming.

"Breath," she told herself and returned his wave.

Chapter Twenty-Five

Jenna turned north and noticed the majestic mountains surrounding the little town. Snow still topped the peaks despite being summertime and reached up into a smoke-filled hazy blue sky.

Ziggy explored as far as her leash would allow her to go

"It really is a sight to behold when you can see it," Paul sauntered to the truck. "I don't think I will ever get tired of the view."

He opened the door for Jenna and pushed aside books and garbage piled on the seat. She climbed in, and Paul scooped up the dog and handed her to Jenna before he moved the other side of the truck and slipped in. Food wrappers from a local drive-thru littered the floor, and Ziggy jumped down to investigate.

"Sorry, about that," he reached down and grabbed the garbage. He held the trash, not sure what to do with it.

"Don't sweat it," Jenna laughed. "You aren't the only one that lives in your car and besides, better to be on the passenger floorboards then on the highway."

Paul nodded and threw the garbage in the back. The paper fell among books and loose pages already littering the bench seat.

"Next time I think to invite taking someone in here, I should probably run out and clean it up," he smiled, and the sound of his laugh filled the cab.

The drive was short, less than half a mile, yet on the other side of the town. They pulled up to a large building right out of a horror movie with a wrap-around deck dominating the front, complete with porch swing. The actual house stood three stories high, book-cased on each side by round turrets. Lilac bushes ran along the front of the deck, and a four-foot white picket fence marked the front yard. Over the gate, a wood arbor sported a plaque that welcomed visitors to the "Mountain View Home.".

"We're here," Paul parked on the curb in front of the house.

Jenna opened the door, and Ziggy lept out. They walked to the door, being pulled by the little dog. Jenna stopped and looked up at the house. She wanted to move in, after all, she was an orphan now.

An older woman met them at the door and let out a squeal as she hugged Paul. They laughed, and the woman introduced herself as Hettie, the housekeeper, and part-time home mother and disciplinarian.

"I'm the one they call when Patty can't bring herself to punish one of the kids," she smiled with a glint in her eye. "I raised four kids of my own, so I have no problem with punishing or correcting someone when they need it."

The trio entered the house, while the sound of children playing made the house feel alive. A few preteen boys sprinted down the stairs, while they hollered about who would be the first one to reach the backyard.

"You two stop running down the stairs before someone gets hurt and quit your wallering before I find something for you to put all that energy into doing," Hettie warned. The boys stopped and started to amble down the stairs, though still goading each other in whispered voices.

Hettie offered refreshments and disappeared back into the depths of the house while Paul led Jenna to a living room, just left of the front door. A fireplace commanded

166

one of the walls, while comfortable plush furniture screamed for someone to jump in and get swallowed up. Jenna resisted the call. She and Paul walked like adults to the couch and sat down. Hettie reentered with a pot of tea and talked about how lucky it was as she just put on a pot of water for herself with plenty of extras. She poured three cups, handed them out, and planted her ample backside down on the other side of Paul.

Patty descended the stairs and ran over to hug Jenna and Paul. She retired into an overstuffed chair across from the sofa.

The conversation consisted of small talk and the status of the fires, which were almost contained.

"I heard the resort just received the okay to reopen in three days after they have an inspector up there just to do a survey," Patty disclosed and glanced at Jenna. "Will you be going back there?"

Jenna looked at the cup of tea in her hands. She shrugged her shoulders.

"I really don't know," She admired the child paintings tacked to the wall and family pictures on the fireplace mantel. Religious books and easy-read children's books covered the wood coffee table in front of Jenna.

"Yeah, I heard that there might be some firefighters coming down from the front line to decompress before shipping back home," Patty reached for her tea and blew on the cup before taking a sip. "And I'm wondering if they are going to stay at the school, or what the plan is."

"Well, I don't know that we have any other options, and I'm pretty sure that they know the score," Paul leaned back on the couch, his hands behind his head. Jenna watched him and let out a small gasp.

Two girls rushed through the house towards the kitchen and like the boys before, Hettie squawked the house rules to them. Patty reached over and touched Hettie's arm.

"I don't know what I would do without you," she chuckled to Hettie.

Patty looked at Jenna and asked if she would like a tour. Jenna nodded, and the two women rose. Jenna followed her host up the stairs and down the hallway. More children's artwork hung in cheap frames on the walls, and Patty explained that each room held four children, and with four bedrooms and four bathrooms, she was at capacity with 16 residents. They entered a back bedroom, and Jenna saw a small, nondescript bed with no toys or decorations. She looked at the sign over the bed and noticed the name, Molly. Jenna looked over at Patty with a questioning look.

"I've tried to get her to put up posters of anything, or even to have a toy or two, but she doesn't want anything," Patty walked over and touched the edge of the bed. "When she first came, she just sat on the bed, and now she at least will leave the room, but still she doesn't really engage."

Patty looked down at Ziggy sticking out of Jenna's pocket, put there for convenience more than hiding.

"Well, until Ziggy came along," Patty reached over to scratch Ziggy's ears. "I can't believe what this dog has done for her. I think she is outside with one of the other girls in the backyard."

"Well, maybe I can send her a picture of Ziggy to put up," Jenna stated, the sight of the sparse living space causing her stomach to ache.

Patty smiled and touched her arm.

The tour continued, the third floor was Patty's living space with a bedroom, bathroom, and little office.

The duo returned to the main floor, and Jenna observed the modern kitchen, a library full of books, a dining room with a large wood table in the middle and then back to the living room. Two more bathrooms completed the house tour, and Jenna marveled at the house and how organized it seemed to be.

"All Hettie I assure you," Patty assured Jenna.

"What do you say we go out back and I let you meet some of the kids?" Patty grabbed Jenna's arm and gently pulled her towards the back door.

Children, tired of being cooped up in the house, played loud games in the fenced yard. A few boys climbed up a wall while some girls swung. In the back, Jenna spotted Molly as she sat in the grass. Ziggy noticed his friend and squirmed out of the pocket. Jenna caught her mid-jump to the ground before she sat the dog on the ground. Ziggy jetted across the yard as fast as her little legs would move, as she avoided her obstacle course of children and toys.

"Ziggy!" A shrill squeal trumped all other noises as the dog lunged at the little girl. Molly's joy polluted the air just as the smoke had the last few days. She hugged the little dog while Jenna crossed the yard to join. Other children surrounded Molly and asked questions. Many reached out to touch the black fur of Ziggy's back.

"Hi Molly," Molly looked up, her eyes filled with excitement and pure adoration for the dog. She thanked Jenna for bringing Ziggy to see her. Her eyes filled with tears.

"Does this mean you are going home and taking Ziggy?" she fought to keep control, and it broke Jenna's heart. She told the child not yet but knew the day was not that far away. She sat down next to Molly and pet the excited little dog.

Jenna stayed for lunch, and the atmosphere relaxed her. Even before cancer, family dinner was just Jenna and her mother, including Thanksgiving and Christmas. Occasionally, her mother invited a stray person from church or Jenna brought home from school, but it was never like this. Never the chaos of passing food or loud chatter. Jenna leaned back in her chair and took in a deep breath. She was sure this was what real families were like, and she smiled.

The day turned to early evening, and Paul announced they needed to get back to the school for dinner service and to discuss with his staff the possibility of the addition of the firemen.

On the drive back to the school, Jenna quietly watched the houses and business speed by.

"Isn't there some way Molly could have her own dog, I mean, like Ziggy," she turned, and her eyes pleaded with Paul for answers.

"I don't know," he shrugged. "I think getting an emotional support animal is more than they can afford there."

Jenna watched the scenery go by.

"What if someone bought one for her?"

"I think it could cause problems," he shrugged.

The rest of the trip was silent; Paul glanced at Jenna, and she just looked away. He ran his hand through his hair and turned to her. He opened his mouth, shut it, and turned

170

back to watch the road in front of him. She put her hand on the armrest and rested her cheek on her fist.

Once back at the school, Jenna opened the door and leaped out of the truck. She mouthed a thank you and Paul couldn't help himself from staring at her pink lips.

"Anytime, and I mean that. All you have to do is ask, and I'm happy to take you again."

She walked quickly towards the building, her long strides putting distance between them. She could feel his eyes on her as she slipped into the building.

Chapter Twenty-Six

At dinner service, Paul announced another bus departing for Portland that evening and anyone interested should see him or one of his helpers. He also gave the news that the resort could be opening in two days, pending tomorrow's inspection and the gym erupted in applauds.

Jenna listened to Paul's smooth voice and knew it was time for her to decide. She felt the hard bench below her and imagined relaxing in a comfortable bed if she chose to go to Portland.

"Or we can go home," she whispered to Ziggy, to an empty house full of ghosts and memories

But she was going to have to do something, moving into the school was not an option.

Dinner was brought into the cafeteria, the smell of roasting meat floated and mingled with aromas of fresh baked rolls and coffee. Jenna sat down and decided to wait until the line was smaller. Next to Paul, Jenna spied the woman she recognized as the one outside of Paul's office yesterday. Visions of the woman adjusting her clothing filled her mind. She watched the woman respond to something Paul said to another person and her quick flirty smile bludgeoned Jenna. The woman reached out and touched Paul's arm, and he turned away from the girl without smiling back or even really acknowledging her.

"I would have thought he was more of a gentleman than that," she said to Ziggy in her lap, and the animal stared at her with big brown eyes.

Paul scanned the crowd and appeared to search for someone. A smile grew on his face as he spotted her. Jenna looked down, a warmth spreading from her cheeks to her forehead.

Jenna's stomach growled as a group of well-built men walked into the cafeteria, and several gasps filled the cafeteria. The smell of wood smoke fell off them like a snake shedding its skin. Jenna raised her head, ogled the specimens. The men joked loudly and talked to anyone that would listen, a jolly feel entered the room with them. One of the men held back and played with some of the boys who started a pickup game of catch.

Slowly, Jenna stood up and placed Ziggy in her pocket for safekeeping while she walked towards the food.

"And folks, we are being joined by some of the brave men who helped to get the fire under control," Paul waved at the group.

People cheered and applauded.

The men advanced to the buffet and piled plates high with food.

"Hey there," a dark-haired firefighter stopped just before running into her. "Sorry."

Jenna looked up into his two dark eyes and caught a joy and playfulness in the orbs.

"No problem," Jenna's cheeks burned as she rushed towards the buffet table.

"Hey, not so fast," the man caught up to her just as she reached the end of the line.

Jenna looked up at him and noticed the small lines around his eyes and the corner of his mouth. Soot was permanently stained on his hands and smudges of ash still streaked his cheeks.

"Yes?" Jenna checked to see if she had forgotten something back at her seat. Why else would he chase after her like this? He stood at least six inches taller than her, and she could see his six-pack abs under his tight tank top. A Celtic band circled one arm in dark blue ink.

"I just saw you back there with your little dog, and you looked like you were alone, so I thought I'd see if you would mind if I joined you?"

Jenna smiled, and looked down, afraid to look him in the eyes, and nodded. They reached the front of the line and were rewarded with many assorted casseroles and dishes.

"So you have been here a few days, what's good?"

Jenna pointed out some of the dishes served yesterday she enjoyed and whispered about some of the ones she thought were just okay. A lump in her throat forbad her from much more than a few words at a time. They piled their plates and moved to one corner of the cafeteria.

Well, Jenna, I hope you don't mind, but if I sit with you."

Jenna shook her head and giggled. She looked into his face, his bright brown eyes shining in a face that sported a scruffy beard.

"So, tell me all about you," the man waited.

Jenna smiled and asked him his name. He laughed at his mistake, and Jenna was drawn into this person's contagious happiness.

"Of course, I'm Mike," he gushed. "And I guess I will tell you about me, then."

He told her he had been a firefighter for the last few years, and during his tenure, he witnessed destruction not only in Oregon but also in Washington and California. He talked about joining the volunteer fire department and found a certain sense of meaning and accomplishment after helping people in peril. He helped to save their precious homes and memories threatened by fire demons.

"I guess you could say, it was my calling," his chest puffed out in pride.

Jenna told him the short story of her life and introduced him to Ziggy, who took an instant liking to the man. The dog jumped up to lick his nose. Jenna found an easiness with Mike she rarely felt. They continued to talk as people finished their dinners and wandered out to the night's activities of a movie in the gym and a church service in one of the classrooms.

They talked with daylight starting to fade into history. People wandered in and out, but they didn't notice.

"I think I need to take Ziggy outside," Jenna stood and realized she didn't want to leave. Mike volunteered to go out with her, and she enthusiastically nodded. She noticed Paul as he talked to the coed from yesterday and again as he watched her and Mike walk into the night air. The stars smiled down on them, and an almost full moon winked behind a few clouds.

"I never get tired of looking at that," Mike gawked at the night sky.

"Of course, tonight, I don't think I could ever get tired of looking at this either," he stared at Jenna.

Jenna turned to Mike, and he reached out and touched her cheek. Finding no resistance, Mike moved in closer to Jenna, his body just inches from hers. He put his hand on her waist and pulled her in closer, his face coming down to hers, his lips slowly and gently touching her lips. Jenna gave into the kiss, and let Mike's touch awaken feelings she didn't realize she missed. She leaned into him and allowed his hands to move up and then down her back. A slight moan escaped his lips, and she felt his touch going lower down her back. She pulled away just as a tug on the leash reminded her Ziggy was here.

"I'm sorry, Mike," amazed at herself for stopping. "I don't think this is a good idea right now."

Mike backed up and wiped his grinning swollen lips with the back of his hands. He ran his hand through his hair and smiled down at Jenna, his eyes dilated to the point of being mostly black instead of brown.

"Okay, you are right, but I really want to see you tomorrow then," he reached out and grasped her hands.

Jenna felt her cheeks burning.

"I would love that."

They agreed to meet up after breakfast, and hesitantly parted ways, Mike hung onto her hand tightly. He finally dropped her hand and watched as she walked towards the building, almost pulling Ziggy as the dog strained against her leash.

He said something after her, but she couldn't quite hear it. She refused to turn around and go back to find out what it was. She may never get back to her own cot tonight if she did.

"You like him, then?" Ziggy looked up at her with bright dark eyes and a small smile.

"Okay, I just hope you are a good judge of character then," she let the dog trot into the building as they made their way down the hall to their sleep quarters.

Chapter Twenty-Seven

Jenna sat on the edge of her cot and fished around in her luggage for clean clothes. She dropped the bag to the floor and put her head in her hands. How did she get here? This was not the plan. The itinerary never included sleeping in a school or lost luggage.

She picked the bag back up and rummaged around again.

"You know the definition of crazy is doing the same thing and thinking you will have a different result, but there has to be at least a shirt or something in here," she whispered. Ziggy laid at the foot of the cot, and her ears twitched with the sound of Jenna's voice.

Her hand bumped a hard object she recognized as her cell phone. She pulled it out and impsected the dark screen. She plugged the charger into a nearby outlet, and the phone jolted to life, dinging with numerous voice mails, text messages, and emails. She pulled up the first text.

"Sorry 4 ur loss, call me," from her high school best friend.

"Call me if u need a shoulder," a college friend wrote.

"I'm here," a third text arrived from a church friend of her mother.

Jenna poured over the numerous texts from people who wanted to help her cope with her mother's death. A tear fell down her cheek. Were they there the entire time, and she was too wrapped herself to see it? She thought of the church women whispering encouragements into her ear while she watched the ornate pine box being lowered into the hole.

She set the phone down and walked back to her cot. She plopped down and looked at her hands in her lap. Ziggy strolled over to her and laid down in her lap. Jenna wondered if the actual obstacle she faced was herself all along.

"I need to find a way to interact with people," she ran her hand through the dog's fur. She didn't have to be strong when so many people wanted to catch her and make the falling less painful.

"Just like Wendy talked about," Ziggy inched her way up towards Jenna's chest.

"Maybe I should let my guard down and really see where Mike and I can go," she whispered to the dog. Ziggy answered with a quick attempt to lick Jenna's nose. "I guess that means you are fine with it."

The phone battery got stronger, and she called her voice mail. Twelve messages poured out of the phone from concerned people. The final message came from the airline and let her know they found her bags and to call a number to let them know where to send them.

"I just don't know where we are going to be," she said to the little dog. "I will get back to them tomorrow. I don't think that anything has to be decided tonight."

She pulled Ziggy closer and shut her eyes. Mike's smile lit her mind, the feel of his touch permanently dented on her skin. She thought about the kiss and reached up to touch her lips. She wandered off into sleep as Mike's face morphed into another one with lighter colored green eyes and a kind smile.

Paul couldn't help but notice Jenna sitting with the fireman. He saw the way she looked at him, her shy smile and a twinkle in her eye. He made himself busy and desperately thought of anything else. The weather. The fires. Anything, But his eyes wandered over to the couple sitting in the corner. He clenched his teeth, and a slight growl escaped his lips.

"Pastor Paul?"

The college-aged girl walked up to Paul, and he cringed.

"Hello," he forced a smile. "What can I help you with?"

She sidled up to him and placed her hand on his arm.

"I really enjoyed our time together yesterday," she slinked closer. "And I hope we can do it again, very soon. You really gave me some things to contemplate."

The hairs on his arms stood up, and he moved his arm out of her reach. Something about the way she talked to him it made him feel dirty. He turned away. He hadn't invited her to join him on his run.

He turned and faced her.

"You know, Rachel, I don't get to run much, at least not on a schedule," he needed to be diplomatic. "But I think it might be better if you talked to some of the athletic youths in the church and started a running club."

He smiled at her.

"I could talk to the youth director, and we could set up something like prayers ever five miles, or dinner with praise after the run or something," Paul was proud of what he was suggesting.

The coed smiled and took the hint. She picked up a few plates and said something Paul couldn't quite hear. He let out his breath as she walked away. He felt like he dodged a bullet. Rachel always seemed to be there with short bouts of conversation and questions about faith, love and finding the perfect person for her, but all the while, he felt he was being set up him up for something.

He turned back to the last place he saw Jenna and the fireman and his heart dropped to see they were gone.

He wanted just one more look at her but instead watched the fireman walk in.

"Well, at least I know she isn't with him right now," he kicked at a box on the floor.

The fireman sauntered around the room and flirted with some of the attractive young women helping to clean the room, including Rachel. Paul sat down. If the other man took an interest in the coed, both problems would be solved in one scoop.

Paul looked up to the ceiling and said a quick prayer.

"Sorry God, that wasn't a good thought. If he can make her happy, then that is what I want. Please forgive me for my own selfish emotions."

Paul stood up, walked back to his makeshift office, and gathered his things to leave. He passed through the cafeteria one more time on his way out and smiled as he noted the fireman and Rachel in a very animated conversation.

Chapter Twenty-Eight

Jenna rolled over in her cot and lost herself to sleep and her dream.

Jenna strolled with Ziggy past the house she used to babysit at and after that the house her best friend lived at. She couldn't dawdle too much since her mother needed her medication soon. She couldn't be late and cause her mother pain. Ziggy frustrated her as the dog sniffed every tree they passed.

"Come on you little monster," she pulled at Ziggy's leash.

The animal focused on a discarded newspaper. A picture on the front page stared back up at her, and she crouched down to get a better look. She picked up the printed paper, and despite the black eyes in the photo, Jenna knew they were green.

"Be quiet, don't laugh so loud," a girl's joyful snickering woke Jenna from the dream. She rolled over and squeezed her eyes shut. She reached into the depths of her mind to read the headline over the picture, but the time passed, and she was awake. She opened her eyes and took a deep breath. She rolled to her back and watched as a ray of sunshine spotlighted dust particles dancing in the beam. She pictured the particles back home, and it felt as if years passed since she watched them from her own bed, in her private room.

Ziggy crawled up the crowded cot and laid her head on Jenna's chest. Jenna laughed and gave up on any more sleep.

She sat up and grabbed the clothes she finally found balled up in the bottom of her carry on. After three days, this shirt and pair of jeans were it. She put Ziggy on her leash and walked to the back of the building. The sound of the shower caught her ear, and she noticed steam seeping from an open window. She slipped into the gym locker room.

Two women's voices echoed around the cement room and bounced around the maze of lockers.

"I heard the resort got clearance last night and we can all go and get out of this nightmare."

"Oh, it hasn't been so bad," the second commented. "I mean, last night those firefighters really sparked me up."

They laughed and noticed Jenna. One of the women scowled at her for eavesdropping.

She motioned to her partner, and they both turned off the water, grabbed towels, and left the area.

Jenna swallowed hard and looked at the floor.

She left the room and sauntered back to the cafeteria where she spied Patty. She approached her friend.

"Hi, um, is Molly with you?" Jenna looked around for the child. Jenna's heart fluttered, and she scanned back to the shower area.

Patty smiled and asked if she could take Ziggy to see the children. Jenna nodded, and she handed Patty the leash. Jenna walked towards the showers.

"Hey," Patty caught up to her friend. "Why don't I get Molly to take Ziggy outside, and I can stand watch while you shower?"

Jenna let out a sigh of relief and smiled.

"And I even know where they hide the towels," Patty had a mischievous glint in her eyes.

After a few minutes, Jenna stripped and jumped under the warm stream of water. The liquid ran down her body and washed away three days of dirt and grime. Her mind wandered to her time here, Paul and Mike; images of the pure joy on Molly's face when she saw Ziggy and Patty's hugs. They played like a movie on her closed eyelids. She moved further under the spray, and thought about sleeping in a soft, warm bed, large enough to really stretch out at the resort. She fantasized about sitting in front of a TV with freshly popped popcorn.

She let the water caress her back and again she thought about Paul.

She squirted shampoo in her hair. She could hear the messages on her phone. She did have people at home that cared about her.

"But what do I have in common with them anymore?" The suds ran down her back and into the drain.

People reached out to her during her mourning time, but could the relationships withstand time? Could she rebuild friendships with people she really didn't know anymore?

Jenna emerged from the shower and quickly dressed. Outside the room, Patty greeted her with a smile and a dancing dog.

"I think your dog was stressing out when she couldn't see you, though Molly distracted for a little while." Patty held Ziggy out in front of her. Jenna took the dog and held her close. She looked around the hall.

"Molly had to go back to the house to get a few things she forgot, "Patty pet Ziggy's head as the dog cuddled into Jenna's arms. "She will be back pretty soon."

Jenna moved to a table and set Ziggy in her lap.

"So, I hear the resort is up and running, and they are going to be having all you people be bused back up there in about an hour," Patty reached over and stroked the dog. "I'm going to hate to see you go."

"Me too."

The women sat side by side, the quiet in the room saying so much.

"Mama Patty,!" I shrill scream broke the silence.

Molly ran to Ziggy and dropped down to her knee. She crowded into Ziggy's space and went nose to nose with the little Pomeranian. She rubbed her head and cooed while the dog licked her face, and Molly burst into joyful laughter. Jenna watched the scene, and her shoulders dropped and bit her lip. In a matter of hours, she would separate the fast friends. Molly picked up the dog and held her close. Patty placed her arm on Jenna as Jenna's chin quivered. Patty nodded and squeezed Jenna's arm.

"I know you have to go," the child's tears started to fill her blue eyes. "I made this for you and Ziggy, so you won't forget me."

Jenna placed her hand on Molly's arm as the child showed the dog a drawing she had made.

"That's me and mama Patty and you," she pointed at the figures on the paper. She sniffled and continued.

"And of course, that is Ziggy," she pointed to a dark black circle with four legs and two triangle ears.

"I'm going to frame this and hang it up in my house where Ziggy and I can see it every day," Tears threatening to leak out of Jenna's eyes.

"It's okay," Molly looked up at Jenna, still holding the dog close to her. "I was just wondering if it would be okay if I

185

wrote Ziggy letters and maybe you could send me pictures sometime?"

Jenna smiled and told Molly she thought that Ziggy would really like that.

"We are all going to miss you both," Patty said and looked away. She turned back to Jenna. "I know it has only been a few days, but really, you have somehow made a difference here."

Patty reached out and pulled Jenna into a tight hug.

"I just hope that maybe you will come and see us again. I'm positive we can find a room for you to have at the house."

Jenna's tears won the fight and started to fall down her cheeks. She nodded and held Patty tighter.

"I will make a point of coming back when I can," she said into Patty's ear. "Even if it means I have to fly."

The women burst into laughter.

Jenna pulled out of the hug and asked Molly if she would take Ziggy outside. The child cheered, and the three walked into the sunshine. A bus pulled into the parking lot, and Jenna and Patty watched in silence while Molly played with Ziggy in a little grassy patch.

"I think we may look at finding a way to get her a dog," Patty revealed to Jenna. "It's tricky though since we can't really get her a dog and not get pets for the rest of the kids."

"What do you think is going to happen to Molly when I leave?" Jenna squeaked.

"I don't know," Patty dropped her head. "I'm not sure what I have to do. I just hope that the progress won't be gone with you and the dog."

Patty turned from Jenna and looked into the sky.

"I just hope I wasn't wrong in letting her get so attached," Patty grabbed Jenna's hand. "I didn't really think this out, and she was responding so positively that I guess I just didn't want to think of this moment. I hope she doesn't just think this is one more living thing that deserted her."

Patty looked at Jenna's concerned face.

"But I don't regret it," she squeezed Jenna's hand

Patty stopped talking and scrunched her brow. Silence invaded the area as both women were lost in thoughts, regrets, and hopes.

"But you know, I'm sure that in the long run, we will look back on this as a good thing and a very educational step on how to connect to some of the harder kids, like Molly," Patty pulled her hand from Jenna's. "I think you being here has been wonderful, and I wish you would stay."

Jenna smiled and looked again at the child and the dog.

The conversation turned to less important things as they each avoided talking about the bus and Jenna's departure. This bus would leave soon with her on it.

Chapter Twenty-Nine

Paul sat at his desk. How could he say goodbye to someone that woke his heart back up? He looked at his open Bible; another day of no words for his sermon. He looked at the picture of his wife on the desk and reached out to touch it. He looked closer at her smile and into her eyes.

"Did you set this up?" he questioned the image. "I could so see you doing that, not wanting me to continue to be alone. Are you sure I am ready?"

He shut the Bible and walked to the door. He folded his hands together and bowed his head.

"God, you have got me through some pretty rough times. Please help me to know what to say and to know what your will is."

He shut the door behind him, and he walked out and grabbed his keys off the table. He rehearsed what he would say when he saw her.

"Help me to find the words," he said as he got in the truck and was on his way.

Jenna walked back into the school, her eyes rimmed in red. The image of the little girl holding on tight to a tri-colored Pomeranian and fighting back sobs haunted her. Nothing could mend this broken heart, and the sight played over and over in Jenna's mind. She could still picture the desperation in Patty's eyes as she looked at Jenna for answers.

"Hey, gorgeous," Jenna spun around and saw the fireman. She forced a smile.

His happy expression changed to concern, and he led her to a table. He instructed her to sit as sobs stuck in her throat. She looked up at the ceiling and wrapped her arms around her stomach. He sat down next to her and listened as Jenna sputtered how she felt. Mike rubbed her back as Ziggy whined to be picked up. He scooped up the dog and placed her on his.

"I think you did more good than you know," he put his hand under Jenna's chin to look into her eyes. "Don't beat yourself up over this."

Jenna leaned into him and felt his arms slink around her.

"I know, but it is so hard to see right now."

A loud squeal came from the speaker being turned on.

"Hi, folks," Paul's smooth voice filled the room. "Just an update. The bus going up to the resort is here and will begin loading the luggage in about 45 minutes. If you would rather go to Portland, there is another bus that will be here in about 2 hours. We are going to be cleaning up the school and start to shut things down, so if you want to use the locker room showers, this is your last chance since they will be closed and locked in about half an hour."

Paul searched for Jenna. He scowled and bit his lip as he caught sight with her and the fireman.

"Of course, if you are not ready, we do have a van going up later this afternoon," Paul looked directly at Jenna.

"I have to get ready to go," she told Mike, and he nodded.

"You know," Mike rubbed her arm. "I secured a room at the hotel here in town for the next four days, so if you would like, I would be happy to come up to the resort and spend some time with you," his eyes shined with a hopeful look. He held his breath and waited for an answer. "But only if you are okay with it."

Jenna smiled and nodded.

The two stood up, and Mike placed Ziggy on the floor. He leaned in and kissed Jenna gently on the top of her head before he pulled her into a hug. They stood together for a moment before he released her. They exchanged phone numbers and promises to talk again very soon.

Jenna walked out of the door and could feel his eyes on her. She turned as he walked out the opposite door.

"Well, Zigs," she addressed the dog at her feet. "I'm not sure where this is going, but I promise to not stand in my own way."

The dog looked up at her and seemed to smile.

Jenna walked into the classroom, her home away from home for the last three days.

"So, would you rank us five stars?" Jenna recognized Paul's voice from behind her.

"Well, I'm not sure," she turned around and took the bait. "I've stayed in better, but then again, I've stayed in worse too."

Jenna pulled her carry-on bag from under the cot and sat down on the bed. She smiled at Paul, and he returned the smile.

"You know, I've really enjoyed getting to know you," he sat down next to her.

"I'd say this was one of the best experiences I've had in a very long time." Jenna turned and looked into Paul's green eyes as Ziggy jumped into her lap.

Jenna felt the warm of Paul's leg next to hers. He moved his hand to reach out to her but pulled back. She watched and moved her hand to closer to his but stopped before reaching his,

"I saw you with the fireman, he seemed interesting in you," Paul's voice was flat and informative. Jenna nodded and told Paul about Mike. Paul looked at the dog in her lap and without thinking reached out to scratch Ziggy's head.

"Do you think that we did damage to that little girl?" Jenna stared into Paul's eyes for answers. "Do you think that yanking Ziggy away from her could do her more harm?"

Paul shrugged his shoulders.

"We won't know that until you are gone, but in my professional opinion, it was more success than failure," he reached out and touched Jenna's arm. "I think that Ziggy has shown us that Molly is capable of bonding with something or someone again. That maybe she is starting to come out of her shell and going to be okay."

"Or will she just think that Ziggy is one more thing that left her?" Jenna's shoulders slumped, and she dropped her gaze to the floor.

Paul gently squeezed her arm, his touch sending electricity through her body.

"She has lots of people around here that really love her and will be here for her. She will get through, I promise."

Jenna nodded and stood up. She put Ziggy's leash on the dog and put her on the floor.

"I have to go."

Paul stood and took her bag from her hand. Together they walked towards the parking lot. At the bus door, Paul again reached out for Jenna's arm and gently took hold of it. Again, his touch sent shivers through her, and she Jenna turned and looked into his eyes.

"I just want you to know," he said quietly, "you have made a difference here; to Molly, to Patty and to me."

He looked into her eyes and Jenna searched for a spark, anything that said he was feeling it too.

"If you ever need a friend or anyone to talk to, I'm here," he smiled at her. "And I'm not talking about as a therapist that was recommended by your counselor, but as a real and true friend."

Jenna reached out and hugged Paul. He held her close as the bus driver coughed, and the couple parted.

"I don't think this is the last time you see me," Jenna wiped away a tear. "You all have made an impact on me, and I'll always be indebted to you for that. I was a mess when I came up here."

Jenna looked up into his eyes one last time.

"You have helped me see I have a future. I don't know what it is, or where I'll be, but you have helped me to see past the hole I was in. And I value the relationships I made here more than words could express."

Jenna picked up Ziggy and stepped onto the bus.

"You know, it could be here," Paul whispered.

She watched him through the window as she walked towards the back of the bus and found a seat. She continued to stare at him as he stopped at the school door and watched the bus pull out of the parking lot, onto the street and away.

Chapter Thirty

A stream ran along the road, and pines hugged the creek until the trees faded back into a forest. Had it really been four days since Jenna watched the same scenery from a bus window? But this time, the trip couldn't have been more different. She squirmed in her seat and Ziggy raised her head from Jenna's lap. A few people in front of her murmured among themselves.

"We will be there in about 15 minutes," the bus driver's voice filled the vehicle. "And I know they are anxious to help you start your vacation.?"

Soon, they rolled into the parking lot, and Jenna stared out the window at the facility. Her eye's widened at the size of the hotel in front of her. An overly cheerful woman boarded the bus and introduced herself as Sarah, the social planner and concierge for the resort. She boasted of the many amenities the hotel offered, from massages to seaweed wraps and long guided hikes in the nearby forests. Sarah informed the group of dining room times and menus while people gushed with excitement at the activities. Jenna turned from the speaker and looked at the surrounding trees. Among the foliage, she could see Patty, Molly, and Paul. She reached down and rubbed Ziggy's chin. Ziggy looked up with big bright eyes.

"I wonder if Molly will be okay?"

With the sound of the child's name, the dog twitched her ears and scanned the area.

Sarah called names off her clipboard and handed out keys. Jenna picked up her only bag and plodded to the front of the bus; Ziggy held tight in her other arm.

Jenna explained it was an emotional support animal, and Sarah asked to see papers.

"Well, I am going to have to have them faxed here since the airline lost my luggage," Jenna held Ziggy tighter.

Sarah smiled and marked a few things on her board before she handed Jenna a room key. Jenna placed Ziggy on the ground and moved to the side.

After Sarah read the last name, she asked the group to gather in a circle for some instructions.

"The resort is offering anyone the chance to stay past their original check-out date due to the circumstances. If you would like to take advantage of this offer, please see me or our front desk."

Jenna looked down at Ziggy.

"What do you think? "Ziggy continued to sniff the ground. "It has been a long week, and I just don't know."

Ziggy looked with a doggy smile and trotted to another area to explore.

"What do you know, your just a dog," Jenna commented.

"You don't have to decide right now," Sarah continued over the bullhorn. "Just please let us know as soon as you can if you would like to stay. We sincerely want to thank you all for deciding to stay after the disruption of your vacation."

Sarah put the bullhorn down and began to direct people to their rooms.

Jenna found her room on the ground floor near the back of the building. The smell of fresh lavender and vanilla assaulted her as she examined the space. A basket of fruit and nuts ruled a small table just inside a sliding glass door which led to a small fenced yard set up for Ziggy. Jenna crossed the room to look at the gift and read the note from the hotel, thanking her for staying. She removed Ziggy's leash, and the small dog ran around the room, nose to the floor. The place passed the dogs survey, and Ziggy jumped up onto the large soft bed. She walked up to the pillow and plopped herself down. Jenna crossed the room and laid down next to her, sinking into the soft comforter.

"Better than the cot?"

Ziggy crawled up and cuddled closer to her.

"Yeah, it does seem that perhaps tonight we will actually get good sleep."

Jenna reached to the nightstand and grabbed the menu. She glanced over the assorted gourmet goodies and found herself thinking of the homemade casseroles at the school, made by people wanting to help other people in need. She stood up and looked at herself in the mirror and contemplated going to the dining room. She looked at Ziggy. She could leave the sliding door open and let Ziggy run around the small yard while she was gone. The canine could chase butterflies and play while she dined with no threat of escape or being taken. She replaced the menu and reached for the remote control. With the push of a button, the TV sprung to life, and resort advertisements filled the screen, emphasizing massages and saunas; manicures and pedicures; and guided hikes. A cheerful person appeared on the screen and informed viewers on how to sign up for pampering or adventures. Jenna threw her bag on the bed and opened it.

"If I'm going to the dining room, I probably need to dress up a little," Ziggy rolled over on her back and begged for a tummy rub. Jenna laughed and obeyed.

She began digging in her bag and pulled out a shirt. Underneath it laid the picture, Molly drew for her. She pulled the drawing out and smiled with tears in her eyes.

"We are just going to have to make sure to video chat or come see her again," Ziggy appeared to smile, still sprawled out on her back.

Jenna dropped down on the bed and reached over to rub the dog's stomach again.

She picked up the phone and ordered dinner for the two of them, a hamburger for Ziggy and a beautiful piece of salmon for herself. It arrived shortly afterward.

"You would have thought I never fed you," she laughed as the dog wolfed down the meal.

Minutes bled into hours, and the setting sun cast long shadows on the pink-flowered wallpaper. Jenna moved to her side as she fought to keep her eyes open. She lost the fight until a notice ring from her phone woke her up.

"Just was thinking of you and wanted to say a quick hi," Jenna furrowed her brow not recognizing the phone number.

She stared at the message.

"BTW, it's Mike." She smiled and put the phone aside.

"Should I answer?" The dog stood up and walked over to Jenna. She placed her head on Jenna's arm and looked up with big dark eyes.

"Where could it go anyway. In three days, we are going home."

Sarah's announcement resonated in her head, and she stopped. "Of course, we could stay longer, but I don't even know where he lives."

She picked her cell phone and texted him back.

196

"Hi, got to the hotel, and in a room. Just relaxing and watching a little TV," she typed.

"Would you like me to come and see you?" The message barely sent before his answer appeared.

She answered with a no. She explained she needed to relax and planned to just cuddle with Ziggy. He accepted her plans, and they made arrangements for him to come by the following day.

"I am going to have to get more clothes or find a washing machine," Jenna stated as she plugged her phone into a charging cable and crawled underneath the covers. She channel surfed until a 1970s sitcom caught her attention and she watched until she dozed off.

Chapter Thirty-One

Jenna woke up as Ziggy ran around, chasing sunbeams.

"You are so strange," she sat up and stretched.

A paper peaked from under the door of her room, and she picked it up. She scanned today's activities from the thick, expensive paper with calligraphy written words as she walked over to the bed and sat down.

"I wonder what they are doing in town," she mused out loud, and Ziggy stopped to walk over to her. Jenna looked down at the dog and patted her lap for Ziggy to join her on the bed. "I bet they are going back to their regular lives."

She petted the dog and leaned back against the headboard and thought about the town people. She opened the nightstand drawer to throw the card into and spied a Bible.

"I wonder if Paul is writing his sermon," she looked into her dog's eyes. "I really need to send the church an offering as a thank you." The dog answered with a panting smile.

Jenna showered, dressed and ordered breakfast. She opened the door to let Ziggy out to play for a while. Her phone was flashing, and she picked up her phone and found a text from Mike.

"On my way, be there in about an hour."

She smiled and put the phone down. She pulled her bag on the bed and looked for anything clean to wear,

and settled on the outfit she wore her first day.

"This isn't too bad."

She shook her head and placed a call to the airline and instructed them to send her missing bag to the hotel. She couldn't wait to be reunited with her missing clean clothes.

Jenna put Ziggy on a leash and walked to the lobby. An overly perky girl stood at the front desk. Jenna informed her of Mike's impending arrival and asked her to direct him to the pool where she planned on getting some sun. The girl agreed, and Jenna walked towards the patio. She didn't know why but wasn't ready to have Mike come up to her room.

On her way to the pool, Jenna picked up a magazine from the gift store and wandered out to the pool. She opened the pages and was shocked to see a familiar face staring at her from the glossy pages. She knew the dark eyes from when they had looked deep into hers. She knew the full lips and what it felt like to have them pressed against hers.

She delved into the article about the hero firefighters who combated flames on the West Coast. The report emphasized the sacrifices the workers endured as they helped to save people and homes from a never-ending barrage of nature. It spoke of fallen heroes and broken people.

"I'm not sure I would totally agree with that article," a voice startled Jenna, and she snapped the magazine shut. She put it down, the face from the pages now looked at her from the other lounger.

"So, you don't like being a hero?" Jenna teased.

"That part, I like," Mike smiled. "I just don't know how true it is."

The couple talked and enjoyed the warm sun beating down on them from a clear blue sky. After a few minutes, Mike suggested they go for a hike, and Ziggy jumped in excitement at the word "walk." Jenna agreed and picked up the few belongings she brought down with her. Mike slung his backpack over his shoulder. Jenna left the magazine on the chair, but not before she asked Mike to autograph it. With a chuckle, he obliged.

They strolled down a path that the brochures advertised led to a waterfall. The couple fell into a comfortable pace while they talked about the article and firefighting. The talk turned to Jenna's mother and the loss, Jenna finally felt she could trust Mike.

"Well, I know it wasn't a good reason, but I have to say that I'm glad you are here," he stopped and pulled her into him. He lowered his face to hers and gave her a deep kiss. She wrapped her arms around him and let him hold her tight.

After a few minutes, he pulled away from her.

"I have wanted to do that since the moment I got here. I couldn't get that first kiss out of my mind and wanted to make sure it was as good the second time," He reached out and touched her cheek.

"By the way, it was."

Jenna smiled and blushed. She noticed that his touch didn't electrify her like Paul's did, but he was here, and Paul wasn't. Besides that, Paul someone already.

"I really wanted to get you alone, and to show you that I may be a tough fireman, but I have a romantic side too," he winked at her, and they resumed their walk down the path again, this time her hand in his while Ziggy ran ahead.

They reached their destination, and Mike pulled out cheese, crackers, meat, and a bottle of wine from his backpack. In one of the pockets, he pulled out a thin, rolled-up blanket.

"And I didn't forget you," he smiled at Ziggy and pulled out a rawhide bone.

They sat in the shade of a large Oak tree, while the sound of the waterfall created the music for their date. The smell of the forest perfumed the air while they talked about their lives and dreams. Mike scooted closer to her. He leaned towards her and planted another kiss, touching her arms and legs. He started to push in closer, and Jenna pulled back. Mike sat up, straighter, and reached for the wine.

"More wine?"

Jenna took in a deep breath and nodded. She watched as he filled her glass and noticed a peculiar discoloring on the ring finger of his left hand.

"What is that?" she asked before she could think to stop herself.

"I mean, it is okay if you don't answer." Jenna backtracked. Was this all too good to be true?

"Oh, that is what happens when you are married for a very long time and take the ring off after 7 years," he shrugged his shoulders.

Jenna waited for more, but silence fell on the couple.

"It is a long story," he broke the quiet.

Mike laid back and rolled to his side.

"I guess I should probably explain that one," he finally conceded.

He explained he married his high school sweetheart when he was in his early 20s.

"The one I told you about when I was talking about being a volunteer firefighter," he took in a deep breath. "We were happy and even bought a small house in a small town. I got a job at the local dairy as a milkman, and she worked at the grocery store, nothing special. We even started to talk about having a family."

He rolled onto his back and folded his hands behind his head.

"The first time I got called to a fire, I remember being so excited and scared. I didn't know how scared she was too, but she seemed to understand," he kept talking. "That was when I found my passion for being a fireman, she begrudgingly stood behind my choice, though I didn't know it was begrudgingly until later."

He told how they lived a comfortable life, as he got more and more involved in the fire department, while she wanted to be a mother. Their attempts to start the family failed.

"Then I got the call to go to fight some fires in California," his face changed as he relived his story. "So, I went. I honestly don't remember if I talked to her about it, or just told her I was going, but I knew no matter what, this was my chance."

He rolled over, drained his glass of wine, and poured another cup.

"Anyway, what I didn't know was the day I left, she found out she was pregnant, but she didn't tell me," he rolled back over on his back and looked up at the sky. "I don't know if she felt it would make a difference, or if she wanted to tell me in a special way when I got back, but it didn't happen."

Mike shut his eyes.

"During my time fighting the fires and saving other people, I wasn't there to save my wife from the pain of a miscarriage," he whispered. "She couldn't get a hold of me because I was in the forest, and when I got home, she told me she couldn't handle it. She wanted to know why other people were so much more important than her and why I would save other people but not be there to save her. I didn't understand. I thought, 'what is the big deal?', it wasn't like she was far along and knew the baby or had felt it move or anything."

Mike sat up and stared into the forest.

"Anyway, so, she divorced me over it," he downed another glass of wine. "And I still think she totally overreacted."

Jenna sat silent.

"So, that was like six months ago, and I guess it will take more time for my perma-ring to fade," he stared down at his hand.

The two sat, no words between them as birds sang in the trees. Ziggy laid on the blanket, panting.

After a while, the chit chat returned, and they talked about the weather, the time in the town and going home. Jenna expressed her anxiety at returning to a place that only had sad memories.

"Then don't go," Mike offered, but Jenna realized no matter how much she liked him, this was not going to work. His newly divorced state was too recent, and she didn't think she could be with someone who was called away to danger so often.

Jenna smiled and stated it might be a good time to start back to the resort. Mike, confused with the sudden switch in mood, sadly agreed.

On the walk back, Mike stopped and pulled Jenna into him.

"I'm sorry," he whispered into her ear. "I don't know what it was that made you upset."

Jenna pulled back.

"You didn't upset me," she looked down at Ziggy. "But I'm just not sure that I should get involved so soon after all that has happened."

He looked at her with sad eyes, Jenna continued.

"Not at this time," she looked at him. "You're still coming out of a long-term relationship, and I don't know how ready you are."

He began to dispute the fact, and she put up a hand to stop him.

"And I don't know if I am ready for a relationship either, and with a man whose job takes him away all the time," she pulled her hand back. "I'm not sure I can handle that either at this time in my life, and I don't want to hurt you like she did."

Mike pulled her face up to his.

"Mike, it's better to face that now," she looked down. "I'm not saying that we shouldn't be friends, and maybe see where that goes, but as far as romance, I think we may need to hold off on that."

Mike dropped his hands from her face and slowly nodded.

"Friends then?" he said, and Jenna smiled as she nodded.

"Definitely," she reached up and kissed him on the cheek.

They walked back to the hotel in silence, and Mike said goodbye once they were back at the resort. He asked if he could text her in a few days.

"If I'm still in the area," he smiled.

"Please do, even if you are not in the area," Jenna reached out and grabbed his hand. "I want to know how your life is and how you are doing."

Mike pulled Jenna into a long hug before kissed her head and walked away. Jenna watched him cross the parking lot and get into his truck. Mike never looked back.

Chapter Thirty-Two

Paul leaned back in his chair and closed his eyes. An image of Jenna filled the inside of his eyelids

"She is gone," he commented to the empty room.

He watched her get on the bus and saw the bus leave. She was gone.

"Okay, God," he prayed. "Help me to find your words to guide my flock."

He sat back up and looked at the empty page on the computer.

"But she said she didn't think this was the last time," he said to the computer. He thought of others in his life that said the same thing, and then disappeared.

"Why would she come back? It had been only four days, not enough time to really form a life-long bond." Paul pulled the keyboard closer to him.

But it was the same only four days for him, and he knew he felt more than he expected.

The phone interrupted his thoughts, and he lunged to stop the ringing.

"Paul, I need some advice," Patty's voice sounded desperate as she told him of an inconsolable Molly.

"But at least she is letting her emotions out," he walked to his desk. "She's not just burying them as she did in the past."

Patty agreed but asked him to come and talk to the child. He agreed, and they hung up.

He left and questioned what he could say to the little girl while his heart was also hurting.

"Help me, God," he parked in front of the house and walked to the house. He crept up the stairs, not sure how he could help. Patty met him at the door and ushered him in. He spied Molly on the couch, and she turned her gaze from the window to Paul, her eyes rimmed in red. Without a change in expression or a word uttered, she returned her eyes to the window.

"Hi, Molly," he sat down next to her. "I hear you are sad." The child looked up at him and nodded.

"You know, I'm sad too," he touched her arm. "And I sometimes don't know how to make the sad go away."

Molly turned back to the window again.

"Do you think this is the way that Ziggy would want you to be?" She shook her little blond head.

"I think that Ziggy would want me to be happy, but I can only be happy when Ziggy is here," she replied.

"Well, I understand that, but right now, Ziggy has a home far away and people that love and need her," he stroked her arm.

"But why can't Jenna and Ziggy live here with us?" the girl looked back at the minister. "Jenna told me she is an orphan, too, so maybe she can move in."

He stopped and knew he couldn't answer the same question he asked himself. He remembered when Jenna questioned her place in the world and wanted to scream that her home was here.

"I know it's hard when we make friends and then they have to go, but she promised to write you letters and send pictures of Ziggy," he reminded the child.

He watched a fresh set of tears stream down the girl's face, and he fought the urge to do the same.

"Tell you what," he whispered. "I forgot my phone at home, but if you like I will come back tomorrow and we can call her. How does that sound?"

Molly offered the minister a weak smile.

"Go home and get your phone now," she commanded and grabbed the pastor.

"Let's give them some time first, and I'm sure that we can call them tomorrow and I just bet you that Ziggy is going to be thrilled to hear your voice."

"Maybe we can even do a face to face thing so I can see him," Molly looked hopefully at Paul to see if he agreed.

Paul smiled and knew he needed to figure out how to video call, but he would anything to see the little girl smile again.

Patty thanked him as he stood and left. She hugged him and held on tight. He could feel the tension on her body.

"I know it was only a few days, but I'm pretty sure that Molly isn't the only one who misses them already."

Paul pulled away, nodded, and left.

Once home, he gathered his phone.

"I hope you are okay, sorry I didn't write sooner," he texted to the number Jenna gave him.

Paul waited for a response, but none came.

Images of Jenna embracing the fireman played in his mind like an old movie.

"Stop it," he growled.

He put the phone back on his desk, turned off the light, and called it a night.

Chapter Thirty-Three

Another note under the door, another day of pampering. Jenna picked the letter up and looked at the date on top. The end of her vacation loomed near, and she wasn't sure she was ready to go home. Time flew the four days bunked up in a school. She pictured the people she met. Despite the short time together, they became significant to her. This trip was definitely not the relaxation she paid for, but maybe it was what she needed after all.

"I'm so dying to know what Wendy is going to say about all this," she plopped down on the bed next to her dog, "She said to be more social, and I think I've gone above and beyond,"

She made friends in the town and even involved herself in a little romance. Yes, Wendy should be proud of her.

She looked down and a second note informed her of the arrival of her missing bags from the airlines.

"Thank God," she surveyed the outfit she was wearing and smiled.

"I think I did pretty good with only three shirts, and two pairs of pants," she looked over at the dog on the bed. "But it is going to be nice to not have to wash sox and panties in the sink tonight."

She walked to the bed and scratched Ziggy's head and noticed the light on her cell phone blinking.

"Do you think it is from Mike already? I just don't know what we have left to talk about. What do you think?"

She picked up the device and smiled as Paul's message popped on the screen.

210

"How you doing? Just thinking of you," she read and noticed he sent it last evening.

"Doing good, finally getting my lost bag..miss you all," she typed back and waited to see if she received a quick response. After a few seconds, her wait paid off with a new message.

"Wondering if it would be okay if Molly and I called you later in the day?"

"Sure, what time?" Jenna smiled and broke out in a subdued dance.

"I think they really miss us," she grabbed Ziggy and hugged the little dog close, spinning her around the room. She swayed to an imaginary song with Ziggy as her partner. The dog squirmed to be released and once free, danced around the bed.

"Would 1pm be okay?"

Jenna picked up the hotel itinerary and scanned the assorted activities despite already knowing the answer

"OF COURSE!" she wrote back.

"Then, 1pm it is!" the words jumped on her screen.

"I can't wait."

She waited a few more minutes, but no more texts came. She put the phone down, though not letting it out of her sight, just in case. Finally, she gave up, and she started to plan her day, making sure to leave the time between 12:45 and 1:30 open. She set the alarm on her watch as she took it off to jump in the shower. As the water cascaded down on her, she sang a song off-key.

Paul awoke with his phone, still in his hand. The night before he crawled into bed and jumped with every chirp it made. Every few minutes, he picked it up and looked at the screen, only to be disappointed with a new email advertisement for something he didn't need.

Tired of the endless disappointments, he almost ignored the chirp early in the morning that woke him, but he still grabbed at the phone.

This time, it was what he wanted to see. He smiled and responded, thrilled be connected with her. He read her final text and put his phone aside, he didn't want her to think he was too eager, despite the fact he was.

Paul rolled over.

"How am I going to wait that long?"

He rolled over again and looked up at the ceiling.

"I give up."

He stood up and began his morning ritual. A smile crept onto his face as images of the damsel in distress at the airport clouded his thoughts.

"As long as I'm not too late to the party."

His hands ran through his wet hair while his mind continued its internal movie; the way she looked in the fireman's arms, and her kiss-swollen lips when he walked her to the bus.

"Should have been me that caused that," he rinsed off and walked out of the shower to find something to occupy his time until he could talk to her.

The day inched along as Jenna found things to keep her busy. She ate breakfast in the dining room, while the clock ticked along. She returned to her room and gathered Ziggy to go for a short hike. Owner and dog enjoyed lunch by the pool, and her alarm finally went off at 12:30 as butterflies were set free in the pit of her stomach. She gathered her things and started back to her room.

She passed the front desk, and the man behind the counter called out to her.

"Ma'am, did you get our message that your luggage has arrived?" he waved. "Would you like someone to bring it to your room?"

Jenna walked up to the agent and spotted her mother's sizeable purple bag. She smiled, and she was on her way up anyway. He pulled it from behind the counter for her and handed her an envelope from the airline. She thanked him and pulled the bag behind her up to her room.

In her room, she threw the bag on the bed, proceeding to unzip it.

"Let's see what is in here," Ziggy jumped up on the bed to see if she could help.

She opened the bag which emitted a foul-smelling sending Ziggy into a frantic happy dance. Jenna withdrew a baggie of dog treats and threw one to her pet which Ziggy devoured in mere seconds.

Jenna continued to unpack the bag before she refolded the clothing and replaced them in the luggage for now.

"Might as well keep them in there for two days, unless you want to stay," she looked at the dog for the decision she didn't want to make.

Ziggy laid down on the pillow to supervise.

Jenna stretched out on the bed, and the alarm on her phone sounded the time. She bit her lip as she waited on the bed, her hands crossed over her over-anxious tummy. Ziggy wandered over and sat in a sunbeam near the glass doors.

"Oh my gosh. Why am I so nervous? It isn't like I have never talked on the phone or even that I don't know these people. What is going on with me?"

The dog answered with a shake of her head and a yawn.

"You are right. These are our friends, only friends. I mean, he has a relationship, no matter what you think or feel."

At precisely 1 pm, the phone rang. Jenna grabbed the phone and answered.

"Is Ziggy there?" a small voice asked. "I can't see you. Did we do this =right?"

Before Jenna answered, a voice from behind the child spoke.

"Now, Molly, didn't you want to say hello to Jenna?" Jenna's heart skipped a beat when she recognized Paul's smooth voice.

Paul took the phone and asked if they could do a video call so Molly could see her one true love, Ziggy. They agreed, and after Jenna fumbled with the phone, they figured it out and were looking at each other. Jenna looked into Paul's eyes, and no matter how many times she saw them in her memories or dreams, it never captured the actual depth and feeling he showed through his dark orbs. Her eyes teared up, and she switched the camera to Ziggy so he couldn't see her.

"Oh yeah, I see you now!" the girl giggled. "Hi, Jenna, I really miss you. Does Ziggy miss me? Look at the stuffed animal Pastor Paul brought me. Doesn't it look a lot like Ziggy?"

The overexcited child put a plush toy bearing a strong resemblance to the dog in front of the phone camera, and Jenna turned the phone, so she could see it, her composure back in check.

Jenna laughed and assured the child the dog did miss her too.

"But just because I have stuffed Ziggy doesn't mean that I love real Ziggy less," the child wanted to make sure Ziggy didn't feel replaced.

Behind Paul and Molly, Patty stood, and after a few minutes, Jenna was walked into the living room of the home. Paul propped the phone on the coffee table, while Jenna propped hers on the little table by the door. The group talked about the hotel and about what was going on in the town. Molly continued to call out to Ziggy with the little dog dancing around every time the child said her name. The conversation dwindled, but Jenna didn't want to say goodbye.

"Well, I have work I've got to get done," Paul looked away from the phone. "I'm having a heck of a time coming up with a sermon and only a day or so to get it together."

Jenna nodded, and despite protests from Molly, they said their goodbyes. Jenna closed the phone, moved back to the bed and laid down. Ziggy jumped up beside Jenna and laid her head on her arm.

"You miss them too?" Jenna scratched Ziggy's head. Jenna's heart hurt, and she didn't have the energy to move.

"How is it that I feel so attached to these people," she looked into the dog's eyes for answers.

Jenna didn't need another massage or to lay by the pool. She didn't need to be coddled anymore.

"Maybe it was never pampering we needed." She thought of the people in the town and how they cared for her.

"Maybe it is time to go home after all," she said out loud. "I know I'm supposed to leave on Sunday, but I just don't know why I even came here."

She rolled over on her side and stroked the black fur of her companion. A tear fell down her cheek and onto the luxurious cotton sheets.

Slowly she dozed off.

Chapter Thirty-Four

Paul hung up the phone while Patty consoled an upset Molly. She held the child close to her while Molly fought tears.

"We can call again in a few days if Jenna says it is okay," Patty fought back her own tears.

"I'm sure that Ziggy wants me to call her back," the child pleaded. "And I promise that if you let me see her again, I will do any extra jobs you want me to do."

Patty forced a smile and rubbed the little girls back. Molly stood up and ran up the stairs to her room.

"Was that a good idea or a terrible one?" She walked over and sat down next to Paul.

"I still think it was good. Molly needs to know that not everyone leaves and doesn't come back," he rubbed Patty's arm.

"But what if Jenna doesn't come back?"

Paul shrugged.

"I hope that isn't the case, but it is in God and Jenna's court now," he put his hands in his lap and looked down. He looked towards the last place he saw the child and stood up to leave.

"I have to go."

Patty nodded and walked him to the door.

Driving home, Paul passed the coffee shop and wondered if he could have a phone friendship with this woman that had opened up something inside him he thought was gone.

Jenna woke from her dream. She didn't remember the details, but something felt off. She stood up, walked into the bathroom, and threw water on her face. She reentered the room and picked up the activities list and planned her evening. She looked at the clock.

"Wow, I must have been tired," she walked over and opened the door for Ziggy to go out. She called the dining room and asked for dinner to be sent to her room.

"I want to go home," she threw the list of massage choices, movies, and games down on the nightstand. She looked at Ziggy.

Jenna picked up the hotel phone and dialed the front desk number. A cheerful voice answered, and Jenna asked for the agent to order a car to pick her up in the morning to take her to the Portland airport. The voice on the other end expressed disappointment that Jenna would not be staying longer.

"Is there anything we can do to make it better for you," the voice asked. "I know it hasn't been the best time, but we would love to have the opportunity to see if we can turn your vacation around for you."

Jenna assured the voice it wasn't anything to do with the resort or the service, the excitement of the last few days had taken their toll, and she just wanted to be in a more familiar place to decompress. The voice said they understood and would have a car waiting for her after breakfast service in the morning

Jenna hung up the phone, not sure if she really wanted to go home, but knew she needed to get out of here.

"I can't go back there. He is involved with someone else. Can I be that close to him and just be a good friend. I just think maybe I want more. Let's just go home and lick our wounds."

Ziggy crawled into Jenna's lap and put her two paws on the woman's chest. She ducked her head under Jenna's chin in a cuddle position. Jenna stroked the dogs back.

"I know," she nuzzled the dog. "I'm not sure where we belong anymore either."

Dinner arrived, and Jenna sat at the table, looking at the untouched food. The TV served as background noise.

Jenna laid down on the bed. She thought about home, about her house, her car, and her neighborhood. She picked up her phone and scrolled through the outpouring by the community. What did any of them know about her? And she noted that the texts and calls stopped about two days after her departure. Didn't anyone wonder where she was or if she was okay?

"Including me," she looked up at the ceiling. "Do I even know who I am anymore?"

She shut her eyes.

"Well, Zigs, today is our starting place for a new life, what do we have to lose. We could start a great adventure."

Ziggy crawled back onto the bed and cuddled in close to Jenna.

"Or I could fall flat on my ass."

She hugged the dog.

"Just you and me, kid," she slowly gave in to sleep.

Paul arrived home and walked up to his office. He needed to write his sermon, but how could he when all he could think about was Jenna. He started to flip through his

Bible and prayed for a sign. He set the book down, and the pages fell open to 1 Corinthians 13:4-8

"Love is patient and kind; love does not envy or boast; it is not arrogant or rude. It does not insist on its own way; it is not irritable or resentful; it does not rejoice at wrongdoing, but rejoices with the truth. Love bears all things, believes all things, hopes all things, endures all things. Love never ends."

Paul started to laugh.

"Could you be any more obvious," he said out loud.

He sat down at his desk and wrote as the words came at a rapid base.

Chapter Thirty-Five

The morning alarm shot through the quiet air, but Jenna woke up hours ago. She laid in the bed and stared at the ceiling.

"What was it all for?" she sat up as the hotel phone started ringing. Her heart beat faster as she picked up the receiver with thoughts of Mike and Paul. A computer voice informed her to wake-up. She put the phone back in the cradle and swung her feet over the side of her bed.

"Well, today is the day we start real life."

The little dog looked up and yawned.

"We're going to have to sit down and really figure some things out."

She stood up, grabbed the large bag, and threw it on the bed.

"I don't know if I should get a job, though I really don't have to." She pulled a fresh blouse and pair of shorts out of the luggage. "Maybe I should think about volunteering somewhere, like maybe at an orphanage or something."

She walked over, opened the sliding door for Ziggy. The dog looked at her, yawned again and put her head down on her paws.

"Okay, lazy," she laughed. "I get it, you want to go home and just lie around all day, but you know, I feel motivated."

She walked into the bathroom and turned on the shower.

Showered, dressed and ready to go, Jenna called the front desk to have someone come and get her bags. She set them by the door, and moments later, a knock on the door caused her to jump. The bellboy entered, grabbed the bags, and took them away. Jenna looked at her watch, the time to go was close, and she still wanted to grab breakfast.

She looked around the luxurious room and slowly left with Ziggy circling her as far as her leash would allow her to go. The resort lived up to its reputation as a comfortable and exquisite place to stay, but it was time for her to go home.

A quick bite and short sit in the lobby later, Jenna watched her car pull up to the front of the hotel, and she bid the hotel staff goodbye as she got in the back of the vehicle. Ziggy crawled up in her lap for the ride back to civilization.

The car sped off the mountain while Jenna watched the same scenery she viewed when she came up to the resort. A sign stood on the side of the highway and pointed to another road. If the car turned, it would take her back to Paul, Patty, and Molly.

"But the vacation is over," she stroked the dog's fur.

The car continued down the freeway, and the Columbia River appeared on Jenna's right, while pine trees dotted the left. The driver attempted small talk about the area, and the recent forest fires and Jenna answered his questions but didn't say much else. The man understood, and the car became silent.

The car pulled into the airport, and Jenna quickly put Ziggy in her kennel. The driver removed Jenna's baggage from the trunk and bid her a safe trip home.

She entered the terminal and walked up to the counter, where a friendly woman greeted her.

"Yes, well, I have a flight in a few days, but would rather get home today," Jenna searched the pockets of her bag for the information she printed before the trip, so long ago. The counter agent asked her name, hit a few keys on the computer, and looked up Jenna's information.

"I'm sorry, but we are full," the airline agent chirped.

"Seriously?" Jenna's shoulders slumped, and the woman gave her a sympathetic look while confirming her statement. Jenna bit her lip and took in a deep breath.

"We had a lot of people stuck here with the forest fires, and we couldn't get the planes in or out due to the smoke," the agent painted a smile on her face. "So we are full."

Jenna stood at the counter while she comprehended the words.

"When can I get home?" Jenna fought tears threatening to fall. The woman hit more buttons, told Jenna that her scheduled flight would be the first time. Jenna nodded and moved out of the line.

"Think there are any other flights?" she peered into the mesh window of the kennel. "And how do we find out? Or do we just get a hotel room and figure it out from there?"

Ziggy stared back with bright eyes that seemed to say, "you know what I want, and I think you want it too."

Jenna plopped down in a chair and skimmed the area. Memories of sitting in a similar chair flashed through her mind and of a handsome stranger as he helped her navigate this same airport. She smiled and felt numb.

Jenna stood up and walked to a board with hotel listings on it. She picked up the attached phone, dialed and after a few questions, hung up the receiver after being told no pets.

"I suppose I could push the issue, but why. If they don't want you there, I don't want to stay with them," she looked down at Ziggy.

Hotel after hotel told her the same thing, 'no pets.'

"You know, if I dug your papers out, they would have to let you," she hoped Ziggy wasn't getting a complex from all the animal rejection.

A small advertisement caught her eye. The glossy picture of the hotel stated it was in the heart of the forest with plenty of activities nearby like hiking trails and antique shopping.

"That sounds good," Jenna commented. "We could stay there and maybe see Patty and Molly. Would you like that?"

She picked up the phone, called the hotel and was ecstatic to find an empty room.

"You are mighty lucky," the person on the other end said. "We had lots of people get evacuated from the mountains here as well as the firefighters, but they are all leaving today, so we have plenty of rooms."

Jenna gave him her credit card and hung up the phone before realizing she didn't have a way up there. She called a car rental company and made her way to the lot. She picked out a nice little car and grabbed a map.

"Well, here we go, good or bad," she commented as she pulled out of the lot. She didn't know if this was crazy, but she knew she needed to do this.

Chapter Thirty-Six

Paul stood at the pulpit and looked down at the rows of pews. Today they were empty, but tomorrow they would be filled with families and friends. He picked up the papers and straightened them out. He started his sermon.

"A popular saying is 'if you love something, set it free. If it comes back to you, it is yours, if it doesn't, it never was," he waved his hands to emphasize his speech. "So, how does that relate to God? This is an example of God's ultimate gift to us, free will. We are children of the Father, and he will always search us out, but he won't ever force you to come back to him."

Paul looked back down at his notes and scowled. He picked up a pen and jotted down some notes on the pages.

"Jesus had a story about this sort of thing, the Prodigal Son," Paul paced and continued to tell the story of the lost soul.

"When he returned to his family, he was greeted with open arms after leaving to search for something more."

Paul wrote more notes and continued to talk about the different types of love and how each is represented in the bible.

Lost in his sermon, Paul didn't notice Patty slip into one of the last pews. She watched the minister talk of God and the power of love. Paul finished his sermon, and Patty stood up and clapped.

"Sounds really good and really personal," she walked up the aisle.

"Yeah, maybe a little," he gathered his papers and straightened them into a neat pile. "I just don't know how it got to this."

Patty sat down in the first row. Paul walked down and sat next to her.

"I don't know how someone can make such an impact in such a short time," he rolled his shoulders and messaged the back of his neck.

"But it happened," Patty put her hand on Paul's arm.

"Besides, it was really apparent she is getting cozy with one of the firefighters, so even if there ever was a chance, I think I waited too long," he dropped his head. "Maybe that was a God telling me what was right. I was asked to be there in a professional capacity if she needed me, and I wasn't sure where the line on that was."

"I saw the way Jenna looked at you, so if there is someone else in the picture, I'm sure it's just a divine place-keeper until you realize it was okay to move on and be happy," Patty squeezed Paul's arm before leaning back in the pew and stretched her legs.

Paul took in a deep breath and sat back. He looked at the altar and proceeded to tell Patty how he felt. She nodded and listened. At the end of the narrative, Paul looked into Patty's eyes for an answer.

"I don't have one," she leaned forward and placed her elbows on her knees. "I think you know the answer and are too afraid to do it."

Paul mimicked Patty's moves and looked down at the floor.

226

"I just don't know what I'm thinking or feeling or what. This is the first time I've allowed myself to feel this way since, well, since you know," he shrugged.

"Look, Paul," Patty sat up and shifted towards him. She put her hand on his. "It's been a while, and I'm pretty sure Karen would be fine with you finding love again. She would never have wanted you to be alone this long."

"I know, but for the last seven years, every time I've looked at a woman, all I saw was Karen."

Patty smiled and shook her head.

"Paul, it's time, and I know God has a plan. Maybe Jenna is his way of letting you know you can open your heart now, and that is all it is, or maybe she is the one, I don't know, only God knows."

Paul nodded and stood up. He placed his hand on Patty's shoulder and mouthed a 'thank you' as he walked out of the room.

Patty looked at the altar.

"Please, God, let him be okay."

Jenna raced down the highway, the same woods she just left, blurred in her peripheral vision. Ziggy relaxed in the passenger chair while she chewed on a treat Jenna picked up for her.

"Well, I can't believe we're doing this," she glanced over at her companion. "But for good or bad, here we go."

Jenna watched the road as her mind wondered what the therapist would say about this.

"Am I ready for this?" she put tapped the brakes on the car. "Am I just trying to replace mom?"

She glanced back at the dog who answered with panting. She recalled going to church summer camp as a child, and the wonders of nature and God filled her. She thought about friends swearing they were there until they were old women, but by a few months, those relationships faded like her tan, the distance too great to continue the closeness they felt alone at the camp. Once home, life returned to the way she left it.

She turned off the freeway and onto a back highway. Ziggy jumped up and looked out the window as if she could smell where they were headed. Soon small farms and business began to populate along the road.

"We are almost there," she chirped to Ziggy, her stomach in knots and her hands tightened on the steering wheel.

Jenna found the hotel, five blocks further into town then the school, but still easy to find. Jenna pulled the car into the nearly empty lot and attached Ziggy's leash. She went into the office building and picked up a key to her second-floor room. The clerk beamed, letting her know it was near the pool and away from the main drag. She grabbed her bags and walked up to her room.

"Jenna?" a deep male voice said her name from the floor below her. She turned and saw Mike.

"Are you stalking me?" he said with a laugh, walking up the stairs and standing beside her.

"No, I promise," she matched his laugh. "What are the chances I would see you here?"

"Well, pretty good since this is the only hotel in the town," he climbed the stairs. "But what happened to the fancy hotel you were staying in?"

She opened the door, invited him in. She sat her bags on the bed and surveyed the small room. The bed was the only place to sit, so she suggested they go and get a bite. They walked down the street after the hard decision to leave Ziggy in the room. They entered a small café, and the aroma of fried food and coffee filled the air. Jenna's stomach growled, and she realized the last time she ate was hours ago. The hostess seated them in a booth in the corner.

"So, what the heck are you doing here?" Mike shook his head and grinned.

Jenna laughed and explained what happened at the airport.

"And there weren't any hotels in Portland?" he said in disbelief.

"Not if you have a dog," she said. "And I'm from a small town, so this hotel seemed to be screaming my name when I was looking for somewhere to stay.

Mike smiled and nodded.

"And you really wanted to see me again,"

"That is just an added bonus," Jenna said and as she reached across the table and put her hands on his. She pulled her hands back when the waitress returned and took their orders.

Mike leaned closer to her and reached out to hold her hands. She sat back.

"You know," Jenna stopped for a minute to form her words. "I like you, and I hope we can be friends, but I'm trying to figure out what I'm going to do when I get home, and I don't think getting into a relationship right now is right for me."

Mike sat up straight, the smile on his face remained the same.

"I know, you told me." he smiled, but his eyes showed other emotions. "I like you too, but I'm not ready either. I haven't been single that long and I know the life I've chosen is a hard one for whomever I'm with."

He looked deep into Jenna's eyes.

"I wish we were in a better spot in our lives, both of us because I think that we could be good for each other," he said.

Jenna nodded.

The food came, and the conversation became lite chatter and joking around.

After dinner, they walked back to the hotel.

"I'm leaving early in the morning," he said as he gathered her hands in his.

They stood outside her door.

"I'm going home for a few days and then back to work up in Washington."

"I hope you keep in touch," Jenna moved closer to Mike.

Mike leaned down and kissed Jenna's lips, and she kissed back, but they both knew this was a kiss goodbye.

Opening the door, Ziggy rushed out of the generic hotel room.

Jenna's followed her out and after a few minutes, called her back in.

She jumped on the bed and looked at the clock. It was early enough to call Patty, and she picked up her phone. She scrolled through the list and hit the call button. The single ring on the other end of the line ended as Patty picked up before the second ring.

"Hey there." The excitement in Patty's voice oozed through the phone lines. "I'm happy to hear from you."

After a few minutes of pleasantries and catch up, Jenna stopped.

"How would Molly like to see Ziggy? The resort just wasn't working for me, so I checked out."

Jenna waited for a response, her heart beat faster, and a slight sweat broke out when an answer didn't come immediately. She held her breath. What if they didn't want her to come back?

"And you stayed here?" Patty squealed.

Jenna confirmed it, and her heart jumped in her chest.

"Was there a reason? Like maybe a handsome minister."

Jenna felt her cheeks heat up, and a smile creased her face. She stood up and paced around the room.

"We are just friends," Jenna interjected before her heart or voice could betray her.

"Well, how 'bout you and Ziggy come by anytime. I know I'd love to see you and I know Molly would love to see that dog, so in other words, get your skinny butt over here!"

They hung up the phone as Ziggy danced around the room.

"Well, I guess I'm, going to have to share you a bit longer," Jenna picked put the happy dog.

"How much do you really understand." Jenna laughed as Ziggy answered with a sloppy kiss to her cheek.

Chapter Thirty-Seven

Jenna spotted Molly as she pulled up to the house. The child stood at the gate and watched traffic. The child's face lit up, and she started to jump around as Jenna parked.

"They're here," she raced to the porch and then back to the gate.

Jenna reached for Ziggy, gathered the dog, and exited the car. The dog squirmed to be put down.

"I'm beginning to wonder who you like better," Jenna laughed into the dog's ear. Ziggy turned and licked Jenna as if an answer to her question.

"I know, it's you and me," she leaned over the fence and placed Ziggy on the ground. The little dog couldn't contain her excitement and wagged her entire back end, not content with just a tail.

"She missed you," Jenna watched the child fall to the ground to be next to the dog.

"You want to watch her for me while I go in and talk to Patty?" The girl's wide smile answered Jenna.

Jenna walked to the porch and left Molly and Ziggy as they chased butterflies.

"Molly, you make sure that Ziggy doesn't get hurt and don't open the gate so she can get out, okay?" Patty yelled from the front door.

"She will be fine," Jenna gave the other woman a hug. "Ziggy was pretty well trained not to wander off when I got her, so I'm not worried."

Patty asked Jenna to come in and showed her to the living room. Freshly brewed coffee mingling with the aroma of baking sugar cookies. Jenna accepted a mug of coffee. Cream and sugar laid out on the table in front of her as she sat down.

"I hope you didn't do all this just for me," she looked at Patty.

"Well, the coffee, yes," Patty nodded. "But the cookies were a project with the older girls, so keep that in mind when you take a bite."

Despite the warning, Jenna took a bite, and the morsel melted on her tongue.

"You may have some great chef's in this house," she moaned.

After a few minutes of catch-up, Patty placed her cup on the table and looked directly at Jenna.

"So, you know, one of my pet peeves is seeing two people that care about each other and are too caught up in their own issues to recognize what's going on," she stared intently into Jenna's eyes.

"I told Mike a relationship with him is just not going to work," Jenna looked down at her hands in her lap. "I don't think my feelings are strong enough to sustain being together when he is off fighting fires all over the west coast."

Patty reached out and put her hand on Jenna's hands.

"And besides, he is newly divorced, and that spells disaster all around," she continued to look at her hands as Patty pulled her hands back. "But I don't think it would be a relationship that would be good for me."

"And you sort of like someone else," Patty picked up her coffee and took a sip. "Because I know you know that is not who I'm talking about, though I'm glad to hear you came to your senses about Mike."

"I don't know what you're talking about," Jenna reached out and took a sip of her coffee. She hoped that would end this part of the conversation but knew she couldn't be that lucky.

Patty looked out the window at Molly and Ziggy as they played in the sun with a few of the other children.

"You know, I really believe that dog just knows who needs help and jumps in," Patty watched the group. "First with you and now with Molly. She's quite a little animal."

Jenna nodded. They sat in silence as the sound of happy children and a barking Pomeranian leaked into the room.

"Okay, look, Jenna," Patty shifted to face Jenna. "Paul's a great guy, and he's been through a lot, so the fact he likes you says a lot about you."

"He's a nice guy," Jenna nodded. "But he is in a relationship right now."

Jenna's voice betrayed her disappointment.

"No, he isn't!" Patty's face showed confusion.

Jenna told Patty about the girl coming out of the office.

"She was really flush and winded, and he was dressing, so either they are involved, or he isn't the man I thought he was," Jenna looked at her hands again and bit her lip.

"Oh my gosh! No way!" Patty jumped up and waved her hands as she spoke. "Oh my gosh! I know all about that! That was Rachel. She is one of the college students in the young adult program."

Patty's eyes flashed desperation. She needed Jenna to understand Rachel and Paul's relationship.

"He's always telling her to talk to her youth pastor, or the women at the church, depending on what she is asking about that particular moment."

Patty sat back down and burst into laughter.

"I bet she'd love that someone thought she and him were, well, more than acquaintances," she shook her head, "but the truth is, they are nothing more than minister and parishioner. I know that Paul sometimes feels guilty for avoiding her, but what is he supposed to do?"

Jenna perked up and sat up straight.

"Look, let me tell you about Paul. I think there are some things that you should know," Patty turned serious. "It's probably not my place to say to you since it's his story, not mine, but I think once you hear it, you may change your mind about a lot of things."

Patty told Jenna Paul's history.

"Paul married a wonderful woman named Karen," she looked out the window. "I believe they were college sweethearts, though I'm not sure. They owned a little house in Portland, where she was a school teacher, and he was an accountant."

Jenna pictured a comfortable life.

"Then Karen got pregnant," Patty smiled. "After nine months, they had a daughter, Alexie."

Patty told her about the happy the little family spending time together and enjoying life as Alexie grew into this beautiful girl.

"Then, the unspeakable happened. Alexie was five years old," Patty took a sip of her coffee. "Karen was on her way home from the store one night, and Alexie was in the front seat with her. Karen decided to take the freeway home, something she never did, but she was tired and just wanted to get home. A few miles later, a semi-truck driver fell asleep at the wheel."

She cradled her cup in her hands.

"I don't think she even saw the truck coming from behind until she was hit."

Jenna's stomach clenched.

"Alexie was killed instantly, and Karen spent the next six months in the hospital," Patty put her cup on the table. "That's when Paul started to go to church, asking why, begging to know what the point was. He didn't know if he believed in God, but he wanted answers."

Patty stopped talking and a deep breath.

"Karen couldn't believe Paul would turn to a God who would take her precious baby away from her. They grew apart, but Paul figured they would come full circle. He found solace in God and saw a therapist to help him work through the pain and guilt," Patty paused and took a sip of her coffee.

"Karen found a different way to escape the pain."

Patty wiped a tear from her cheek.

"One day, he came home, and there was a note on the bedroom door for him to not come in and call 9-1-1. He turned the handle, but the door refused to open. It was locked. He beat on it and tried to knock it down. Screaming at Karen the entire time."

Patty stopped and gathered her thoughts.

"Finally, he called emergency, and they went into the room. Karen was hanging there, and Paul was never the same. Something inside him turned to God. He dedicated his life to the Lord, partly to see if he could find some answers and partly because maybe he could find the grace for God to forgive Karen and let her rest in peace."

Jenna sat stunned, and the silence pushed down on her. She couldn't find any words until finally, the silence was broken as Molly ran into the house, a smile plastered on her face and out of breath.

"Oh, Jenna," she jumped up and down. "Thank you for letting Ziggy come over. Can I take her to my room and show her the stuffed animal that Pastor Paul got for me?"

Jenna forced a smile and nodded. Molly ran outside and returned, carrying the little dog. Ziggy panted a smile, and it was apparent she loved the attention.

After the child left, Jenna turned to Patty.

"I had no idea," she shook her head. "That's terrible. I think I may have been like Karen when mom died, blaming God and asking why, but not suicidal. I admire Paul for finding solace in his religion."

"Look, he doesn't tell his story to anyone, and I bet there are people in his congregation that don't know," Patty looked at Jenna. "He downplays it and looks at it like it was a growing experience, part of his story, but not something he lets hold him back. He's always said if you keep yourself locked in the past, then you're giving away the gift of the present and the hope of the future. He also lives a pure life, full of things that make him happy. He says he owes it to Alexie and Karen to live a full and happy life to make up for the ones cut short."

Jenna felt tears in her eyes. For the last few months, she asked herself what she was going to do and how could she move on, but here was someone who went through worse and now lived a full and happy life.

"I know he likes you, and I know that this is the first time since Karen that he has been open to something like this"

Patty reached over and touched Jenna's shoulder. "And I'm pretty sure you like him."

She took her hand back.

"I don't need to be a rebound," Jenna looked at Patty.

"It's not like that. It's been seven years," Patty assured her. "He's been attracted to women, but you are the first one to open up something more intimate in him."

Jenna blushed.

"So, why not just do this, come to church with me tomorrow and listen to him speak," Patty leaned towards Jenna. "Just look at him knowing his story and see if you can see anything that would make you believe he isn't frank and sincere in everything he does."

Jenna nodded and said she would like that.

"And tell you what, I'll even let Molly skip church so she can watch Ziggy," Patty's eyes twinkled and a smile creased her lips. "If you are okay with that, of course."

Jenna smiled and agreed.

"Thank you for telling me," she returned the smile.

"You know, we are all broken in some way," she put her hand on Jenna's. "We just have to go through it and move on. This town seems to be full of the people that cling together through the tragedies each one of us has been dealt with. We hold each other up and pick up those that can't get up for themselves."

Jenna smiled.

"You know, you belong here too."

Jenna felt moisture on her cheeks and leaned in and hugged Patty.

The night wore on, and Patty reached over and turned on a lamp as the room got darker.

The conversation started to falter, and Jenna said she needed to go. Patty walked her up the stairs to Molly's room and entered. They found Molly and Ziggy curled up in a ball together asleep.

"They tired each other out," Patty whispered. Ziggy raised her head, opened her eyes, and yawned. Jenna gathered the dog as Molly rolled over into the spot the dog once occupied.

The women walked downstairs, said goodbye and Jenna promised to pick Patty up in the morning.

Chapter Thirty-Eight

Paul sat at his desk and looked again at the picture of Karen and Alexie. He took the picture just a few weeks before the accident. They were at the ocean, and the smell of the salty breeze blowing off the water still haunted him. He felt the sand between his toes. He recalled his talk with Alexie about the seagulls who circled overhead. They made up a story about what the two birds were talking about. Karen sat on a towel as she read a book. Later they walked on the beach and watched the sun sink into the ocean.

He loved that memory above all the other ones. It wasn't about what they were doing, it was about doing it together.

"You know, Karen," he picked up the photograph. "I'll always love you, nothing can change that. Not even the fact that you weren't strong enough to stay with me."

He replaced the picture in its place on the corner of the desk where he could see it whenever he worked.

"What do I do?" he looked into the eyes of his wife. "I think Patty is right. I think you'd want me to find love again, and I think Jenna proved I can feel those feelings again."

He stood up, crossed the room, and looked out the window. Jenna crossed his mind, and he wondered what she was doing right now. Was she with the fireman, cuddled up in front of a fire on a beach somewhere? Or at the resort enjoying a massage? He wondered if he ever crossed Jenna's mind.

He moved back to his desk. He turned off his desk lamp and left the room.

Jenna grabbed dinner at a drive-thru and arrived back at the hotel. She gathered the bags and Ziggy. She proceeded to her room, the soft, lumpy bed called her name.

"I don't know about you, but I think that I'm going to be glad to go home," Jenna threw a burger in the dog's dish. She looked around the room, at the same sort of bed and dresser in hotel rooms everywhere. It didn't matter how luxurious it was, or dumpy, it was still impersonal. Jenna was homesick.

After dinner, Jenna took Ziggy for a quick walk before she switched the TV and crawled into bed for the night.

"I bet mom would be really proud that I'm going to church tomorrow," she cuddled Ziggy. "I know you never knew her, but God was significant to her."

She told the dog stories of her mother, and laughed at funny memories, as well as shedding a few tears.

"Yes, she would love you," she pulled the dog into a hug. "She wasn't much for pets, but I really think she would have made an exception for you."

Jenna dozed off, still thinking of her mother, burrowed down into the soft covers while her mother's smile filled her mind.

"I love you, mama," she whispered. "Thank you for watching over me. I know you're there."

Jenna rolled to her side, and slowly put a leg over the side of the bed. The wake-up alarm screamed from next to her, and she swatted it as Ziggy jumped down on the floor.

"I don't know if I really want to do this," she sat up and stared down at the dog.

She rose to her feet and got ready. Once out of the shower, she tossed her luggage on the bed.

I don't even think I have anything to wear," she said as she investigated the garments

She threw a shirt and pants onto the bed before she settled on a light pink blouse and khakis.

"Well, this is the best I brought," she dressed and looked in the mirror. "It's just going to have to be okay."

She finished with a light blush colored lipstick. She scooped up Ziggy, grabbed her keys, and exited the room.

"Still not sure," she commented quietly as she started the car.

The drive seemed faster as Jenna continued to question what she was doing.

"Hey you," Patty waved as she jumped down the steps of the porch. Next to her, Molly danced around her arms, outstretched to grab Ziggy. The two reached the car.

"The others left about half an hour ago in the van," Patty slipped into the car with a smile. "So we'll meet them there."

"So, what are you thinking?" A small chuckle escaped from Patty as Jenna shrugged, the corner's of Jenna's mouth in a war with themselves not to smile. She bit her lip, turning her face away from Patty and pulled out into traffic.

The front of the car remained quiet while Molly sang to Ziggy in the back seat

They pulled into the church parking lot, and people milled as they greeted one another.

"We are very casual," Patty explained, as Jenna's noted several people dressed in jeans and tee-shirts. "You'd think just the opposite, but I guess when people saw the minister at church events in jeans and decided the good Lord doesn't care what you wear as long as you love him."

Molly led the trio, the leash held tight and proud in her hand. The group advanced to the door, while Patty instructed Molly to play with Ziggy in the side yard until after services. Molly ran off with Ziggy at her heels. People greeted Patty with hugs and handshakes.

"You are very popular here," Jenna smiled at her friend.

"Well, you know how small towns are. Everyone knows everyone and their business," she held her arms up to let in another parishioner pass by her.

Patty directed them to a seat in the middle, but a shake of the head by Jenna redirected them to a position in the back corner. The choir began to sing as the congregation stood and joined in. The pre-sermon section of the service sped by, and Jenna could hear her heart speed up as Paul walked to the pulpit. She gulped at the lump in her throat.

Chapter Thirty-Nine

"Good morning, friends," Paul's voice boomed out into the sanctuary. He paused as some of the audience wished a good morning back. He cleared his throat and looked at his notes.

"As most of you know, this week we had the pleasure of helping people stranded by the forest fires. I want first and foremost to thank all that helped. I feel it was a success, and I see a few faces this morning I met during this trying time," he looked out and Jenna slumped down in her seat.

"I know we reached people, and I believe we showed them love, and I pray they pass it along."

The congregation clapped.

"During my time with our new friends, someone asked me how a loving and merciful God could bring such painful things to his people. Isn't he a God of love?" Paul stopped and took a deep breath. "That's a common question when there is a loss, whether loss of homes or families breaking up. Or even the death of a loved one. It's a question I hear over, and I can't give them the answers they want to hear. Though I believe there is a purpose, saying it is God's will isn't always received openly since usually it's the last thing people want to hear."

He walked away from the pulpit and started to pace in front of the altar.

"When death is involved, people don't want to hear they will again see their departed loved one in the Kingdom of God; They want to see that person now, hold them now," his voice shook, and he looked at his notes, pausing for a heartbeat. "I know because I've been one of those people with those same questions."

Paul stopped and looked out to the people.

"A lot of you know my past, know I had a child killed in an auto accident and a wife who turned her back on everyone, and took her own life. She was unable to bear the sadness of loss," he swallowed. "I know what it's like to question God. I remember asking what the point was."

Paul moved back to the pulpit and stopped.

"But it just maybe it wasn't God's plan, but was a product of our very own free will," he said.

He smiled and shook his head.

"Free will, one of the most interesting of gifts from God."

He wiped his brow with a tissue.

"In Proverbs 16:9, we are told us, 'In their hearts, humans plan their course, but the Lord establishes their steps.' So, why not make the steps different for a different outcome? But again, he gave us the gift of free will."

Paul paced in front of the altar, holding his hands out like he was doing the math on his fingers.

"Free will is both an empowering and a dangerous thing," he commented. "God loved us enough to give us freedom, the chance to do as we please, whether that's pleasing to him or not. He wants us to come to him, to love him, to worship him, because it is in our hearts, not because he makes us. He wants us to come to him, though he is always just within a small whisper away."

He walked back over to his notes.

"In chapter three of Peter's second letter to the early Christians, verse nine, he wrote, 'The Lord is not slow in keeping his promise, as some understand slowness.

Instead, he is patient with you, not wanting anyone to perish, but everyone to come to repentance'."

"It reminds me of the saying, if you love something, set it free. God sets us free," Paul raised his hands, "and shows us his love by giving us that freedom, even with the understanding and knowledge that some of his children will never return."

"So, how can a loving God allow bad things to happen? That was the question," Paul said with a short laugh. "And the answer is, he allows it because he loves us enough to give us free will, and hopes we accept the love he has for us, enough to return to him."

He walked from behind the pulpit and addressed the crowd.

"But Pastor Paul, what about the free will of the victims? What about the pain the family of the grandmother lost to heart disease? That wasn't free will, that was God's will."

He dropped his head and walked back to the pulpit.

"Okay, that is a harder one," Paul said, looking back out. "That was me. Why did he take my family? I didn't do anything wrong. I didn't fall asleep at the wheel. Why me? Was my family just collateral damage?"

He stopped again and took in another breath.

"I know my wife and daughter are in paradise and waiting for me, but I didn't always feel that way. I went to therapists who just taught me how to cope, but couldn't answer the questions I asked. I went to religious leaders who said it was His plan and what human had the right to question God."

He looked out and grasped the stand in front of him.

"But I did question."

Paul nodded and moved away from the pulpit.

"Maybe it was part each of our journey's, which isn't a good answer either," he chuckled, his hands folded in front of him. "But maybe, just maybe, it is a wake-up call. A call to his children to lean on Him when we are troubled. What did Job do to lose his family? Here we have those same questions being asked in ancient time. I don't know what I would be doing or where I would be living had this tragedy not occurred and led me here."

"Job was tortured, and God allowed it. Why? Job never lost his faith, and in the end, he was rewarded after he repented for his questioning.

Paul looked out at the faces, and he had their attention.

"Job 42:1-6: 'Then Job answered the Lord and said, I know that thou canst do everything and that no thought can be withholden from thee. Who is he that hideth counsel without knowledge? Therefore have I uttered that I understood not; things too wonderful for me, which I knew not. Here, I beseech thee, and I will speak: I will demand of thee, and declare though until me. I have heard of thee by the earing of the ear" but know mine eye seeth thee. Wherefore I abhor myself, and repent in dust and ashes'. Job 42:12-13: 'So the Lord blessed the latter end of Job more than his beginning: for he had fourteen thousand sheep, and six thousand camels, and a thousand yoke of oxen, and a thousand she asses.'"

He opened his hands as if pleading to the group.

"Even as we trudge through our trials, God never deserts us, no matter how far we have fallen, he will still show us that love, even during a tragedy. As stated in chapter ten, verse thirteen of Paul's second letter Corinthians, he states,

'No temptation has overtaken you except what is common to mankind. And God is faithful; he will not let you be tempted beyond what you can bear. But when you are tempted, he will also provide a way out so that you can endure it."

Paul moved to the front of the pulpit.

"I have to remind myself of these things every day, free will and God's love. I've suffered tragedy, and I've experienced joy. I've felt the pain of the loss of loved ones and ecstasy of unexpectedly finding love again, and with each turn, I have felt the hand of God pushing me forward. I have had to pray to do his bidding and not exercise my free will and wander off the path he put me on. Are you on the path he put you on, or are you on the path of your own free will? To walk his path is not giving up your free will, but merely working as a team with the Lord.'

He moved back to behind the pulpit.

"Free will is not a bad thing, it's a gift from a very loving father, letting his child out into the world to experience the wonderful things God put on this earth for us to experience; Like love, family and friends, the feel of a new child in your arms, or watching a young couple commit their lives together. As Paul wrote to the Galatians in chapter five, verse 13, 'You, my brothers and sisters, were called to be free. But do not use your freedom to indulge the flesh; rather, serve one another humbly in love'."

Paul put his hands together on the pulpit.

"It's free will when a person gets behind the wheel of a car when they are not fit to drive. It's free will when a person takes too many pills or puts a gun to their head and pulls the trigger," Paul paused. "It's free will to question

God, but it is also free will when a person picks up this book."

Paul held his Bible up for all to see.

"And it is free will to read the words. It's free will to get on your knees and ask for help, and it is the ultimate in free will to ask Jesus to guide you; to be your shepherd, to give up that free will and rely on him."

Placing the Bible back on the pulpit, he continued.

"So, in conclusion, I quote Joshua, chapter 24, verse 15, 'But if serving the Lord seems undesirable to you, then choose for yourselves this day whom you will serve, whether the gods your ancestors served beyond the Euphrates, or the gods of the Amorites, in whose land you are living. But as for me and my household, we will serve the Lord'. Do you use your free will and serve the Lord? Are you willing to give your life to Jesus, and to let him guide you, thus trading in your own free will for a ticket to a glorious kingdom? The decision is up to you, that is your free will."

Paul paused, letting his message sink in.

"Let us pray."

The congregation lowered their heads, and Paul asked God for forgiveness and guidance in the coming week.

Jenna looked around and peeked up at Paul. She looked at Patty and debated if she should ask if he knew she was here. The sermon seemed directed at her. Patty reached out and put her hand on Jenna's knee and squeezed.

"Sometimes God works in very mysterious ways," she leaned over and whispered.

The crowd said 'Amen' in unison, and the room buzzed with the people talking and laughing. Worshipers gathered their belongings and filed towards the door.

Chapter Forty

"Do you want to go and check on Molly and Ziggy?"
Patty stood and reached for her jacket.

Jenn sat and glowed in the aftermath of the sermon.

"Are you sure he didn't know I was here?" she gazed at
Patty.

"I didn't tell him, and in fact, I was in here yesterday, and
that was not the same sermon I saw him practice," she
pointed towards the minister who was talking to people at
the front of the sanctuary. "I don't know where that came
from, except to say God works in mysterious ways."

Jenna looked at Paul and spied Rachel among the group.
She muffled a giggle as the girl reached out to take Paul's
arm, and he slyly moved just out of her reach.

"She doesn't see it. He thinks of her as a child, and you as
a woman." Patty leaned in and whispered in Jenna's ear.

"Do you want to go and talk to him?" Patty gently pushed
her back towards Paul.

"I don't know if I should, he looks busy," Jenna didn't
move. She bit her lip and took in a breath. She wrapped her
arms around her stomach and was glad she hadn't eaten
yet. "Maybe I can talk to him later today, or maybe
tomorrow."

Patty shook her head at the other woman.

"You know, even if you are just friends, and I believe any
relationship the two of you have, would be good. You can
still just go up and say hi," Patty's hands motioned for
Jenna to take the first step forward.

Jenna nodded and took a tiny step.

"Let's go check on Ziggy first," she turned and jolted towards the door. "I'm sure Molly's doing a wonderful job, but really, I need to make sure."

Jenna rushed into the sunlight. She took a deep breath of the fresh air as Patty caught up to her.

"What is going on?" Patty grabbed Jenna's arm. "Three days ago, you and he were fine. Just before you left, I saw you chatting like old friends, and now, for some strange reason, you seem afraid to see him. What gives?"

Jenna rounded the corner and spied Ziggy and Molly as they played in a fenced area with other children. She stared at the happy youngsters as Ziggy's frantic barks filled the air.

"Okay, well, a few days ago we were just friends," Jenna took in a deep breath and looked at Patty. "I liked him, but he was taken, so no pressure," she stared off into the distance, not really looking at anything, but avoiding the Patty's demanding gaze.

"Now if I believe you, which I do," she turned and put her hand on Patty's crossed arms. "Everything changes, and I don't know how to talk to him or act."

Jenna gave Patty a pleading look.

"I think this is a situation of ignorance is bliss," Jenna looked down at the ground.

"Poppycock!" Patty loudly exclaimed and threw her hands in the air. "He's the exact same person he was three days ago, and I'm not about to let you leave here without at least waving at him. You can wave, right?"

Jenna had no choice in this, no free will from Patty. She took in a deep breath and held out her hands to Patty. The older woman took them in her own hands and smiled back.

"You have nothing to worry about. Don't make this hard. God won't give you more than you can handle right now."

Jenna looked at Molly in the yard and back over at Patty.

"This would be easier if I could walk away from here," she whispered. "But I like these people. They feel like family, and I need that right now. I don't want to screw that up."

Patty crossed her arms across her chest and stared at her.

"Okay, I'll go talk to him, but when he's done with everyone one else," Jenna stood up straight "I don't to be in the way, and I don't want to interrupt someone that may really need his guidance."

Patty nodded, and the two women stood in the grass while cars slowly exited the parking lot behind them.

They crossed the yard, and Molly looked up as the two women approached her, her happy face turned to apprehensive as she realized her time with Ziggy was nearing its end.

"Can I just have a little more time?" she begged. Jenna nodded, and the two women sat down on a bench.

"Okay," Patty waved her hands towards the empty parking lot. "It's time."

Patty stood up and offered a hand to Jenna.

"Look, I'll buy you lunch right after," Patty pulled the younger woman to a standing position, and placed her hand on Jenna's back.

Paul stood with his back to the door. He spoke quietly to a woman at the reception desk. The woman stopped talking and motioned towards Patty and Jenna. Paul turned, and his grin converted to a broad smile

"Oh my goodness," he advanced towards Jenna with open arms. "This is such a wonderful surprise."

He wrapped her in a hug and held tight. After a moment, they separated, and a smile covered his face. His hands still held her shoulders, and Jenna wasn't sure her knees would keep her standing.

"I thought you were staying at the resort, what happened?" he pulled her into another hug while Jenna explained her disillusion of the hotel.

"Well, their loss is without a doubt our gain," he pulled away from her.

He touched her arm and guided her to a small round table. Patty followed, and they sat down.

"So, how long are you here?" he reached across the table and took her hands in his.

"I go home tomorrow afternoon," Jenna looked down at the four intertwined hands.

"Well, then, let me take you to dinner tonight, please," Jenna looked in his eyes and saw his sincerity. She nodded, and they set the time to meet later at Patty's home.

The group bid goodbye, and the women walked out of the building, turned the corner to gather Molly and Ziggy before heading home.

"Not so bad," Patty commented with a sly smile. "And you get a free dinner."

Jenna smiled and kept walking.

Chapter Forty-One

Molly jumped around excited after Jenna asked her to "doggy sit" Ziggy for the evening.

Patty and Jenna walked behind the bouncing girl and entered the house. The sounds of yelling children wafted in from the back yard, and fresh baking meat perfumed the home.

"Ah, home," Patty dropped her jacket and purse on a table and plopped down on the couch. She grabbed Jenna's arm as she descended into the plush sofa and pulled Jenna down.

"I have no idea what to wear, and I'm not even sure if this is a date, or just, like, a friendly get together. Do I dress for a nice dinner or a cheap meal?" Jenna's voice was higher and faster than usual.

She put her hand in her lap and concentrated on breathing. Patty grinned and turned her body towards Jenna.

"I really like him," Jenna confessed. "But I'm leaving tomorrow, and I know you say he likes me, but where could it possibly go? I keep wondering what it'd be like to have a romantic relationship with him, but then I remember I live in a whole other state."

Patty put her hand on Jenna's back and rubbing slightly.

"Look, it is going to be okay," her hands moved in small circles. "This isn't something that has to be decided tonight or even tomorrow. Just let it flow. Get through tonight and then tomorrow get through tomorrow. If we need to address other issues or setbacks, we deal with them as they come up. Just relax."

"Maybe my coming back was a huge mistake," Jenna put her chin in her hands and glanced out the window. Molly played a game with Ziggy. "Maybe I made a huge selfish mistake."

Jenna fought another round of tears

"Why would you say that?" Patty pulled back and looked at her friend.

"Look at Molly," Jenna pointed to the girl. "She's going to be heartbroken all over again when we leave, and now I'm going to have to say goodbye to you and Paul all over again. I could've gone home, or even just stayed in Portland, and not put all four of us through this again."

Jenna put her hands over her face and shook her head. Patty reached over and pulled Jenna's hands down so she could look her in the eyes.

"You have given Molly a gift that is better than gold. She gets to see Ziggy again and a lesson that true friends come back and don't desert you,," Patty squeezed Jenna's hands. "And you have given Paul hope again that he can be happy and fall in love. And you have proved to me I have a wonderful new friend."

Jenna looked out at Molly again.

"I wish I didn't have to leave her." Jenna hadn't wanted to admit her attachment to the girl, but she could no longer deny it. The weight of reality sent a searing pain through her heart.

"But what judge is going to let a single lady with no job and just overcoming a death have guardianship over a child, especially one that has gone through what she has."

Patty sat back, her face mixed with happiness and confusion. Jenna looked at Patty and hoped the older women would disagree with her.

"Do you think that maybe she could come and stay with me sometimes, just as a vacation," Jenna watched the girl in the yard. "And of course, I want you to come as well."

Patty nodded and stated she would see what could be done.

They sat in silence for a few minutes, as both stared out the window at the happy girl and dog.

"So what are you going to do to support yourself?" Patty interrupted the silence.

"I don't know," Jenna shrugged and shook her head. "I don't really have to work, my mother left me quite a bit of money. In fact, enough that I really don't have to find a job, but I need to find something to do, some way to get out among people. Something to occupy my time."

The conversation stalled. Jenna stood up and suggested she go to the hotel and gather a few things for tonight's date. Patty agreed and hugged Jenna as she left the house with a promise to be back in less than half an hour.

Jenna pulled out her limited wardrobe.

"Well, I have this in case of a mixer," she pulled a short black cocktail dress out of her bag. She held it up to her body and looked in the mirror. She wrinkled her nose and threw it in a pile on the bed.

Next to the dress, a pair of black pants and one pink and one blue blouse laid already separated from the clothes herd.

"Well, one of these are going to have to do," she waved her hands over the garments and grabbed a pair of black kitten-heeled shoes.

She flung the clothes over her arm and headed out the door. Patty would know what was right. She glimpsed at the clock and made a mental note that in two hours, Paul would pick her up. She grabbed her stomach with her free hand. Anything to make these butterflies go away.

"Okay, just breathe. He is a nice guy, and it's just a nice friendly dinner," she reminded herself.

"Hey, you in here." Jenna's voice bounced up the stairs.

"Yeah, come on up," she shouted back.

Jenna entered the room and dropped her items on Patty's bed.

Patty picked up the black cocktail dress and felt the soft silky material. A delicate and intoxicating aroma of fabric softener and perfume fell off the gown in a wave.

"This is perfect," Patty exclaimed. "It is gorgeous, please, put it on!"

Jenna slipped out of her clothes and dribbled the form-fitting dress on. The soft shade of black brought out the warmth and uniqueness of Jenna's auburn curls and green eyes.

"Oh, he is going to be in shock," Patty smoothed down the skirt on Jenna. "You look incredible."

Patty pushed Jenna down on the chair at her vanity, and squirted out foam from an aerosol can into her hands. She rubbed her hands together and proceeded to massage the substance into Jenna's hair. Patty separated Jenna's coils into soft, bouncy spirals, all the while, she explained that one of her early adventures was helping elderly people get beautiful for mixers at senior homes.

Patty stepped back and smiled approval. She grabbed a makeup palette and began applying a soft smoky color to Jenna's eyelids, a pale pink blush to her cheeks, and a mauve tint to her already full lips.

"Okay, what do you think?" she handed Jenna a mirror to inspect her work. Jenna sat, staring at the image in the mirror and almost didn't recognize the woman who stared back.

"You are a miracle worker," she uttered in awe, "but this is not good."

She put the mirror down and dropped her head. Patty sat down next to her and took the mirror from her hand. She reached for Jenna's hand to offer comfort.

"I don't understand," she said.

"I can't ever repeat looking like this, so from here on out, I would just be a disappointment. All downhill," she whispered, a slight smile crossed her lips.

Patty pulled her hands back and gave a mock slap to her friend's arm. The two women laughed, and Jenna grabbed the mirror from the counter in front of her and looked again.

"You missed your calling," she said, a huge smile lighting up her face.

Chapter Forty-Two

Paul pulled out his non-work royal blue suit and brushed the dust off the shoulders.

"The last time I wore this, was our last date," he looked at the picture on his nightstand of Karen and Alexie.

He still heard Karen's soft voice when she told him he didn't have a choice, he was going to the play with her. The play was written by one of her friends and titled 'Movin' On,' about a man going on his first date after the death of his wife. In the play, the wife continued to visit him from beyond. With each move towards the future, the character was pushed back to the past by the ghost.

"Ironic," he touched the material.

"What am I doing?" he threw the suit on the bed and sat down next to it.

"Am I really ready for this?"

He recalled the conversation Karen, and he shared on the way home. She asked him what he would do if he were in the main character's shoes.

"Well, I would just have to adjust to being single," he reached over and put his hand on her knee.

She quickly told him it was not what she wanted.

"Yeah, well, there is no way I could ever feel about someone else the way I feel about you," he squeezed her knee. "When you have perfection, there is no going back."

She smiled and placed her head on his shoulder.

Paul shut his eyes and put the jacket to his nose and breathed in; her perfume still a faint odor on the shoulder. He noted the scent was spicier than the floral smell Jenna wore.

"Maybe I was wrong, and there is someone," he stood up and looked in the mirror.

He hung the suit back in the closet and pulled out a polo shirt and dress pants. He looked at the suit again.

"Not tonight," he closed the closet door. "But don't go too far away."

He changed, grabbed his keys, and rushed out the door.

Jenna squirmed on the couch as she looked at her hands. The clock on the wall counted away the seconds. With each tick, Jenna felt her heart thump in her chest.

"He will be here on time," Patty walked into the room from the kitchen and sat next to Jenna

Jenna stood up and paced. The sun got lower in the sky, and children's voices drifted in from a back room along with the aroma of macaroni and cheese. Jenna's stomach growled and gurgled. She crossed her hands across her chest and wrung her hands together as silence filled the living room. Voices from the diners laughed, complained, and fought. She shut her eyes and envisioned the large table surrounded with kids of all sizes, as they wolfed down meals. In her mind, kids slipped Ziggy morsels under the table, and the dog happily took the offerings.

"A Rockwell painting," she muttered and sat back down. She looked at her watch again. Patty sat quietly beside her and didn't seem to register the chaos in the other room.

The clock's ticking grew louder as seconds became minutes, both too quick and too slow.

"Nervous?" Patty broke the silence, and Jenna nodded.

"Well, remember, it's just Paul."

Jenna looked out the window at the red and pink sky.

"I know, it's just Paul, and you are right, but I'm still not sure this is a good idea."

"Well, as you said before, if it doesn't go well, you are leaving tomorrow afternoon anyway," Patty picked up a pillow and inspected the stitching.

Jenna glanced at her friend, and Patty refused to meet her gaze. She looked back towards the window and looked at her own reflection. She saw how perfect she looked sitting there. She didn't want to leave, and it seemed Patty wanted her to stay, but this was a vacation, not real life. Things always looked idyllic on vacation.

She remembered other friendships and romances from vacations long ago each one fizzled out once everyone was back home.

"Just a shipboard romance," Jenna quoted the words her mother comforted her with.

"Or the love of your life," Patty's voice interjected into her thoughts. "And you could decide to get a job and move here."

Jenna smiled, and Patty returned with the same.

Paul's white SUV pulled up to the curb.

"Oh goodness," Jenna put her hands on her stomach.

Patty chuckled and rubbed Jenna's back one last time as Patty passed her to let Paul in. She instructed Jenna to sit still and assured her she looked beautiful. Jenna took in a deep breath and listened as the two voices mingled in the hallway. Paul rounded the corner, stopped, and stared at Jenna with wide eyes.

"You look amazing," he gasped, and Jenna broke into a wide smile. A pink blush inched across her cheeks, and she dropped her head. He moved into the living room and reached for Jenna's hands.

"Wow," he pulled her up to a standing position.

"Well, you two need to get going," Patty clucked. "We'll take good care of Ziggy, and I've got your number if anything happens."

Patty looked over at Paul with the best mother-face she could muster.

"And don't have her out too late," she teased.

Jenna grabbed a sweater Patty held out for her.

"Bye, Jenna," Molly called from the doorway as a happy Pomeranian squirmed in her arms. Jenna waved, and Paul placed a hand on the small of her back to guide her out the door. Patty walked slightly behind the couple.

"Have a good time, and don't worry about anything," Patty whispered in Jenna's ear as the couple walked out.

"Remember, it's just Paul."

Paul and Jenna arrived at a small Italian place hidden behind a bowling alley. Neon lights told the world they were open as well as advertised assorted beers.

"This is supposed to be the nicest place in town," Paul looked across the seat at Jenna, his eyes almost apologetic. "I have no idea if it is any good, but it was recommended by one of my office workers."

Jenna shot Paul a reassuring smile.

"Remember, I'm from a small town also, and dining options are limited there too," she chuckled. "At least it isn't a truck stop and gas station."

They laughed nervously and exited the SUV. The smell of garlic and fresh bread floated on the air like puffy white clouds as a young man dressed in a black and white plaid shirt and black pants led them to a table in the dimly lit restaurant. The waiter held out Jenna's seat for her and once seated, handed her a menu as he listed off the "daily specials." Jenna opened her menu. In the middle of the table, a candle was shoved into a wine bottle. Paul asked if she would like a glass of wine and after her nod, ordered two drinks. The conversation stalled as both looked over the list of pasta dishes.

The waiter returned with the bottle of wine and poured a small taste for Paul to sample. He picked up the glass, held it up and looking at the red liquid. He swirled it around and then took a sip, while Jenna sat and watched with a smile.

"I really have no idea what I'm looking for, or what it is supposed to taste like," he leaned over and whispered. "But it seems okay to me."

Jenna wondered if the twinkle in his eye was for her or just a reflection from the candle flame,

"I wouldn't have a clue either."

The tension dissipated much like the wine.

They shared life stories over breadsticks, achievements, and failures over salad; and fears and joys over Chicken Parmesan. With each course, they got more comfortable with the other person.

"This really is a pretty good little place," Jenna admired the poster's of Italy scattered on the walls. "I would have to rate it a definite five-star."

The check came, and Paul put a credit card in the folder, though no one rushed to grab a coat or stood to leave.

"So, what are your plans when you get back home," Paul held his breath as he waited for her answer.

"I don't have a clue," Jenna sighed. "I suppose I'm going to have to find a job or something to do with my time."

He looked over at her, and his eyes glowed in the firelight, and she felt her heart beat a bit faster.

"Have you thought about continuing with health care?" he reached out and took a sip of his wine.

She shrugged. She wasn't sure she could put herself in the position she just left.

"I just don't think I'm strong enough for that," she looked down at the table. "I'm not sure I want to nurse someone just to watch them die. I honestly don't know how you do it."

"Well, it isn't easy. Sometimes I have to go see people that I know don't want me there," Paul rolled the stem of the glass in his fingers and watched the liquid swirl in the glass. "Though I keep up with the local sports teams or current music scene so that I can use that to break the ice sometimes."

Jenna smiled. She didn't care what they talked about as long as they kept talking. His smile sent shivers down her spine, and she wondered what it would be like to be in his arms.

"There have been many times that I showed up, and the person didn't want to hear about God," he continued. "So, I usually just ask if we can talk about whatever they want. I try to make them understand that I'm there to be whatever it is they need from me, whether that's prayer, scripture reading, or sports talk. When it's time to leave, I let them know that I'm here if they want me to come back. That simple, really"

"I wish I could do that, but how do you not become emotionally invested?" Jenna looked at Paul for answers.

"I do get emotionally invested, you have to," Paul took a sip of wine. "But I remember that this is not my decision. I don't have the right to tell them what to believe or what to do. This is their journey, and I can only give them the help that they are willing to take or ask for. I leave it in God's hands."

Jenna nodded.

The conversation started to lag, and Paul glanced at his watch.

"Oh wow, it's already nine o'clock. I think they want us to leave," he whispered to Jenna, and she noticed for the first time they were the only ones left in the dining room, and the staff was trying hard not to get caught watching them.

"You know how these small towns are," Paul winked at Jenna, "they shut down early, usually at dusk, and sometimes even earlier."

Smiling, she stood up and grabbed her purse.

"Boy, do I know," Jenna laughed. "It's exactly the same where I live."

Paul threw some cash on the table, put his hand on Jenna's back, and guided her out the door.

Chapter Forty-Three

Paul parked behind Jenna's rental car as the streetlights began to pop on, and the dusk added a sense of fantasy to the situation. Jenna closed her eyes and debated on pinching herself just to make sure this wasn't a dream.

Paul turned and faced her. He put his arm on the back of the seat and leaned in towards her.

"What time are you leaving tomorrow?" he looked out the window as a few raindrops fell onto the windshield.

She looked at his face and slightly moved towards him. She stopped and pulled back as she turned her attention to her hands folded in her lap.

"I need to be on the road about eight in the morning. My flight is at eleven something," she looked up to see if she was looking back at her, but he stared out the window.

"Have you thought about staying a little longer?" he shifted his body to face her. He stared into her eyes, and she looked down to avoid the magnetic pull. "I bet Patty would be more than happy to let you stay with her if you need a place to lay your head."

"I wish I could, but I have to go home and take care of things," she glanced up at him. "Maybe I can come back sometime? I just think it is time for me to get back to my real life."

She took a deep breath and concentrated on the smell of the impending storm and the pasta leftovers in the back seat. She studied the houses and street. How could she even be thinking of just picking up and leaving the place she lived her entire life, and the people she grew up with? She thought about her mother. How could she leave her alone in the cemetery with no one to visit her? Who would put her favorite flowers on the grave for birthdays and holidays?

She needed to go home.

"I get it," he sighed. "But could I still call you? Maybe help to start planning your trip back?"

"Of course," her heart beat faster.

They sat in the car, and he reached for her hand. He rubbed the top of her knuckles with his thumb as he looked out the front windshield. He inched closer to her.

"You know," Jenna filled the silence. "It's okay if life starts to get in the way. I mean, the long-distance just doesn't work, and you have a life here, and I have a life there, and.."

She stopped before she finished the sentence.

The incomplete sentence hung in the air. What life did she really? She knew people back home cared, but the last year proved they were not the type she longed to talk with each day. Were there friends there who wanted to be and an active part of her life? Had she shut them out? She shared histories with them, but was that enough to reconnect?

She looked over at Paul and knew she wanted to talk to him every day.

"It's okay, I know what you mean," Paul interrupted her thoughts, "real life."

He pulled back his arm and turned forward. Shadows cast by the setting sun and warped by the light rain, ran wild in the cab like ghosts of the past.

"Paul," Jenna turned to him. "I hope we stay in contact. I really do value your friendship, and it would break my heart to think I didn't have it."

He nodded and assured her he would always be there for her.

"You know," she dropped her head. "I wish I was staying longer."

He rotated to face her.

"Then do. What's stopping you?"

Jenna saw hope in his eyes.

"I just can't. I need to figure out what I'm doing with my life," Jenna looked down, shaking her head.

"This has been a great vacation, despite everything, but let's face it, you have a life here, and I have a life...."

Did she really have a life somewhere else?

"So, this is it?"

"I think it has to be," Jenna nodded but wasn't convinced herself.

Jenna leaned over and fell into his arms. Her body awoke with the shock of his touch and she could stay that way forever, if not for real life getting in the way.

Without a word, she sat back up, opened the door, and exited the car. She ran to the porch, and behind her, he started the vehicle, but the SUV didn't move.

Once at the door, Jenna turned to look towards Paul one more time. She stood still and grasped the handrail. She felt the light raindrops on her skin as she watched the truck pull away from the curb and onto the street, traveling slowly away from her.

"Please, just let me know what the right thing to do is," Jenna prayed her first words to God since her mother's death. "Please, let me see him one more time if it is meant to be."

She drew in a deep breath and entered the house. With the slam of the door, she wondered if she was also closing the door on her possible future.

Chapter Forty-Four

"How did it go? You're home late, so that must be a good sign!" Patty rushed to Jenna, with a smile pasted on her face.

Jenna stood in the doorway; her shoulders slumped. The smile on Patty's smile vanished at the sight of her distraught friend.

"What happened?"

Jenna dropped down on the couch, leaned forward and put her hands over her face. Patty sat down next to her and rubbed circles on Jenna's back. A pot of jasmine tea sat on the coffee table with two cups.

"I just blew it," Jenna shook her head. "But it wasn't going to go anywhere anyway."

Patty sat next to her, and Jenna dropped her hands to her lap.

"He was so sweet, and the restaurant was nice," Jenna looked over at Patty. "The conversation was good, and he was a gentleman the whole time."

Jenna stopped and gathered her thoughts.

"It was actually one of the better dates I've been on," she shrugged and swallowed. "But on the way home, he asked me to stay a few extra days, and I let my mind take over. I got scared. I started thinking that if I stayed, there were so many things that could go wrong."

Jenna leaned back into the couch and closed her eyes.

"I kept thinking to myself, 'what is he hiding?' and then I started to wonder what was I hiding?" she sat up and scooted to the edge of the couch like a bird ready to fly. She opened her eyes wide and looked directly at Patty. "I mean, right now, we are both on best behavior, but what if he doesn't like something about me that I can't change. What if something he thinks is cute now, becomes ugly in time?"

Jenna wrung her hands in her lap. Her words coming faster and faster. Patty reached out and placed her hands on top of Jenna's.

"And what if I sold my house, and left my hometown and friends to be near him?" Patty saw panic in Jenna's eyes. "What would I do? I would be lost and with no one to catch me."

"I would be there," Patty stated. Jenna turned and stared at Patty.

"I know," she forced a weak smile. "I'm just not ready for this. I'm still trying to figure out what to do with my life. He and I just met, like, what, a week ago."

Patty nodded and reached out to pour hot liquid into the mugs.

"But that doesn't mean you can't get to know him better." She handed one of the cups to Jenna

Jenna nodded and took a sip of the tea.

"I know, and I'm looking forward to that," Jenna wrapped her hands around the mug. "And maybe he's my knight, like in the fairy tales, but there are so many obstacles. How can I know if what I'm feeling is real, or could it be that someone is showing me kindness, and I'm reading more into it? What if he just wants to be friends and isn't ready for a relationship and I'm making all these fantasies up in my head that are wrong."

Jenna stopped for a breath.

"And what if you are right about what the two of you are feeling?" Patty put her own mug down on the table untouched "What if you go back home, get settled into life there, and let all these negative things fester in your mind? What if you never give him a chance? And from what you told me, who is going to be there to catch you back home?"

Jenna looked at Patty, her mind racing with scenarios, both good and bad.

"Yeah, true and I'll give him a chance, but I need to be realistic. Sure, we can get to know each other in calls and emails, but really, it's the day to day stuff that binds you, like what if he doesn't like the way I keep my house or the way I want to decorate. That's something you only get to know by physically being together. Or what if he likes only spicy food and I like sweet and savory?"

"I understand, but I know there is something between you two," Patty sat back, her hands at her side. "I see it in both of you. There is a reason you came here, and a reason that he is finally opening up to romance and believe me, he is scared too."

"Maybe it's as simple as that, something brought me here so that he would realize his heart was healed enough that he could find love again," Jenna put her cup down and turned towards Patty. "And maybe the lesson here for me is that I can open up again to people. It is probably that simple."

Patty shook her head.

"You can believe what you want, but I believe that this is God's plan for the two of you to find each other. I honestly think that the lesson wasn't just opening back up, but in finding the right person."

Jenna looked over at her friend, a hopeful look in her eyes.

"I think that the timing was from God. I think that any other time or any other circumstances would have resulted in a different outcome, but I think this is the pot of gold at the end of the rainbow, a gift from God, and I hate that it is being rejected," Patty scooted to the edge of the seat. "I understand your fears, I really do, but please, take this leap of faith."

Jenna slowly shook her head and looked out the window.

"I'm just not sure I can," she turned and faced Patty, tears sparkled in her eyes. "I think I need some sort of sign, and I just haven't seen one."

Patty threw up her hands and gave up the campaign.

"Okay, well," she sighed, "how about we have one last breakfast before you leave town tomorrow?"

Jenna smiled and nodded. Patty yelled to Molly, and the little girl appeared in the doorway, Ziggy clutched tight to her body, eyes red.

"I know I have to say goodbye now," she whispered in the dog's ear, "and I know I promised not to cry, but I'm going to really miss you."

She walked over and held the animal tight. Jenna reached for Ziggy, and the child kissed the dogs head one more time. Molly turned and ran from the room as the dog left her arms. A sniffle echoed off the walls.

"Now I really feel bad," Jenna stroked Ziggy's soft coat. "I wish I could do something, but I really need Ziggy."

"She will be fine," Patty patted her shoulder. "And I'm going to look into maybe getting the house a dog or something. Ziggy has been wonderful for her, but it's also a good lesson for her, especially if she can video call and see her."

Jenna assured Patty she would call at least a few times a week for the child. Jenna rose from her seat and turned to her friend.

"I have to go," she leaned down and hugged Patty. "I just want you to know, I appreciate you, and I really don't think this is the last time I will see you."

Patty stood, reaching out and stroking Jenna's arm.

"I know," she whispered. "We will figure out something."

Jenna nodded and looked out the window.

"And you can invite Paul if he wants to come," Jenna looked at Patty with longing in her eyes. Patty said she would call him and ask.

"I know he takes Monday's and Tuesday's off as his weekend," she escorted Jenna to the front door. "So, unless something major is happening, I'm sure he would love to see you off."

They stood in the entryway and set up a place and time the next day for Jenna's going-away meal.

Chapter Forty-Five

Jenna arrived at the hotel with a heavy heart. She changed into her nightclothes and crawled into bed. Ziggy jumped up and snuggled in close to her.

"I just don't know what to do," she held tight to her little companion. "I guess we go home and just take this one step at a time."

Jenna rolled to her side and placed her hand on the dog's soft back.

"If I just had some sign, one way or another," she explained to the dog.

She closed her eyes and listened to the sound of rain on the open window and the cars as they drove by. Ziggy stood up and moved to the foot of the bed and laid down as Jenna watched the shadows on the ceiling.

"Just one sign, God. Not even a big one, just a little one, but please, tell me what to do."

She gave into her tired body and the encroaching sleep.

Paul crept into his house and surveyed the room. He saw the place for the first time despite living in it every day for the last few years. He smelled the scent of time and apathy and looked for any sign of the person he was. For so long, his life consisted of helping everyone around him or letting people know God's word. For the first time, he realized part of what he saw was an attempt to not think about himself or his needs.

The light blue couch and matched the comfortable chair and were just furniture he picked up at the local thrift store after getting the job as minister. The walls were bare except for a single piece of artwork over the couch and painted for him from a church member. The neat kitchen and bathroom lacked any sort of personalization except for the dishes, and even those were from a church member. It was their style, not his. He walked down the hall and to the bedroom, the only furniture a bed and dresser the last tenant had left behind, though at least this room had a few pictures of his family. He looked across the hall to his office, the only room reflecting a part of him.

He sat on the bed, thinking about the house he shared with his family.

After they signed papers on the first home, they painted the living room walls green and the kitchen yellow. The furniture took weeks to find as he and Karen went from store to store looking for just the right type and color. On the walls, they hung oil paintings of the ocean and beaches from a local artist. Down their hallway, Karen mounted photographs of their little family. It was their home, and it reflected who they were.

"What does this house say about me?" he looked at the plain white walls.

"Could I have that again?" he asked the ghosts of his past that haunted him.

He laid down on the bed, closed his eyes, and let sleep take him away.

A morning sunbeam spotlighted Jenna in her bed, while a little wet nose nudged her and brought her to the surface of awareness. She sat up in the bed, and the squirming little dog jumped up and attempted to lick her.

"Okay, you need to go out," she moved her legs over the bed and pulled on a pair of sweats, and a shirt. She slipped on her shoes and took the dog out for a brief walk. The smell of coming rain filled her senses and brought back memories of the night before. Ziggy finished, and they returned to the hotel.

"Oh, look at the time," Jenna stepped into the generic room. "We have about an hour to get packed up and out of here."

She jumped in and out of the shower, dressed and began to pack her belongings.

"How is it that it seems I have so much more?" she asked the little face staring at her from the bed. "I know we didn't buy that much."

She instructed Ziggy to stay in the room, while she ran her first bag out to the car, dodging raindrops.

"I have no idea what I did with my airline information," she admitted to the dog while she ran through the pockets of her carry-on. She pulled items out and laid them on the bed, "but I'm sure it will turn up, and I will look closer after I get us ready to go."

Ziggy answered with a small excited yip.

"Well, I don't really have to have it, everything is electronic now," she gave up and shoved all she took out of the bag back in. "But I think I would like to have it. A security blanket thing, you know."

Ziggy rolled over on her back, begging to have her stomach rubbed.

"You are incorrigible," Jenna chuckled and gave the pooch a quick little bit of attention.

"Anyway," Jenna went back to her packing. "I'm not going to worry about the paper. I know I have it. It's probably in the side pocket, and I'll look for it after we see Patty. I hate being late."

Jenna grabbed the dog, did one more look around the room for lost items, before she grabbed her carry-on. She rushed out the door and into the parking lot. She looked up at the building which had been home for the last few days one last time and felt a strange feeling of loss.

"It's going to be good to be home," Jenna nodded her head. She wasn't sure about that anymore.

With the car loaded and checked out of the hotel, Jenna rushed to meet Patty at the cafe. She entered the establishment, and her stomach growled softly at the aroma of grilled eggs and hashbrowns. Across from the door, she spied Patty, alone at a small table. In front of her, a fresh cup of coffee steamed and a second cup across from her called to Jenna.

"Oh my gosh, you read my mind," Jenna scooted into the booth. She plopped her heavy overstuffed purse next to her on the inside of the enclosure. A subtle movement within the bag made Patty grin as she realized Ziggy joined them.

"She is fine, not the first time I've had to hide her," Jenna grinned as Ziggy's furry little head popped out of the top.

"Oh well, I do have her papers in there saying I need her," Jenna gave up trying to hide the little animal. "I just think if she sits there quietly, no one will notice anyway."

Patty agreed, and the two looked over the menu. A waitress appeared, and the women ordered their meals.

"So, is it just us then?" Jenna's eyes scouted the small room.

"Yes, I'm sorry, it is," Jenna's face fell, and she took in a deep breath.

"I called him last night to see how he was feeling and asked him if he wanted to come. He said to tell you he is really going to miss you, but he was busy today with something important he had to take care of. I even asked him if it could wait and I would call you to see if we could do breakfast earlier, but he said it was an all-day project and he couldn't get out of."

Jenna looked out the window, as the waitress brought them their food.

"I guess I made the right decision to go home then," she looked at her plate. "I guess this was the sign I prayed for."

Patty opened her mouth to talk but shut it without a word leaving her body. Jenna dropped her head. She was not going to cry. Patty took a bite of her eggs, and the conversation stopped. Jenna took a deep breath. What did she want? Could she be this close to Paul and yet, so far away? Could Patty hear her heart beating so loud?

"Well, I'm here, and I want you to stay.

Jenna looked into Patty's eyes, and Patty reached across the table. She covered Jenna's hands with her own and smiled. "And I don't know if you should count Paul out yet. I don't think it is personal."

"Or maybe it is just his way of separating, like with that girl."

Jenna turned and swiped at a rebel tear. She forced a smile and looked at Patty.

"I know you are here, and I appreciate that more then you will ever know," she took in a deep breath. "But to stay here and not be a part of his life would hurt too much. Maybe in time, I will get to know him as a friend and these feelings won't be as strong, but for now..."

The sentence was left unfinished, and neither person needed to be completed to understand. With the statement, she finally could accept her own feelings.

They ate, and the conversation changed to what life would be like for Jenna when she returned home. Jenna spoke about possibly going back to school or finding a job in an office.

"I think that I need to be around people,' she confessed. "I think that would be good for me. Maybe even date or something."

Time moved forward, and before either was ready, Jenna announced it was time for her to go to the airport. Patty paid the bill, and the friends walked together into the parking lot with their arms around each other. Jenna opened her car door, put her purse with the dog onto the seat, and turned to Patty.

"I'm going to miss you."

Tears filled her eyes, and she let them fall. Her arms reached for the other woman and Patty pulled her into a hug. Jenna melted into the woman's embrace. Though not much older than Jenna, Patty filled the large hold her mother's departure created in her heart. Jenna felt Patty's tears drop into her hair and felt her tears on her cheek. She pulled away and looked at Patty.

"I will call you tonight, and we'll keep in touch, like every day," Jenna promised, and Patty nodded.

Jenna slipped into the car and started the engine, but didn't want to shut the door and make it officially over.

"We will see each other again, I know it," Patty reached in and patted Jenna's shoulder. "This is not forever."

Patty pushed the car door shut, and Jenna put the car in gear. Jenna watched her friend grow smaller in the rearview mirror as she pulled out of the parking lot and onto the street.

Chapter Forty-Six

The road to the airport seemed to take longer than Jenna remembered, and she watched brief bits of scenery rush past her. The same trees and same river dotted the landscape just as it did days before. They appeared less brilliant now, perhaps worn down by the fires, maybe because it was a week later in the season. Perhaps it was her.

"I don't understand why he couldn't at least come and see me off," Ziggy laid in the passenger seat, and the dog raised her head as she listened to her owner's voice.

"I know he probably has things he has to do on his day off, but really, he couldn't spare just half an hour?" Jenna's voice grew louder, and the little dog dropped her head down to her paws. She looked up with sad eyes at Jenna.

A milepost sped by, and Jenna was one mile closer to her uncertain future.

"He could have asked if we could get together before his things. I would have met them earlier or something." Angry tears started to sting Jenna's eyes. "I was just looking for some sort of gesture."

Ziggy stood and started to walk to Jenna. She stopped and put her head down on Jenna's leg. The sound of tires on the road was the only noise in the car as Jenna's words hung like laundry on a line drying in the sunlight. Another milepost sped by on the side of the road.

"Do you want to listen to some music?" She reached down and hit the on button on the radio. "Something to get my mind off of things?"

A sappy voice filled the space with a song about lost love.

"Oh, hell, no!" Jenna said, swatting at the radio. "Silence it is then."

A few seconds later, another milepost marked another mile further down the road.

Jenna pulled into the car rental return, settled her bill and proceeded to the airline ticket counter where an overly cheerful agent typed her name in the computer to pull up her reservation.

"I'm sorry, ma'am, but I'm not finding you in here," the smile on her face morphing into a concerned look. "And you don't have your confirmation code or some other thing that can help me to find you?"

"Oh my gosh! Your kidding!" Jenna scanned the counter and at the other travelers waiting their turn to talk to the agent. "I was here three days ago, and they found me no problem. The agent told me there was no space on an earlier flight and I was better just keeping my flight today than trying to change it."

The woman kept pounding on the keyboard.

"I'm sure it's here, and that it's just a matter of the computer acting up," the agent forced a smile on her lips in an attempt to make Jenna feel more at ease.

Jenna stood and watched the woman get more frustrated.

"I might still have a copy of my flight schedule in my bags, I'm sure I printed it out, I'm just not sure which pocket it is in, for sure," Jenna leaned down and unzipped the front pocket of her bag. She ran her hands around in the pocket and pulled her hand out empty. She unzipped another pocket with the same results.

"Not that bag." Jenna drew in a deep breath and closed her eyes just for a moment.

The agent stopped typing as she watched Jenna dig around in her bags. Jenna moved on to another pocket and still found nothing.

"Three down, only three to go," Her worried voice betrayed her attempt to not show the panic as it began to set in.

"I know I have it here," she unzipping a pocket on the side and was rewarded with the feel of folded up pages. With a triumphant "Woohoo," she freed the folded papers from their material prison, and as she did, another envelope took advantage of the release and escaped also. Jenna handed her printed itinerary to the agent and crouched down to retrieve the envelope. She scooped it up and looked at the white surface. She instantly recognized the neat writing of her name across the surface and the existence of another note. She stared at the envelope, and her heart thumped in her chest. She rubbed the back of her neck. It seemed so long ago since she found the other letters from her mother. She couldn't stop staring at the paper until the sound of her name forced her back to the present.

"Jenna?" the agent said. "I found out what happened."

The woman keyed more information into the computer, and Jenna folded the envelope in half and stuck it in the back pocket of her jeans.

"It seems that when you were in here the other day, the agent at the time tried to get you on that flight, but wasn't able to," she reported. "But at that time, she also accidentally canceled the flights you had paid for."

Jenna stared at the agent.

"Can I get home?" The agent didn't say a word as she looked at the computer monitor. Jenna noted the hint of concern in her eyes.

"Well, the flight is very full," the agent slowly relayed. "We're still recovering from all the flights that were canceled due to the fires."

Jenna nodded, but sternly reminded her she bought seats on this flight and did not change it.

"I know," the agent's voice began to quiver with an edge of panic. "I'm trying to figure out what we can do."

Jenna shifted her weight to a different standing position.

"Well, we could put you on a flight tomorrow morning and pay for your hotel tonight," the agent offered with a forced smile, still typing frantically. Jenna shook her head.

"I need to get home tonight," Jenna stated bluntly. "I have a ticket, and I'm sorry that your agent screwed up, but I never authorized a change and was in fact, told that she couldn't do anything and to just keep the flight I had, so that is what I did, and now you are telling me that I don't have that flight anymore and I'm going to have to stay here another night, when all I really want to do is to get home."

Jenna longed for the security of her own things around her.

"So, I suggest you get on that computer of yours and make that offer to someone that didn't pay for one of those seats," she demanded. "You can offer the hotel stay to someone else, but all I know is that I'm going home tonight, even if that means you have to figure out a way to put me on another airline."

The agent stopped typing and looked at the screen with a somber look.

287

"I am very sorry, but.."

"There are no buts," Jenna put her fisted hand on the counter. "You're either going to find a way home for me tonight, or I'm going to have a meltdown right now."

Jenna felt the tears as they surfaced and began to blur her vision. Her own voice surprised her.

"I don't know if it says it in there, but I also have a support animal with me and finding a hotel in this area that will allow my dog is not easy," she took a deep breath. "I know because I looked a few days ago."

Another agent came up behind the woman on the computer and asked if there was a problem. She identified herself as the supervisor and listened as the story was told to her. A few minutes later, the two agents discussed the history of the ticket and solutions.

"Okay, let's just get you on that flight," the supervisor smiled. "I understand the frustration you must be feeling, and I'm so sorry you have to go through this."

A few more keystrokes and the woman stuck a tag on Jenna's bags and put them on a conveyor belt behind her. She reached down to a printer, grabbed a slip of paper, and handed it to Jenna.

"Here is your boarding pass," she chirped and pointed out how to get to the correct gate for the flight. Jenna concentrated on the directions, remembering her early experience at this airport.

"I just want to say I'm sorry again and thank you for flying with us," she concluded as Jenna grabbed her carryon bag and kennel. She moved towards where the woman pointed and reached the security line. A nice uniformed man directed her to another line due to Ziggy and Jenna obliged. Jenna threw the contents of her pockets in a bowl to go through the x-ray machine. She stared at the white paper envelope mingled with pocket change and the boarding pass as it passed through the scanner. After being cleared, she grabbed the envelope and replaced it in the back pocket of her jeans. She took hold of her bags, Ziggy's kennel, and rushed to where the supervisor indicated.

Chapter Forty-Seven

Jenna wandered down the busy walkway and smelt Italian food. She gazed into one of the restaurants and noticed an advertisement for alcohol and thought of the neon beer signs the night before.

The overhead speaker broadcast the last boarding call for another airline.

She walked closer to the food vendor.

"We don't have a knight in tarnished armor to help us this time," she looked down through the mesh window at Ziggy. The dog stared up at her and panted, making the dog look like she was smiling.

"Was it really just a week ago?" Ziggy put her paws on the sidewalls and arched her back to reach the top opening.

"Okay, you are right," she nodded to the dog. "If I have a drink, it may make me even more paranoid, better to pass, or if I have to, get a drink on the plane."

She turned back towards the gates.

People pushed past her on their way to assorted gates. The air filled with their chatter and excitement. Other travelers trudged towards the exit, their faces tired and relieved.

Jenna found her gate and sat among the other passengers waiting to board the plane. She reached down, opened the kennel, and pulled Ziggy onto her lap. The little animal stood on her hind legs and tucked her head under Jenna's chin in a cuddle. The bump of the note in her back pocket poked into her back, but after consideration, Jenna decided to read it someplace more private.

"Yeah, we are finally going home, and we can start life," she stroked Ziggy's soft black fur. "I know it's going to be different and even challenging, but I think together, you and I can get through anything."

She scanned the area, and little bits and pieces seemed familiar. She leaned over and examined a row of chairs further down the walkway.

"Do you think those are the ones we were sitting in?"

An announcement boomed through the area as over the speaker for passenger Paul Baker to pick up a courtesy phone and Jenna stopped. She quickly scanned the room to see if anyone rushed over to the phones.

"I still can't believe he didn't want to see me today," Jenna sighed. She looked out the large window at the planes on the tarmac. "I guess I overestimated his feelings. He is a people pleaser, so he probably just knew I needed attention and was being friendly to us."

An announcement over the loudspeaker signaled the boarding of her flight. She put Ziggy back in the kennel, grabbed her bag, and advanced to the jetway. She looked at the pass for the first time and noted her seat was in the back of the plane.

"Well, it isn't ideal, but it is a way home," she took in a deep breath and handed the gate agent her pass.

"Well, hello again," she addressed the smiling man on the tail.

"You going to do better this time," she asked him, and he just smiled at her.

"Oh, why didn't we buy train tickets?" she looked down and asked the dog. Ziggy looked up at her, and Jenna imagined the dog agreeing with her.

"Sure, it would have taken 10 hours, but we could have figured something out," she continued to put one foot in front of the other as people behind her crowded in. "But I guess we're here now."

She found her seat and tucked Ziggy's kennel under the seat in front of her.

"I know, but it is a short flight, and I promise, if you just go to sleep, we will be home before you know it," she talked to the whimpering dog. Ziggy looked up at her with wide eyes, pleading to come up to her lap.

"Sorry, buddy," she said, "I wish I could, but at least it's only an hour flight."

The envelope's corner stabbed her back as it screamed to be read. She pulled out the paper and settled into her seat. She watched more passengers load onto the jet.

An elderly woman scooted into the seat next to her and flashed her a warm smile.

"I just love traveling, don't you," Jenna smiled a response and looked down the plane.

"Are you going on vacation or home?" Jenna's neighbor asked.

"Home," she replied and prayed her short response would send the woman a message. It seemed to work as the woman pulled the in-flight magazine from the pouch in front of them, and scanned the pages. The smell of her perfume sent a nostalgic shiver down Jenna's back when she recognized the same scent her mother wore on special occasions, the same odor the room reeked of after her night of rage.

An announcement over the speaker system welcomed the traveler and informed them they would be pushing away from the gate momentarily, and in the air a few short minutes later. The flight attendants, with their painted-on smiles, showed what to do in the event of an emergency while Jenna fiddled with the envelope.

The plane moved, and Jenna closed her eyes. She took in a deep breath and looked out the small window. The plane stopped and slowly crept forward. Suddenly, it picked up speed, and Jenna felt her stomach lurch as they took flight.

Once in the sky, she concentrated again on the letter.

"How many more, mom?" she turned it over in her hand. "Are you about done?

Jenna held it tight in her hand and thought of her tired and sick mother penning her final words to her daughter.

"Okay, mom, you're right. I appreciate the effort you made to stay with me."

Jenna carefully pulled at the flap of the envelope, not sure she was ready to read this. The sting of Paul's rejection was too fresh, combined with the anxiety of going home. She folded the note and set it in her lap.

A flight attendant offered her something to drink, and Jenna ordered a glass of wine. She looked back at the letter and picked it up again. This time, she did a quick pull of the tab, and the message flew open. She reached in and pulled out the note.

"My dearest daughter," the letter began. "I hope the fact that you have found this letter is a sign that you are taking a trip. WONDERFUL!"

Jenna looked around at the people sharing this aluminum tube with her and noticed other people also surveying the passengers. She carefully refolded the letter, replaced it in the envelope, and slipped it into a pocket on the side of Ziggy's kennel.

"You protect it for me," she commanded the dog who responded with a smile.

Jenna closed her eyes and prayed to fall into a light snooze, but sleep was allusive as she felt each bump and turn of the plane.

"Whoohoo," the woman next to her said with each jolt. "Makes you feel alive!"

"Thank you, God, this is only an hour flight," Jenna whispered to herself and downed her wine.

Chapter Forty-Eight

The plane landed, and Jenna took her fingernails out of the armrests.

The overhead speakers squawked a welcome to their destination and thanked everyone for choosing this airline. Jenna muttered under her breath about being subjected to this torture.

Jenna sat still and waited for the other woman to move. She was trapped as the center line finally began to move towards the exit.

"They won't get to our row for a few more minutes," she gave Jenna a grandmotherly smile. "You might as well just relax."

Jenna sat back down and pulled the kennel out from under the seat in front of her. Ziggy moved around in the crate, panting. Jenna watched the people in front of her slowly move towards the front of the plane.

"Okay, it will just be a second now," her row mate stood and began to gather her belongings.

"It was a pleasure sitting next to you," she stated, and her smile seemed sincere. "I know we didn't talk much, but you didn't make me get up much, and I like to recognize the good things. I could tell this wasn't easy for you, and I hope things are going better. I have to admit, I said a short prayer for you while we were flying."

She looked at the kennel in Jenna's lap.

"And you were the perfect little pet," she touched the mesh window of Ziggy's prison, and the dog licked the wire door, desperate to make contact with her new friend.

The woman smiled while they advanced. Anxious passengers lunged forward as the door opened and Jenna fell in behind her seatmate. She stepped off the plane and onto the ground, resisting the urge to drop down and kiss the floor. Weight fell off her as she felt herself on solid ground. She drew in a deep breath and slowly let it out.

"Another half an hour drive, and we will be home," she said quietly. "Now what?"

She moved further into the seating area and stopped in front of a row of empty chairs. She put the kennel on one of the seats and set her bag next to Ziggy. She stood up straight and rolled her shoulders. More people exited the plane and walked past her. She put a hand on the small of her back, the same place Paul had touched her, and arched.

"Are you okay?"

Jenna smiled at an employee of the airline. She nodded and replied she was just reorganizing. The agent acknowledged her reply and moved on.

Jenna sat down and enjoyed the stillness. She opened the door of the kennel, and an anxious dog jumped into her arms. Ziggy shook and dug into Jenna's chest to be held.

"Wow, you were more freaked out than me," she rubbed Ziggy's head as the little dog's heart began to slow.

She moved the kennel, and the corner of the envelope peaked out of the pocket.

The last few stragglers left the jetway and passed her, followed by the crew. No one noticed the woman and dog as they watched the people leaving. The smell of Italian food drifted in from further down the walkway and music wafted around from speakers above. A soft 1980's love ballads mingled with the smells and put Jenna's mind on memories overload. The song words spoke about love and loss and begged his obsession to return to him.

Ziggy tucked her head under Jenna's chin and got heart to heart with her beloved owner. Jenna held her close with one hand, while the other hand grasped the unread note.

With the dog secure, Jenna managed to free the letter from its confines, open it up and with her free hand, held it up to read.

"My dearest daughter," Jenna read. "I hope the fact that you have found this letter is a sign that you are taking a trip. WONDERFUL! I don't know how long it will take you to see this, but I pray it is because you are getting ready for a vacation, and not because you are just going through my things to send to the local thrift store. Maybe you are on your vacation, and enjoying some much deserved time to relax. Either way, my prayer is for you to get away and start enjoying life and not a trip to Goodwill for me. I'm going to continue to write the way I want it to be, you laying on some sunny sandy beach with a sweet cold drink in your hand. I hope your travel is sooner than later, and I have not been gone for many years. Hopefully, it has only been a short time. I realize I don't know, and that does make me sad, but it makes me more worried to think of you all alone in the house without getting away for some adventure and rest.'

Jenna put the letter back in her lap and stared out large windows at the airfield.

"Yeah, I went like you wanted me to," she sighed, "and look what it got me. I would have been better off just sitting at home."

Jenna lifted the letter back up to continue reading.

"Anyway, I hope whenever you find this, you have had time to adjust to your new life. One I pray filled with joy and love. I pray you have taken time for yourself after the numerous hours you gave me, putting your own life on hold. You have been nothing short of a miracle angel to help me go through this illness, and I have frequently thought of how selfish I have been to allow you to put your own life on hold like this to help me to go through the last stages of mine."

Jenna dropped the note to her lap and stared towards the window. Planes took off flying to exotic locations. She looked at a poster on the wall for Hawaii. Places she would never see if it meant getting back on a plane again.

She pulled the letter back up as Ziggy jumped to another chair, circled a few times and laid down.

"I know we didn't do very many vacations when you were small, it was a chore just to make ends meet when you were growing up, but now you need to go, to travel, to see the world, not for just you, but for the both of us. You need to find out who you are and what you want to do as a beautiful grown woman. You are set financially, I made sure of that, but this isn't about money. This is about the time you need to take to invest in you."

"Invest in what?" she said aloud, and Ziggy looked up at her. The dog's large dark eyes and pulled back ears showed concern for her best friend. Jenna reached out and gave the small dog a reassuring scratch on her head.

Jenna continued to read.

"As I write this, I can hear you saying 'mom, why are you pushing me on a trip so hard?' Or hopefully more like 'I am here, now leave me alone,' with that slightly annoyed tone

298

you always got when I suggested things to you. I remember your voice with more than a hint of aggravation when you finally gave in to going to the prom with that nice boy, James. You had such a wonderful time, and I remember you floating on clouds after that for about a week. I was right then, and I am right now!"

Jenna smiled and dropped her hand and the letter into her lap. She closed her eyes and thought back to her prom night. Her mother was right. She saw the bright lights, smelled the scented air, and relived the moment. She could still feel the way he pulled her close while they danced. She vividly pictured all the girls in their beautiful dresses, and her in the one the church ladies made. She saw the boys, as their demeanor announced to the world how proud they were in their tuxedos. She remembered laughs with friends and feeling butterflies when James dropped her off with a goodnight kiss followed by an awkward goodbye as she slipped through her front door. And as she dreamt of that night, her dates face morphed into Pauls.

"Yes, mother, you were right about that one, but I always had you to come home to," she whispered and opened her eyes. She looked around the empty room.

"Who do I have to come home to now? Who is going to be waiting behind the door dying for details of how it went?" A tear blurred her vision before she allowed it to fall unashamed down her cheek. She took a deep breath, and the other tears retreated for the moment. Ziggy stood up and moved to her lap. She squirmed as she attempted to lick the salty drop from her face. Jenna pulled the little dog in closer, holding her tight.

"It's okay," she reassured her pet. "I just want to get through this letter, and then we will go home."

She breathed deep and thought about home. She visualized herself as she walked back into the dark house and got lost in the silence, acutely aware of the lack of noise except for the ghosts that resided in her mind. She wondered if anyone would have brought her mail in, but really, who even knew she left?

She looked out the big windows again, and at the bright sun. She put the letter away and stood before she shrugged and sat back down.

"Why rush?" she asked the dog. "It isn't like we have any place to be or anyone to see."

She pulled the letter out again and continued to read, the little dog still clutched close to her body like a warm security blanket.

"You may argue it, but sometimes someone has to push you to do things that are good for you," the handwriting began to get sloppy, though still readable, "and it saddens me to know it won't be me.

Jenna wiped another tear from her eye.

"You have probably found other letters," Jenna smiled as she pictured the other notes piled secured in her bag, "and are probably questioning my insistence for you to go on a trip, and I will be honest, it isn't just because I think you need it, which I do, but also because I am hoping you will get out and meet other people. I know I have told you numerous times about how your father and I met, and how it was on a spring break vacation my last year in college. How he sauntered up to me while I laid on the beach with some girlfriends, and the minute I saw him, I knew he was the one I wanted to spend my life with."

Jenna took in a deep breath.

The loudspeaker above called for the boarding of a plane to Los Angeles.

Jenna thought about a father she never knew. The house was littered with his photographs, but she was unable to bring his face into focus other than the images in frames. Over the years, her mother kept his memory alive with stories, but they were unimportant to the growing girl. Days, weeks and years seemed to make him less significant in her life, until now when she no longer would have those stories. Now all the information she owned were from memories of stories her mother told her and her mother's writings. How long before they would fade too.

She went back to the letter.

"I can see you now, rolling your eyes, and shaking your head. 'Mom, really?' I can hear your voice saying as you chastise me one more time about finding someone, but it is going to happen, and now more than ever, I have to believe it. Just open your heart to it, let down your guard. Throw caution to the wind and let your emotions guide your path. Trust your feelings, and don't let your head get in the way of your heart. I know it is scary and I know it can be painful, but I promise, my wonderful daughter, I promise it is worth it. You have to decide that you want to be in love. Chemistry is unmistakable, and great for lust, but love, you have to decide to love someone. Even in committed relationships, there are hard times when it would be easy to throw in the towel, and those are the days you just have to decide that you love the other person. Falling in love is easy, staying in love is a decision and one worth making. I can envision you with a family, and it warms me. Those images help me to find a strange, rare comfort through all of this and some days are the only way I can get through the pain of all this."

She looked at the top of the letter and was pleased to see this note was written less than a week before her death.

"Well, once again, I am going to have to stop writing as I am getting fatigued. I don't know how many letters I have hidden around the house, or how many more I will be able to write. I feel the time is getting closer and closer for me to leave you and this pain. I hope you understand, the last thing I want to do is leave you, but that is not an option. I hope you find solace in these letters and not just painful memories. I love you and know you have so much love to give, so please, find someone worthy to give that love to. I want so much for you to know the joy of a loving partner and children. I want you to know the love of God and know I am not afraid. If it weren't for you, I might even be excited about this new adventure I have coming in paradise. Please, Jenna, my most wonderful and precious child, I want you to live!"

Jenna put the letter in her lap and looked out at the airfield one more time. A lone bird flew by the window and out towards the sun. She carefully folded the letter and replaced it in the envelope. She listened to a far off voice announcing planes arriving and a few minutes later another plane boarding. A few people scurried past her down the empty hallway, not noticing the woman and dog sitting alone quietly. An airline employee walked to the podium behind her and turned on the reader board.

"Well, I guess we need to go," Jenna reached into her purse for the dog's leash. "I think you can walk from here and I bet you could use a trip outside."

She didn't know what it was about this letter that gave her strength, but she felt alive despite everything that happened earlier. She stood up and straightened her back.

"You know," she spoke to the dog. "She's right, it's time we start really living and not just existing!"

Chapter Forty-Nine

Ziggy pulled at her leash, and Jenna searched for a sign that showed her the way to baggage claim. She spied it and marched towards her unknown future. Behind her, her carry-on luggage rattled and strained with the kennel broken down and strapped to the top. Along the way, more people rushed to their destination. The smell of cooking food reminded her she hadn't eaten since breakfast and was getting hungry.

"We are going to do this, Ziggy," she walked out of the security area. "We are going to start a wonderful life full of adventure!"

She followed the arrows to baggage, while the fluorescent lights above made everything flat and colorless. She reached the luggage carousel and reached for her bag as it moved by.

"You look like you might need some help," a strong voice behind her made her jump.

"I don't mean to bother you, but I just want to make sure you are okay or see if I can help you at all."

The words cut through her like a knife, the voice familiar and warm. Jenna spun around to look into kind green eyes. The same eyes she dreamed about every night for the last week.

"Oh my gosh!" Jenna screamed and jumped. "Paul, what are you doing here?"

Paul wrapped Jenna in his arms, as Ziggy yipped and jumped around his ankles. She threw her arms around his neck and pulled him in tight. She wondered if he could hear her heart. Tears escaped her eyes freely, and after a few seconds, she pulled away.

"I'm sorry, but Ziggy really needs to go outside," Jenna's cheeks heated up underneath the salty moisture from her eyes. Paul nodded and walked towards the doors in silence. Their hands brushed against each other, sending electric shock waves through her arms and straight to her heart as he took control of her suitcase.

They exited, and Jenna directed them to a grassy area she remembered from her flight out. He dropped onto the grass, and Jenna slunk down next to him. She gawked at him, unable to believe what she was seeing.

"So, don't get this wrong, but why are you here?"

Paul looked into Jenna's eyes.

"Last night, I prayed about what I should do," he picked a blade of grass and tore it from top to bottom. "I knew I couldn't let you go, and I knew I wouldn't be happy unless you were a part of my life."

Paul looked down and picked another blade of grass and shred it.

"I don't want a long-distance friend, I have those," he looked at Jenna. "I haven't felt this way in a very long time, and I'm just not ready to let have it end."

Jenna nodded, the words from her mother's letter still danced in her mind.

"Throw caution to the wind and let your emotions guide your path. Just believe your feelings and don't let your head get in the way of your heart," her mother words screamed in Jenna's mind.

"I agree," Jenna looked down at Ziggy.

"What do we do then?" Paul leaned towards Jenna.

"I guess I have to see if Patty still wants me to work for her?"

Paul jumped up and pulled Jenna up with him. He grabbed her and squeezed her into him as he let out a yelp. He looked her in the eye and then placed his mouth on hers.

"Exactly what I wanted to hear and why I am here," he pulled away and kissed her lips. "I got my truck, and it is even cleaned out."

"We will make this work."

She cuddled into his arms; her heart next to his and the beats seemed to echo each other. Jenna didn't have any idea how this would work, but she had no doubts it would. She found her home and her place in the world with him. She closed her eyes and said a quiet prayer.

"Thank you, mom, you are right once again."

About the Author:

Terrie Stevens lives with her husband of over 30 years and four dogs, including Ziggy, in a little suburb of Seattle WA. She is the mother of two boys and grandmother of granddaughter, Chloe.

Terrie's history includes jobs as a photographer, reporter and travel agent. She loves travel, family and writing.

Also she is a "12 to the day she dies (Go Seahawks).

This is her first novel and she is currently working on her second one to be out in a about a year.

She is currently on Facebook at @NovelistTerrieStevens, Twitter at @TeriSteven0920 and her email address Fikshunal@gmail.com

She would like to thank all the people that put up with her while she pursued her dream, as well as her constant changes: her family, Nelson, Justin, James, Amanda, Nicole and Chloe; her parents Darlene and Dave. Good friends Phill S, Jeannine D, Rose D, Joan S, Trisha T and Cindy R; minister Terrence Proctor and the CBSR family; and dogs Abby, Ziggy, Sadies, and Taz.

Made in the USA
Middletown, DE
11 May 2020